TO THE STARS AND OTHER STORIES

RUSSIAN LIBRARY

R

The Russian Library at Columbia University Press publishes an expansive selection of Russian literature in English translation, concentrating on works previously unavailable in English and those ripe for new translations. Works of premodern, modern, and contemporary literature are featured, including recent writing. The series seeks to demonstrate the breadth, surprising variety, and global importance of the Russian literary tradition and includes not only novels but also short stories, plays, poetry, memoirs, creative nonfiction, and works of mixed or fluid genre.

■ □ ■

For a list of books in the series, see page 247.

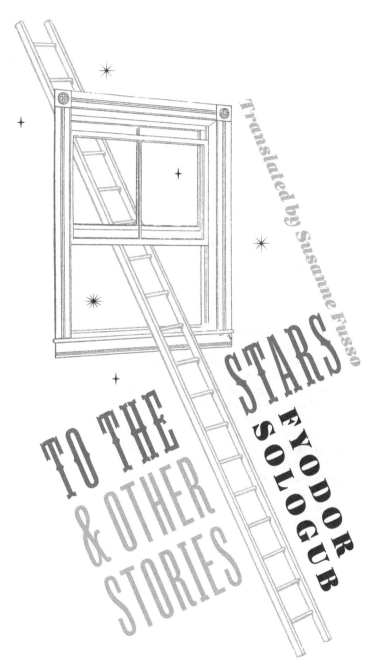

TO THE STARS & OTHER STORIES

FYODOR SOLOGUB

Translated by Susanne Fusso

Columbia University Press   New York

Published with the support of Read Russia, Inc., and the Institute of
    Literary Translation, Russia
Columbia University Press
Publishers Since 1893
New York   Chichester, West Sussex
cup.columbia.edu

Library of Congress Cataloging-in-Publication Data
Names: Sologub, Fyodor, 1863–1927, author. | Fusso, Susanne,
    translator.
Title: To the stars and other stories / Fyodor Sologub ; translated by
    Susanne Fusso.
Description: New York : Columbia University Press, [2022] |
    Series: Russian library
Identifiers: LCCN 2021056208 (print) | LCCN 2021056209 (ebook) |
    ISBN 9780231200042 (hardback) |
    ISBN 9780231200059 (trade paperback) |
    ISBN 9780231553407 (ebook)
Subjects: LCSH: Sologub, Fyodor, 1863–1927—Translations into
    English. | LCGFT: Short stories.
Classification: LCC PG3470.T4 T6 2022 (print) | LCC PG3470.T4
    (ebook) | DDC 891.73/3—dc23/eng/20211119
LC record available at https://lccn.loc.gov/2021056208
LC ebook record available at https://lccn.loc.gov/2021056209

Cover design: Roberto de Vicq de Cumptich

CONTENTS

ACKNOWLEDGMENTS

My attention was first drawn to the work of Sologub by the man who taught me Russian, the late Professor George W. Smalley of the Slavic Department at Lawrence University. Smalley was delighted by the perverse humor of Sologub's novel *The Petty Demon* and loved to quote from some of the more grotesque episodes in the life of the hero Peredonov and his lover Varvara. It has been one of the pleasures of my career to carry on this tradition, introducing my students at Wesleyan to Sologub in a course on Gogol and his legacy. Their enthusiasm and appreciation for Sologub has inspired me to offer this collection of stories as a way for his brilliant stories to reach a wider audience.

Many people have assisted me during my work on this translation. First, I must thank Christine Dunbar, editor of the Russian Library series, for her support and wise counsel. Three anonymous readers of the initial proposal made extremely helpful suggestions that set me on the right track as I translated these stories at the beginning of the Covid-19 pandemic. The completed manuscript was read by three anonymous reviewers who helped me to improve the work significantly. I am particularly grateful to the reader who commented on the entire manuscript in detail. All these readers brought great expertise, stylistic acumen, and collegial generosity to their task. Any remaining errors are of course my own. Thanks are also due to Leslie Kriesel and Ben Kolstad for their careful editing, and to Roberto de Vicq de Cumptich for the elegant cover design.

The scholarship of Aleksandr Vasilievich Lavrov, Jason Merrill, Margarita Mikhailovna Pavlova, and Stanley J. Rabinowitz has been a beacon and an inspiration. My deep gratitude goes to Jason Merrill for providing me with an article I was unable to obtain through my own library.

Irina Aleshkovsky, Olga Monina, Alexandra Semenova, and Roman Utkin have been responsive interlocutors for all my translation queries. Olga and Roman also directed me to important sources that I was previously unaware of. Nataliya Karageorgos, Priscilla Meyer, Justine Quijada, Peter Rutland, Victoria Smolkin, and Duffield White create a collegial atmosphere that has supported my work even under conditions of physical isolation.

As always, Katherine Wolfe and Lisa Pinette in the Interlibrary Loan Office at Wesleyan's Olin Library have been indispensably helpful in obtaining materials for me.

My students at Wesleyan respond to Sologub with infectious enthusiasm, and I thank them all for their insights, particularly Najeeba Hayat, who was inspired by one of Sologub's most outrageous characters to start Liudmila Shoes, a luxury footwear company. I like to think that Sologub himself would have appreciated the wit and beauty of Najeeba's creations.

Regular Zoom conversations with Duffie Adelson, Ayşe Agiş, Nadja Aksamija, Jim Brooks, Lindsay Ceballos, Robert Conn, Kingsley Day, Laurie Frenzel, Olga Peters Hasty, Dave Larson, Joyce Lowrie, Bruce Masters, Jim McGuire, Priscilla Meyer, Olga Monina, Stew Novick, Paula Paige, Nancy Pollak,

Roger Sánchez-Berroa, Alexandra Semenova, Emily Wang, Phil Wagoner, Rieko Wagoner, David Westmoreland, Fen Yao, and Paul Zec helped get me through pandemic isolation, and I am grateful for their unfailing good humor and lively sociability. My brother Jim Fusso and his husband Richard Barry have been sources of loving support through the pandemic.

I am grateful to Wesleyan University for its long-standing encouragement of my scholarship. I thank Demetrius L. Eudell, Dean of the Social Sciences, Nicole Lynn Stanton, Provost and Senior Vice President for Academic Affairs, and Michael S. Roth, President, for their wise and caring leadership throughout the difficult past year.

My husband Joseph M. Siry, Professor of Art History and William R. Kenan, Jr., Professor of the Humanities at Wesleyan, was the best possible person to be in isolation with. He aided me with love and good humor throughout my work on this project, and I owe him my profound thanks.

INTRODUCTION

SUSANNE FUSSO

I take a piece of life, coarse and barren, and I create out of it an
ambrosial legend, for I am a poet. Stagnate in the darkness, or
rage with a furious fire—I, the poet, will erect above you, O dim
and everyday life, my created legend about the enchanting
and the beautiful.

▶ Fyodor Sologub, *The Created Legend*

The short prose of the Symbolist poet, playwright, and
prose writer Fyodor Sologub (pseudonym of Fyodor
Kuzmich Teternikov, 1863–1927) deserves a wider audience for its masterly command of the realist and fantastic modes and
its vision of the power of the individual imagination to transcend
everyday reality. His fellow Symbolist Andrey Bely gave perhaps the
most penetrating description of the art of Sologub's stories in a 1907
review: "His vivid, honed, stinging style, which combines simplic-
ity and elegance, coldness and fire, tenderness and austerity, keeps
getting more and more supple. His anguishing conceptions more

and more convincingly lift the cover of enchantment that all of reality turns out to be. He is the singer of death: but he sings of death with all the tenderness of a prayer, all the ardor of passion; he speaks of death the way a passionate lover speaks of his beloved."[1] Sologub is best known in the West for his novel *The Petty Demon* (1905–1907).[2] Sologub's stories share many of the features that render *The Petty Demon* so compelling for a modern audience: the examination of late Imperial Russian society through a jaundiced eye and the wielding of a magisterial style to describe it in all its grim detail; the frank discussion of a sometimes unconventional sexuality; the poet's talent for play with language and deployment of punning and paronomasia as a vehicle for meanings that transcend the mundane; and a longing for transformation, the celebration of the individual's ability to create an existence beyond what meets the eye, as reflected in the title of his trilogy of novels, *The Created Legend*, or more precisely *A Legend in the Making* (1907–1913).[3]

Sologub's artistic activity belonged to the experimental, modernist milieu of Russian Decadence and Symbolism, which was highly influenced by figures such as Charles Baudelaire, Joris-Karl Huysmans, Paul Verlaine, and Oscar Wilde. But he was born in 1863, when the great Russian realist writers Fyodor Dostoevsky, Leo Tolstoy, and Ivan Turgenev were still alive and productive. As Stanley J. Rabinowitz writes, "Sologub is one of the oldest writers of the 'new' generation; his cast of mind was largely formed while realism was still the predominant literary style and his work reflects evidence of a considerable debt to it."[4] Margarita Pavlova has traced the formative influence on the young Sologub of the French naturalist novelist Émile Zola's "experimental method," the "gathering and documentary study of 'nature' and an objective exposition of events with the exactitude of an official record."[5] One of the most distinctive aspects of Sologub's prose is its combination of realist observation and detail with fantastic elements and the experimental use of language. This aesthetic quality is reflected in the stories in this collection, from the period in which Sologub produced his best short prose, 1896 to 1912. They represent Sologub's favorite and most productive themes and techniques: the world of children and its proximity to death, the Symbolist practice of "life creation," and the talismanic use of language to access other worlds and other levels of meaning.[6]

Sologub was born in St. Petersburg. Both his parents were of peasant origin. His father worked as a tailor until his death of tuberculosis when Sologub was four years old. Unable to support the family independently as a laundress, his mother was forced to return to work as a "single servant" (cook, maid, laundress) in the home of the Agapov family. Although Sologub was given access to the family's books and sometimes taken to the theater and the opera, his childhood was one of poverty, humiliation, and abuse. His mother beat him frequently with birch switches, even into his adulthood. Sologub's sister-in-law Olga Nikolaevna Chernosvitova, who cared for him in his last years and heard his recollections of childhood as he was dying, noted that "it was here [in the Agapov house] that he came to a lasting understanding of and love for the soul of a child, a soul that has been refined by suffering."[7] Although the children in this collection's stories "To the Stars," "In Captivity," and "The Two Gotiks" do not suffer physical abuse, their alienation from the adult world that surrounds them has "refined" their souls, giving them a powerful poetic imagination. In "The Youth Linus" and "In the Crowd," the sufferings imposed by the evil earthly world are both spiritual and physical, and fatal in both cases. Sologub came to regard his mother's beatings as a form of purification for an adolescent "shamed" by the habit of masturbation. There is also evidence that his childhood experience of corporal punishment developed into a sexual proclivity, if only an imaginative one, as reflected in some of his artistic works, like one of the stories in this collection,

"The Lady in Shackles. A Legend of the White Nights."[8] Sologub clearly had a complex relationship with his mother, who lived with him, moving from place to place as dictated by his career, until her death in 1894. In his last months he recalled that although she was illiterate for most of her life, he had never met a woman who had been blessed by nature with such a strong intellect.[9]

Sologub graduated from the St. Petersburg Teachers' Institute in 1882 and served as a teacher in various secondary schools for twenty-five years, in other words from age nineteen to forty-four, a period that overlapped with his mature literary career. His experiences in 1882–1892 as a teacher in provincial towns far from the capital provided him with rich material for his first two novels, *Bad Dreams* (1895) and *The Petty Demon* (1905–1907).[10] According to a biographical sketch by his wife, Anastasia Nikolayevna Chebotarevskaya, he had written his first poem at the age of twelve, and while working as a teacher in the provinces, he was sending poetry to journals in St. Petersburg and receiving rejection after rejection.[11] Finally his works began to be published, and in 1892 he returned to St. Petersburg to take a position as a teacher in the Rozhdestvensky City School. Here he began working closely with the major writers in the Symbolist movement, including Dmitri Merezhkovsky, his wife, Zinaida Gippius, Vyacheslav Ivanov, and others. The editors of the *Northern Herald*, the journal in which he began his serious literary activity, devised the pseudonym Fyodor Sologub for him, probably inspired by Count Vladimir Aleksandrovich Sollogub (1813–1882), an aristocratic writer, government official, and salon host whose background could not have been further from that of Fyodor Teternikov. In 1899, Sologub became inspector (a kind of assistant principal) in the Andreevsky City School. (The position of inspector, an administrator with responsibility for discipline, is the position that the hero of *The Petty Demon* vainly aspires to achieve by fair means or foul, although in his case it would be in the more prestigious *gimnazia*, the secondary school that prepared male students for university study.)

After the dominance of the Russian realist novel in the second half of the nineteenth century, the writers of the fin de siècle turned to poetry as the preeminent genre. Poetry provided the most expressive means for a philosophy and an aesthetic that strove for the transcendent, for a higher reality beyond what meets the eye. Sologub's poetry was esteemed for its polished form and sophisticated use of language. He was often labeled a Decadent, one of the writers who expressed the despair and twisted desires of a generation in decline. In an unpublished essay that confronted the label head-on, Sologub defined decadence less in the conventional terms of decay and sexual perversion and more in terms of linguistic experimentation. His essay "Is It Not Shameful to Be a Decadent?" seems to prefigure the ideas of the Russian Futurists and of associated theorists such as Viktor Shklovsky in its assertion of the power of the word as such: "Decadents use words and their combinations not as mirrors for the repetition of the world of objects, but only as a weapon for arousing in the reader a certain inner process. The futile work of giving perfect images of beauty in literature has been abandoned—art's primordial task of enchantment and ecstasy has been returned to it. . . . Everyday speech, with its dim, worn-out, and unfaithful expressions, is becoming insufficient: the need is appearing to seek fresh, expressive words, tender or coarse, euphonious or harsh."[12]

Over the course of his long career, Sologub wrote poetry, stories, novels, plays, criticism, poetic translations, and journalism. The publication of *The Petty Demon* as a separate edition in 1907 brought him great fame and popularity. *The Petty Demon* is a remarkable novel that weds the nineteenth-century novelistic tradition of Gogol's *Dead Souls* with a supremely Decadent linguistic inventiveness and sexual perversity. It is the story of the provincial *gimnazia* teacher Ardalyon Peredonov, a kind of unconscious and perverted

Symbolist who sees sinister meanings and threats in flowers, animals, the sun, his fellow teachers, and his students. Baudelaire's programmatic and proto-Symbolist 1857 poem "Correspondances," with its person walking through "forests of symbols" that watch him "with familiar glances," could have been written to describe Peredonov's universal paranoia. Peredonov's story is interwoven with that of Lyudmila, a young woman who provides not so much a contrast to Peredonov as an example of another kind of bad teacher, initiating the handsome, androgynous fifteen-year-old student Sasha into the ecstasies of perfumes, punning, and cross-dressing, while giving very little thought to the moral and psychological consequences of her dangerous games for the young boy's development. As Lukasz Wodzyński has pointed out, "Because [*The Petty Demon*] operates on several levels of meaning, it appealed both to the modernists—who recognized most of its subtexts and intertexts and thus could fit it into the group's symbolic universe—and the majority of educated readers, including the intelligentsia, who saw in it a sharp satire on provincial life in Russia."[13] Sologub was so popular and central to the Russian literary life of the time that his collected works were published twice in his lifetime, first in a twelve-volume edition by the Shipovnik publishing house (1909–1911), then as a twenty-volume edition by Sirin that added eight volumes to the Shipovnik edition after that company had closed (1913–1914).

The year 1907 was a personal turning point for Sologub. His younger sister Olga, with whom he had shared his life, died in June. He was forced to retire from his career as a teacher and inspector (possibly as a result of his literary activity, although the reasons for his retirement are not fully documented) and had to move out of the apartment that had been provided for him by the government. And he received a letter from a thirty-year-old woman named Anastasia Chebotarevskaya, asking him to provide her with a short autobiography for a collection of writers' lives she was planning (he refused, saying, "No one needs my biography").[14] He and Chebotarevskaya quickly developed a close relationship, and by August 1908 she had moved in with him to live as his wife (their official marriage took place later, in September 1914). The scholar A. V. Lavrov characterizes their union as marking for Sologub "a new creative and life *dvuedinstvo* [two-in-oneness, or two people operating as one]."[15] Chebotarevskaya tirelessly worked to promote Sologub's interests. Unsympathetic contemporary accounts describe her as forcing Sologub into a tasteless "makeover" of his way of life, having him shave off his beard and get rid of his pince-nez, throw out his old furniture, and start hosting salons that were very different from the strictly literary gatherings he had held before he met her. These new gatherings were attended by a heterogeneous bohemian company of writers, artists, and theater people and featured not just literary readings but also performances and carnivalesque masquerades.[16] Sologub himself called Chebotarevskaya "my constant and active collaborator" and wrote that "she rejoiced at my every success much more than I did, and was excessively grieved by the numerous annoyances that fell to my lot . . . , to which I myself had long become inured."[17] Sologub acknowledged her as a coauthor of several of his plays and of the stories "The Old House" and "The Road to Damascus," the latter of which is included in this collection.

Chebotarevskaya is a compelling figure in her own right. She was the sixth of seven children born to a lawyer who went on to have six more children in his second marriage, after her mother committed suicide when Anastasia was three years old. Despite the family's straitened circumstances, the children managed to get a good education. Anastasia and her sister Aleksandra studied in Paris in a school founded by legal scholar and liberal activist M. M. Kovalevsky, and they both published translations of French literature into Russian. Aleksandra later became a close friend and associate of Vyacheslav Ivanov. The translations by Chebotarevskaya included classics by

Stendhal and Maupassant as well as Decadent works by Octave Mirbeau (1848–1917): *Le Calvaire*, about a passionate and tortured love affair; *Sébastien Roch*, about a young boy sexually molested by a priest; and *Le Journal d'une Femme de Chambre*, about the underside of bourgeois life as viewed by a chambermaid. Chebotarevskaya was also an established critic by the time she began her relationship with Sologub. Chebotarevskaya's coauthored story included in this collection, "The Road to Damascus," has a very different tone from the stories by Sologub as sole author: it is arguably more sentimental and less ambiguous and subtle, but it also has a stronger sense of the internal life of a woman, in this case a woman who has been subjected to psychological abuse by a doctor who prescribes sex as a remedy for unspecified symptoms, no doubt considered to be caused by "hysteria."

Sologub had been sympathetic to the Revolution of 1905 and expressed his support for the ideals of justice and equality in both his fictional and nonfictional works. His background hardly disposed him to be a supporter of the tsarist autocracy, and he welcomed the February Revolution of 1917. He was highly active as an advocate for artists during the period of the Provisional Government (February to October 1917, O.S.). In March 1917, the Union of Practitioners of the Arts was formed, in which Sologub played a leading role. In an article of April 2, 1917, called "The New Class," Sologub defines the intelligentsia as a class apart from both the bourgeois exploiters and the proletariat and predicts that in the new regime, this class, which produces not goods but ideas and forms, will become an "oppressed and lower class" that will then achieve self-knowledge and fight for its own interests. He goes on to argue against the institution of a ministry of art, which had been proposed in March 1917: "Art does not need either patronage, or defense, or money from the government. The only gift art asks for from the government is the affirmation of the freedom of art."[18] The word Sologub uses for *freedom* here is not the commonly used term *svoboda*, but *vol'nost'*, which is derived from the word for *will*, and seems to represent for him a more elemental kind of freedom, one that follows its own will and desire without regard for outside strictures.[19] Sologub used the same word a few days later in an address to the Union of Practitioners of the Arts: "Religion, philosophy, art, and science are not free [*svobodny*]: they are willful [*vol'ny*]. They must enjoy such willfulness not because one or another political party permitted them to exist and manifest themselves, but because such is the nature of the human spirit."[20] This attitude was to be the exact opposite of the position adopted by the Soviet state toward religion, philosophy, art, and science.

The Bolshevik Revolution of fall 1917 was ruinous for the Sologubs and their way of life. Perhaps the best account of what happened in its wake is given in Sologub's own biographical essay on Chebotarevskaya. He describes how his wife heroically endured the poverty, hunger, and cold of the postrevolutionary years, without material comforts and with no outlet for the couple's literary efforts in the increasingly restricted Bolshevik cultural sphere. For two years they tried to get permission to leave Russia and were put through agonizing cycles of permission being granted and then rescinded.[21] Chebotarevskaya had long suffered from what her sister Olga called "attacks of circular psychosis," periods of energetic activity followed by suicidal depression.[22] Sologub writes that after the couple finally received permission to leave Russia in the summer of 1921, "although Anastasia Nikolayevna seemed quite healthy, buoyant, and cheerful, her nervous system had been completely worn out." On the evening of September 23, taking advantage of his brief absence, she left their home and threw herself from the Tuchkov Bridge into the Zhdanovka River and drowned. Sologub writes, "Her body was not found at that time, and only on about May 2 did one of the last ice floes bring her out onto the bank of Petrovsky

Island. She was buried on May 5 at the Smolensky Cemetery. The people who tried to save her on that miserable rainy evening heard her last words: 'Lord, forgive me!'"[23] Sologub wrote in a letter to Merezhkovsky, "She gave up her soul to me, and carried my own off with her."[24]

After his wife's death, Sologub abandoned his attempts to leave Russia, but his publishing career was virtually over. Despite his continued productivity and efforts to publish his work, he was politically untouchable. He continued to write poetry and work on novels, but his public activity was mainly centered in the work of the Leningrad section of the (nongovernmental) All-Russian Union of Writers, where his deputies were the emerging novelists Evgeny Zamyatin and Konstantin Fedin.[25] His archive contains a statement on his view of the results of the revolution that prefigures the vision of Mikhail Bulgakov in *Heart of a Dog* (1925) and *The Master and Margarita* (written 1928–1940): "I never belonged to the ruling classes in Russia, and I have no personal reason to regret the end of the old order of life. But I don't believe in that end. Not because I like that which was before, but simply because in our new times I can feel our old times. I would believe that the old world had died out if not just the form of government but also the form of worldview, not just the order of external life, but also the order of the soul, had changed. And that is precisely what does not exist anywhere or in anyone."[26] Sologub died in December 1927, apparently of multiple cardiovascular, renal, and respiratory causes.

Of the thirteen stories in this collection, six are centered on children, and the "Little Fairy Tales," although not designed for an audience of children, are framed in a quintessentially child-like genre. In his study of Sologub's literary embodiment of children, Rabinowitz writes, "No major writer since Dostoevsky has afforded the child such profound and elaborate treatment as has Sologub."[27] Rabinowitz goes on to describe how focusing on children serves

Sologub's "desire to transcend banality and escape to a higher state of beauty and perfection."[28] The form of escape chosen by Seryozha, the hero of "To the Stars," is intimately linked with the universe created in Sologub's poetry, particularly the 1898–1901 cycle *The Star Mair* (published 1904). These poems speak of an enchanted land of Oile that is revealed by the star Mair: "There, in the shining of the clear Mair, / Everything blossoms, everything sings joyfully. / There, in the shining of the clear Mair, / In the swaying of the luminous ether, / Another world lives mysteriously."[29] Seryozha is tormented by the banality of everyday, sunlit life and by his desire to enter the mysterious, unearthly world of the stars. Sologub's descriptions of Seryozha's moments of escape from the vulgarity of his family's life at their dacha shimmer with poetic unreality, and this contrast is one that his stories return to again and again. Sologub is the master of the fantastic in Tzvetan Todorov's sense, the space in which the reader hesitates between an explanation that adheres to the laws of nature and one that accommodates supernatural events.[30] In stories such as "Death by Advertisement," "The White Dog," "The Kiss of the Unborn Child," and "The Lady in Shackles. A Legend of the White Nights," our experience is made poorer if we decide in favor of either a realistic or a supernatural interpretation. When the magic words in the story "In Captivity" are revealed to be common obscenities, and the mystical events of "The Two Gotiks" turn out to have a realistic explanation, it is a disappointment for the child heroes and the reader alike.

In "The Youth Linus," at one point entitled "The Miracle of the Youth Linus," the supernatural is not explained away. But it coexists with a convincingly imagined reaction of guilt and terror on the part of the Roman soldiers who witness the miracle. It also has the feeling of a parable that speaks to its audience of their own time, not just the mythical past. This story, which the great critic D. S. Mirsky called "one of the most beautiful pieces of modern Russian prose," couches its imagining of Roman imperial might and cruelty in the most elegant Russian, thus presaging the "Pilate" chapters of Bulgakov's *Master and Margarita*.[31] Both Mirsky and Chebotarevskaya interpret "Linus" as an allegory of a Russian revolution, whether the one that had just taken place (Mirsky) or a possible future "great social bloodshed" (Chebotarevskaya).[32] A revolutionary impulse is implicit as well in "In the Crowd," which moves in masterly fashion from its satirical opening to its devastating, brutally absurd end. "In the Crowd" is based on the 1896 Khodynka disaster, a human stampede that occurred during the festivities accompanying the coronation of Nicholas II, in which 1,389 people died. Sologub transfers the action to the provincial town of Mstislavl, clearly a microcosm for Russia, but as the story progresses, the satirical portrait of the town is slowly and inexorably transformed into a monstrous vision of earthly life in general, a life that crushes its innocent young victims in the most literal fashion. As the satirical mode shifts to the apocalyptic, the style shifts as well, from realistically detailed, matter-of-fact sentences to brief outbursts of metaphysical horror. The story is hard to read, but it is a masterpiece, perhaps the pinnacle of Sologub's art in the genre of short prose.

One of the key ideas of the Symbolist writers and thinkers was "life creation" (*zhiznetvorchestvo*), what Olga Matich has called "a merging of writing and life practice": "Besides creating art, the Russian symbolists participated in a grand project of making a utopian *Gesamtkunstwerk* of their lives."[33] For Sologub specifically, the idea of life creation is embodied in the concept of *mechta*, which Jason Merrill has defined as "a daydream that inspires creativity or actually leads to creation."[34] In an illuminating article on Sologub's aesthetic system, Chebotarevskaya draws a distinction between Sologub's concept of *tvorimoe*, which might be translated as "that which is in the process of being created," and *sotvorennoe*, "that which has been created." She writes, "By the former we mean the potential power of the will of the creator over things, over the clay out of which he *creates* images, ideas, *life itself*; by the latter we mean the usual combinations of authorial material."[35]

In the stories included in this volume, "life creation" is engaged in by a man who advertises for a woman to impersonate his death ("Death by Advertisement"), a seamstress who finds a liberating energy in "becoming" a dog and howling at the moon ("The White Dog"), a club of young girls who masquerade as the grieving fiancées of recently deceased men they've never met ("The Saddened Fiancée"), and a woman who invites random men to embody her abusive husband once a year on the anniversary of his death ("The Lady in Shackles. A Legend of the White Nights").[36] David Bethea has asked, "What are the rules of *zhiznetvorchestvo*, that very Symbolist game of 'life creation' that incorporates others, often unbeknownst to them, in making myth (or mythos, literary plot) out of one's personal life?" Bethea claims that Vladimir Nabokov in *Lolita*, unlike Sologub in *The Petty Demon*, shows "the inherent dangers in using other human beings as material to realize one's private dreams."[37] It could be argued, however, that this moral problem is precisely what the story of Lyudmila in *The Petty Demon*, as well as the stories of Rezanov in "Death by Advertisement" and Nina in "The Saddened Fiancée," are about. Both Rezanov and Nina begin by making a game of others' lives. In both stories the game backfires, although Nina finds a new, serious (but still dangerous) purpose for her own life in the course of realizing her "created legend."

Two of the stories in this collection, "Beauty" and "The Sixty-Seventh Day," deal with human nudity (particularly female nudity), which for Sologub was one of the avenues of human transformation. In a 1905 essay, "The Canvas and the Body," he writes that to depict a nude body is to "give a visual symbol of human joy, human triumph. . . . The joy of nudity is that the body is plunged into its native elements. The wind wafts over it, the water embraces it, the earth is tender and soft under its feet, the fiery sun kisses its skin. Movements are free, conventions are cast away."[38] In an essay on the American dancer Isadora Duncan, whose performances had caused a sensation in Moscow and St. Petersburg in 1907–1908, Sologub describes how her bared arms and legs as she danced transformed an ordinary woman (the peasant Aldonsa in *Don Quixote*) into an ideal of beauty (Quixote's vision of the divine Dulcinea): "She dances, giving wings to her bared legs in her dance, raising her bared arms in an amazing movement—and she draws the enchanted soul of the viewer into the rippling movement of her dance. Now he sees the true miracle of the transfiguration of ordinary flesh into an extraordinary beauty created [*tvorimuiu*] before his eyes, he sees how the visible Aldonsa is transfigured into the true Dulcinea, into the true beauty of this world—and he feels the miracle of transfiguration within himself."[39] Although in "Beauty" a young woman's enjoyment of her nude body is confined to a civilized drawing room and is ultimately crushed by banal reality, in "The Sixty-Seventh Day" Sologub provides a verbal equivalent of the kind of "hymn" to the human body, freely wandering through nature, that he had prescribed for visual artists in "The Canvas and the Body." The publication of this story in 1908 gave rise to a criminal prosecution of the journal *The Golden Fleece* on a charge of pornography, and the publisher was fined.[40] This official charge of pornography for a story in which Sologub was offering a "hymn in colors, praise to the human and his Creator" seems to be a real-life counterpart to the inevitable crushing of the ideals of Sologub's characters.

Included at the end of this collection is a selection of Sologub's "little fairy tales," which were published in various journals between 1898 and 1906 and in two collections, *Book of Fairy Tales* (1905) and *Little Political Fairy Tales* (1906). As Adrian Wanner has discussed, these are fascinating, ambiguous exercises in what Wanner calls minimalist prose that in many ways anticipate the wildly creative mini-stories of Daniil Kharms.[41] Couched in child-like language but not at all intended for children, these sometimes frightening, sometimes hilarious parables display Sologub's inventiveness and linguistic ingenuity and are a kind of bridge between his prose and his verse. One of the tales, "Death Taken Captive," can be read as a programmatic statement by Sologub.[42] A brave knight manages to capture death. He offers her a chance to defend herself before he "puts death to death." Death declines to speak for herself but suggests that he ask life to speak on her behalf. The knight sees life, "a buxom, ruddy, but hideous wench," standing before him: "And she started saying such nasty, unholy words to him that the valiant and invincible knight began to tremble, and he hastened to open the dungeon . . . and he never told anyone on earth what he had heard from life, the hideous, unholy wench." Sologub has been braver than the knight: he has told us in these stories what he has learned from hideous life, but he has also told us what the enchantment of art and language has helped him to create.

SELECTED WORKS ABOUT SOLOGUB IN ENGLISH

Hansson, Carola. *Fedor Sologub as a Short-Story Writer: Stylistic Analyses.* Stockholm: Almqvist & Wiksell, 1975.

Khodasevich, Vladislav. *Necropolis,* trans. Sarah Vitali. New York: Columbia University Press, 2019.

Lodge, Kirsten, ed. *The Dedalus Book of Russian Decadence: Perversity, Despair and Collapse,* trans. Kirsten Lodge, Margo Shohl Rosen, and Grigory Dashevsky. Sawtry, UK: Dedalus, 2007.

Masing-Delic, Irene. *Abolishing Death: A Salvation Myth of Russian Twentieth-Century Literature.* Palo Alto, CA: Stanford University Press, 1992.

Merrill, Jason. "Authorial Intent vs. Critical Reaction: Fedor Sologub's *Hostages of Life* and the Crisis of Russian Symbolism." *Slavic and East European Journal* 61, no. 4 (2017): 754–77.

——. "The Many 'Loves' of Fedor Sologub: The Textual History of Incest in His Drama." *Slavic and East European Journal* 44, no. 3 (2000): 429–47.

——. "Plagiarism or Russian Symbolist Intertextuality? Hawthorne's 'The Snow Image' and Sologub's 'Snegurochka.'" *Slavonica* 12, no. 2 (2006): 107–28.

Rabinowitz, Stanley J. *Sologub's Literary Children: Keys to a Symbolist's Prose.* Columbus, OH: Slavica, 1980.

Ronen, Omry. "Toponyms of Fedor Sologub's *Tvorimaia Legenda.*" In *The Joy of Recognition: Selected Essays by Omry Ronen,* ed. Barry P. Scherr and Michael Wachtel (Ann Arbor: Michigan Slavic Publications, 2015; originally published in *Die Welt der Slaven* [1968], Jahrgang XIII, Heft 3, 307–16).

Wodzyński, Lukasz. "The Quest for 'Pure Fame': Fedor Sologub's *A Legend in the Making* and the Modernist Ambivalence About Literary Celebrity." *Slavic and East European Journal* 61, no. 4 (2017): 778–801.

NOTE ON TRANSLITERATION AND TRANSLATION ISSUES

he transliteration of names in the text is based on the principle of coming as close as possible to the correct pronunciation without distracting the anglophone reader too much. In footnotes and bibliography, I have used a modified Library of Congress system for ease of reference in library catalogues. When dates are mentioned that are from the Julian calendar used in Russia before the revolution, they are noted as "O.S." ("Old Style").

Russian names consist of a first name, a patronymic, and a last name. The patronymic is formed from the father's first name plus the suffix -ovich/-evich for men or -ovna/-evna for women. Russian also uses a wide array of diminutives for the first name. For example, in "The Saddened Fiancée," the main character is named Nina Alexeyevna Bessonova, which signifies that her father's first name is Alexey; Bessonova, not Alexeyevna, is her last name. People are referred to either by their first names (or nicknames such as Ninochka, as Nina's mother addresses her), first names plus patronymic, or last names. Only in rare cases is a person (usually a peasant or someone of the lower classes) referred to only by their patronymic. Sologub also uses some unconventional nicknames, such as Paka for Pavel in "In Captivity" or Gotik for Georgi in "The Two Gotiks."

The *gimnazia* was the secondary school that prepared students for university study. I have chosen to use the word *gimnazia*, because its connotations of privilege are not captured by "high school."

Several of these stories take place at dachas. The word *dacha* is sometimes translated as "country house," but it should be distinguished from the manor house on a landed estate (*usad'ba*). In the 1890s and 1910s, when these stories take place, the word *dacha* could connote a range of houses from humble to sumptuous, normally used as summer retreats for city dwellers, and often grouped into settlements on the outskirts of major cities. The dacha could have a connotation of vulgarity, which Sologub at times exploits. See Stephen Lovell, *Summerfolk: A History of the Dacha, 1710–2000* (Ithaca, NY: Cornell University Press, 2003): "The culture of the time regularly presented the dacha as a meretricious, low-grade alternative to the country estate, as at best a stepping-stone to the *usad'ba*" (90).

TO THE STARS AND OTHER STORIES

TO THE STARS

I.

Seryozha felt offended. As always, this made him shrink unattrac-
tively in his short, tight, little-boy's suit, which he didn't like and
didn't know how to wear: when he wore it, his movements were
awkward and sluggish. His heart pounded fretfully and weari-
somely, and he looked with spiteful dark eyes across the bed of multicolored, fragrant flowers at the fence of the dacha where he and his
mama and papa lived.[1] A carriage was standing at the gate. Mama
was preparing to leave and was merrily chatting with some strange
men, who were all lanky and smart-alecky and all dressed like buf-
foons, in Seryozha's opinion. His father was with them too.

Now as Mama kissed Seryozha good-bye, she said, "Oh, my dear
little love-bird, did you want to tell me something? Just wait, I'll be
back soon, and we'll talk to our heart's content, we'll talk about the
stars too."

Seryozha heard the insincere notes in Mama's voice and knew
already that it was just words. Mama was so elegantly dressed, and
she smelled sweetly of perfume, and this annoyed Seryozha.

"My little boy is such a dreamer," Mama said. "Just think, yesterday he was prattling something about the stars, you know, something childish and naive, but poetic, really. My little boy's going to be an artist, don't you think?"

The guests laughed, and Papa laughed without removing the cigar from his mouth, and his laughter made it wobble. Then they all walked away, and Seryozha remained. And now he was standing alone in the middle of the garden and looking angrily in Mama's direction.

When Mama had ridden away, Seryozha's pale but round face went from spiteful to sad, and he turned to the house. The wooden house with its attic story was so beautiful, and the flowers on the balcony windowsills were so bright and fragrant, and the creeping plants that twined around the pillars of the balcony were so green, that Seryozha had an eerie feeling—he felt himself to be alien here—and all this elegance was dark and strange to him. He didn't want to go into the rooms where he knew in advance he would languish among the comfortable, expensive furniture, among the beautiful, inescapable surroundings, where everything was seemly and tiresome.

Sadly inclining his untanned, unattractive face, he slowly plodded into the depths of the garden. There he leaned his chest on the fence and for a long time watched the horseplay of two barefoot boys in the yard. They were the same age as Seryozha, but he couldn't play with them, that was unseemly and forbidden. He was sorry he couldn't approach these cheerful boys. He watched with curiosity as they took turns chasing each other, playing tag.

Running was a pleasure that was forbidden to Seryozha: when he ran, his heart would start thumping hard, and he would stop, panting. But now, when the others were running, he watched them greedily and laughed with the joy their running and shouting inspired in him, and at times his heart palpitated as if he himself were running with the boys. But he tried to restrain his laughter: he would be ashamed if anyone saw him watching the play of street kids with such interest.

The boys stopped their play, stood in the middle of the yard, and held a ringing, strident consultation, as if they were squabbling. Seryozha kept watching them. He found it strange that they were so disheveled and barefoot and yet they weren't at all self-conscious about it. They started running again, but Seryozha's thoughts had wandered.

A shout in the yard made him shudder. The cook Nastasia was shouting frantically and pummeling one of the playing boys, her son, and he was howling desperately. Seryozha squealed from terror and from the other person's pain, which he suddenly felt in himself, and he ran away.

Neither Mama nor Papa returned, even as the day turned to evening. Seryozha was alone almost the whole time, because his tutor, a genially lazy, towheaded university student, was flirting with the fashionably dressed maid Varvara, whom Seryozha didn't like because of the way she would obsequiously look into her mistress's eyes and kiss her hands.

When it had become quite dark, Seryozha stealthily left the house and went to one of the distant paths in the garden. There he lay down on a bench, put his hands under his head and started looking at the sky. It seemed to melt, layer by layer, and gradually lay bare the stars hidden behind it and the deep-blue abyss beyond the stars.

The damp and chill of the July evening enveloped the boy. If the older people caught sight of him in the garden, they would chase him into the house. He himself knew that it was bad for him to lie here, under the damp lilac branches—he was so delicate and nervous— but he stayed on purpose and angrily recalled how Mama had treated him scornfully and how the guests had softly laughed as they looked at his small figure. He also recalled how once Aunt Katya had called him *miniature*, and now that word annoyed him.

"Do such miniatures really exist?" he thought angrily. "And why do all older people always grin and try to say something funny and cheerful? To laugh from joy—that's all right, but they laugh from spitefulness. And from envy because I'm small and they're going to die soon."

He thought that if he were strong, he would make Aunt Katya get on her knees before him and ask forgiveness. But no one else should be there at the time, so that there would be no one to laugh. And he would take Aunt Katya by the ear and say to her, "Watch out, you'll catch it worse next time."

And she would go away meekly, without laughing. And what would he do with those lanky men? Nothing—chase them away, that's all. If only neither they themselves nor the memory of their stupid laughter would keep him from looking at the stars, which they weren't interested in, just as they weren't interested in Seryozha.

The stars, distant and peaceful, looked right into his eyes. They twinkled and seemed timid. Seryozha was also timid, but now he felt that he and the stars were happy. He remembered that his tutor told him that each star is like a sun and has its own earth. But he couldn't believe that out there it was just like here. He thought that it was better out there. He was sorry he couldn't make it there: the earth was large, and it pulled him. If it didn't pull, then he could fly away there, to the stars, and find out what was happening there, whether angels with white wings and wearing golden shirts lived there, or the same kind of people as here.

Why do the stars look at the earth so attentively? Maybe they are alive themselves and are thinking?

Seryozha looked at the stars for a long time and started to forget his annoyance and his spitefulness. It became gentle and clear in his soul. His face with its plump but pale lips seemed imperturbably calm.

The stars burned above Seryozha ever more clearly and affectionately. They did not outshine one another; their light was without envy and without laughter. Every moment they seemed to come closer to the boy. He felt joyful and light, and it seemed to him that he was floating on the bench, rocking in the air. The stars pressed down closer to him. Everything fell silent, sensitively and expectantly, and the night became denser and more mysterious. As if merging with the stars, he forgot about himself and lost all sensation of his own body.

Suddenly the high-pitched sounds of a harmonica came flying from somewhere in the distance and woke Seryozha out of his self-forgetfulness. Seryozha was amazed at something—perhaps at this self-forgetfulness that had just passed—and then he got annoyed at the harmonica that had woken him up, the vile sounds of which jumped and wriggled above the boy. These impudent, squeaky, importunate sounds reminded him of everything that belongs to the day—the guests, the student, Varvara, the boy whose mother beat him and who shouted frantically—and this last memory caused Seryozha to start trembling suddenly, and his heart started pounding painfully. He was enveloped by anguish and a great unwillingness to be here, on this earth.

"But what if the earth doesn't pull me down?" he suddenly thought. "Maybe if I want to, I can detach myself and fly away. The stars pull me, not the earth. Suppose I start flying?"

And it seemed to him that the stars started to quietly ring, and the earth beneath him slowly, cautiously started to tilt, and the garden fence slowly started crawling downward near his feet, and the bench he was on started moving smoothly, raising his head and lowering his feet. He got scared. With a faint, harsh cry he jumped up from the bench and took off running for home. His legs got heavy, his heart was hammering painfully, and it seemed to Seryozha that the earth was swaying beneath him with a muffled sound.

Trembling, he ran into the house. No one noticed him. As always, the lamps were burning in the empty rooms, and people's voices could be heard nearby.

"What was I afraid of?" Seryozha pondered. "I was just lying there, and it turned out that the fence was opposite my feet, and it seemed to me as if the earth was turning."

He wanted to go to where the people were, so as not to be alone. But when he entered the room where he could hear the cheerful voice of his tutor, he saw that he was interrupting the tutor's chat with Varya.

The student turned quickly to the boy, looking strained and embarrassed. His hands were awkwardly spread apart because he had just been holding them on Varya's shoulders. Varya was standing near the table, as if she needed to tidy up something on it, smirking with a lascivious smile and looking at Seryozha with a look of superiority, as at someone who couldn't understand. But Seryozha knew that Konstantin Osipovich, the student, liked Varvara and that he was only joking around with her and would not marry her, because they were not equally matched. Now he suddenly felt it to be unpleasant to look at them. He thought that they had bad faces, both the snub-nosed and pockmarked student and the red-cheeked and black-browed maid. He didn't know what was bad about their faces, but they annoyed and shamed him.

He turned his eyes away from them and looked at the lamp, shaded by a red paper shade with a delicate openwork border. But he recalled the stars, and it became painful to look at the red light of the lamp. He walked over to the window. Misty, smoky earthly lights looked at him from all directions. Nearby at one of the dachas, paper lanterns were burning, probably for some family celebration. These garish, harsh lights made Seryozha feel anguish.

"What's going on?" he said plaintively. "When is Mama ever going to come home?"

"Your respected mommy will be coming home late," Varvara answered in a sweet voice. "You will see her ladyship tomorrow, Master Seryozhenka, but now it's time for you to go to bed."

Seryozha looked at Varvara with spiteful, cold eyes; his eyes glimmered strangely in his pale yellowish face. His lips were twisted in a spiteful smirk, and this caused his cheeks to seem swollen toward the bottom. Spitefulness seized his heart with a distinct languor, similar to languishing from hunger.

"I'll go to bed," he said with a slightly quivering voice. "Are you going to start kissing him?"

Varvara blushed.

"My word, Seryozha, you should be ashamed of yourself," she said uncertainly. "I'm going to complain to your mommy."

"I'll complain myself," Seryozha answered and wanted to say something more, but couldn't because the languor of spitefulness and anguish was squeezing his heart and throat to the point of pain.

"Seryozha, let's cease this," the student advised him, trying to cover up his embarrassment with an authoritative tone and a contemptuous smirk, "and go to bed."

Seryozha glowered at him and silently went off to his own room.

As he undressed, he tried to forget about the student and Varya and all the people. He wanted to dream meekly and lovingly about the stars. He went up to the window, moved the blind a little bit aside, and looked at the sky. It was all sparkling and glittering. The stars were like diamonds, and their shining seemed cold, as if a chilly breath was descending from them.

Bent over and pressing his shoulder to the window frame, Seryozha stood and sadly thought about how it was impossible to get the stars to tell him about what it's like out there—and his cold eyes glimmered in his pale face. But when he was standing like that and looking at the stars, his spitefulness gradually began to yield, and his heart ceased languishing.

In the night Seryozha dreamed of a mysterious and marvelous world, a world located on the clear stars. On the trees in a prophetic forest, wise birds sat and looked at Seryozha, and under the branches of the trees, wise beasts passed slowly by, beasts that had never been seen on earth. Seryozha felt joyful and light with them and with the people of that world, who were all clear and looked wide-eyed and did not laugh.

II.

The day was hot, and Seryozha was sad. He didn't like the heat, he didn't like the bright illumination of the sun, and in the daytime he was always afraid of something. All this heat and light lay oppressively on his chest, and an unpleasant languor and flutter awakened in it from time to time, somewhere near his heart.

Besides, in the daytime they rudely pestered him with instructions and assignments, when he wanted to be alone and think, or they scornfully pushed him away because they didn't have time, when he wanted to talk about what was on his mind. Every day there were strange people at the house, mostly men, smart-alecky and noisy. They all seemed dark to Seryozha, as if the dust from their eternal laughter had stuck to them.

Seryozha wanted night to come again, as soon as possible: he would look to see if the stars were glimmering the same way today that they did yesterday. Again he would feel joyful, but in the daytime—it was anguish! Because everything was alien and hostile. His father was a total stranger. He didn't even know what to talk to Seryozha about: he would stop in front of him, stroke his head, and ask something incoherent and unnecessary, like: "Well, what do you say, Seryozha, how are things?"

And then right away, without waiting to hear what Seryozha would say, he would start talking to the others. As for Mama, sometimes she would suddenly take Seryozha by the shoulders and begin to caress him and talk to him, and then she would become so simple and luminous that Seryozha wasn't even scared of her elegant clothes, and he would trustingly snuggle up to her. But that happened seldom, quite seldom; usually Mama too was a stranger—gracious with the guests and elegantly dressed, exhaling fragrance for them, for all those lanky men dressed in their ridiculous fashions, but with Seryozha she was cold and scornful.

"Yes, even Mama is a stranger," Seryozha thought. "And everything that happens in the daytime is tedious, but the stars are mine; they all look at me and don't turn away. They are luminous. But on earth everything is dark. And Mama is luminous only once in a while. But maybe my soul is somewhere out there, on a star, and I'm only here, by myself, when I'm sleeping, and that's why I'm bored?"

At the usual time Seryozha set off with his tutor, Konstantin Osipovich, to go bathing.[2] Seryozha wanted to talk about his ideas, and he thought that it would be a good time now, because the student was also hot and apparently felt uncomfortable: he was walking lazily and not smiling.

"The sun is dark," Seryozha declared as a start.

The student snorted vaguely.

"It's true," Seryozha continued, trying to be convincing. "It's impossible to look at it. And if you do look, you get dark circles in your eyes. And the day is dark, you can't see anything in the sky. But at night it's luminous. The stars are better than the sun."

"Don't try to fly too high, Seryozha," the student stopped him lazily. "Don't say so many stupid things."

The student's coarseness was disagreeable to Seryozha. But he continued to talk.

"Everyone can see that you have a towel on your shoulder."

"So?" the student asked.

And again, Seryozha didn't like the coarse sound of that "so." He lightly sighed and said, "That means everyone knows that we're going bathing."

"Right," the student affirmed in the tone of a person who is listening to obvious nonsense. "What's your point?"

"Well, we're going to get into the bathing house. It's cramped there, and we'll bathe there in secret, but it's forbidden to swim out into the open."[3]

The student suddenly broke into a grin and started snickering very strangely. Seryozha looked at him in amazement. The student again had a bad face, the same one as last night. Seryozha felt awkward and annoyed, and he started talking about something else.

"What stupid horses there are on the earth," he said, looking at the submissive muzzle of a shaggy cabby's nag.

The cabby was drowsing on the coachbox in the heat of the sun, and the horse was also drowsing. Seryozha remembered the wise animals he had seen in his dream: they watched and knew something, but these . . .

"They're really stupid," he repeated.

"What did they do to bother you?" the student asked, still snickering.

"Don't you get it, they're strong but stupid: they carry people on their backs."

The student started laughing loudly. Seryozha shuddered at this sudden laughter and looked around sadly. And everything all around was sonorous, agitating, and alien: the dachas, the bright greenery, the bright sand on the roads, the bright flowers in the gardens, the elegantly dressed ladies. And alongside the luxury of this life scurried dirty barefoot boys with avid and timid eyes.

In the bathing house, when the cold water made Seryozha feel free and cheerful, he again recalled that people have shame and that it's forbidden to swim out into the wide-open space. And he didn't understand what was shameful about him, when here he felt so light and comfortable, in this water that was cold and calm and held him in its embraces. Out there, on the earth, when he put on his suit, he would again become small and ridiculous, but here he was simple and clear. He quickly beat the water with his arms and legs, squealing from joy and raising clouds of spray over himself. He was seized by a riotous gaiety and at the same time by unbearable spitefulness because it was cramped and he could constantly feel walls under his arms or under his legs. He clenched his teeth, squealed piercingly, and dived under the wall of the bathing house. The water was low, and he had no trouble getting out into an open space.

It was luminous, spacious, cold, and cheerful. There was another bathing house standing right alongside; from it could be heard the voices and yelping of girls. With a joyful, loud squeal, Seryozha poked himself into that bathing house.

There were about five girls, and they were on their own, without adults. When they saw a boy in their place, they started screaming and squeaking and floundering absurdly in the water, turning their backs on Seryozha and splashing him with water. One of them who was a little bolder, a well-grown girl, peered at Seryozha and shouted angrily and scornfully: "He's just a little boy!"

And she started swimming toward him, evidently with hostile intentions. Seryozha hurried to escape to his own bathing house.

He listened silently to the student's reprimands as he dressed, but his eyes were spiteful and shone like a snake's. The student's coarse, clumsy words went right past him, like almost all those empty words that he had already heard so many of. But he thought that the student would of course tattle on him at home, and they would again scold him and laugh, and this made Seryozha sad.

"Laughter and shame every day!" he thought. "What did I do to deserve such a life?"

At home they started explaining to him the unseemliness of his action. Everyone ganged up on him: Mama; Aunt Katya, Papa's sister, a plump lady with a wrinkled yellow face; and cousin Sasha, his aunt's daughter, a slim young lady with a flat, drawling voice. Seryozha listened dully to the words but didn't follow them. He himself knew that what he had done was considered unseemly, but he was quite uninterested in thinking about it.

Mama sighed, half-closed her beautiful dark eyes, and said quietly, not addressing anyone in particular: "He seems restless today, and for what reason, I really don't know."

And then Mama looked at the student.

"Konstantin Osipovich, you should be—" she began and faltered, not knowing whether she should say "stricter" or "more lenient." Finally she finished: "Somehow . . . you know," and she made one of those refined gestures that Seryozha so disliked.

Konstantin Osipovich made a knowing face and remarked sagely, "Extreme nervousness . . . in general . . . his generation . . . and the end of the century."[4]

Aunt Katya spoke in such a sour and weary voice, as if she were the one who was most offended by Seryozha and by everything else: "The children today! Take the Nechaevs' boy, what a horrible thing."

She bent down to Mama's ear and started whispering. Seryozha stood sullenly a little distance away, waiting for them to let him go, and thought brief, spiteful thoughts. Mama listened to the whole secret story with a dejected look, sighed again, and said, "Yes, children. . . . So many worries. . . . Really, you don't know what to do with them. Seryozha, my love-bird, you be sure to abstain from all these kinds of antics. You have to understand, it's not good for you: people scold you, and you get excited. And it's bad for you to get excited. And you should have pity on me, you've completely upset me. I have worries enough besides you . . ."

"You see, Seryozha," his cousin said. "You're distressing your mama, and that's bad."

Seryozha looked at her light-colored dress with its puffed sleeves, ribbons, and pleats, and thought that she was wrong to interfere; it wasn't any of her business. She said something else deliberately and flatly, and her thin lips moved in a repulsive way. The drawling sounds of her voice filled Seryozha with anguish and spite, and his heart again froze and languished. Finally, he interrupted his cousin in the middle of a word and said, "Cousin Nadya got married, but you don't have any suitors this year and you won't have any, because you're made of vinegar."

Mama got angry, turned red, and said, "Sergey, you will have to be punished."

His cousin pursed her thin lips. His aunt exclaimed, "What a spiteful boy you are, Seryozha!"

"There's no choice but to punish him," Mama repeated in a weary voice.

Seryozha looked sullenly at her. He felt his heart beating more rapidly and his cheeks turning pale. He thought, "If only adults could be threatened every day with being punished. Punished!"

"How?" he asked.

"What?" his mother asked in amazement.

"How are you going to punish me?"

"It's not your place to ask how," Mama said irascibly. "I'll call Varvara, and then you'll see how."

"So I'll be handed over to Varvara for execution?" Seryozha asked again calmly.

Mama threw up her hands and broke out into nervous laughter.

"Just try to talk to him," she said in a voice that rang with offense. "No, take him away, Konstantin Osipovich, I just can't. He's growing up to be some kind of idiot."

Seryozha started laughing with the same squealing laughter as Mama and ran out of the room. The heavy red portière caught his closely shorn head unpleasantly with its scratchy fabric. Seryozha suddenly thought that he was always being offended and that anyone else in his place would be sure to burst into tears. But he never cried, and now he even felt sorry that he didn't start crying: Mama perhaps would have started consoling him and caressing him. A burning desire for Mama's kisses and caresses passed through the boy's soul in a hopeless, acrid wave, but he quickly suppressed that desire. His lips pursed fretfully, and his trembling chin pressed to his chest. He reached his own room at a run, collapsed face-down onto the bed, started thrashing his bent legs in the air, and began quietly squealing strange, unattractive sounds. His spiteful eyes glimmered and dilated, and the blackness of their pupils seemed deep in contrast with his untanned face, pale to the point of yellowishness.

III.

Someone touched Seryozha on the shoulder. Seryozha jerked his legs in annoyance and turned onto his back. Konstantin Osipovich was standing over him. The pockmarked, snub-nosed face of the student, with its sparse, soft, reddish beard, was solemn, and this didn't suit him and was ridiculous. Seryozha saw at once that there was something the student needed to do with him, perhaps something very nasty, and the boy felt sad and afraid. He lay motionless, with his arms stretched out along his body and pressing his whole body tightly into the bed. His dark eyes were dry and spiteful.

The student stood over the boy for a moment, frowned, and said, "In the first place, you aren't allowed to lie around in the daytime."

Seryozha silently sat up on the bed, and then stood all the way up. He stared fixedly at the student, from below, into his face, raising his head high in order to do this, and somehow he wasn't thinking of anything during this time. The student frowned even more, tried to find words, and started speaking: "And in every way you have, you know . . . gone nuts . . ."

"Nuts," Seryozha agreed quite mechanically and started inspecting the student's hands, which were large and bony, with thick dark-blue veins.

"Don't interrupt," the student said angrily. "You, you know . . . you said a lot of sassy things to that young lady, and to your mommy too. So it's turned out kind of . . . unsightly. You quite, you know, you behaved quite groundlessly. Well, to act coarsely, that's . . . not a good thing, and it's quite . . . well, in a word, it's unsightly."

The student made an energetic gesture as if he were quickly and powerfully shoving something through a narrow crevice. Seryozha was annoyed that he was dragging it out so long and speaking so incoherently.

"Do I have to ask forgiveness?" Seryozha asked.

The student cheered up. "Well, here's how it is. You sort of . . . I mean . . . just go out there and bow and scrape and kiss their hands."

"I'll even kiss their feet, it's all the same to me," the boy said sullenly.

"Well, that would, approximately, be excessive."

"And they won't whip me?" Seryozha inquired in a business-like tone.

The student smirked as if he had just heard about something very near and dear to him.

"They don't plan to," he answered, "but they should."

He would have liked to throw a scare into the boy, but he didn't dare: Seryozha's dark, spiteful eyes disconcerted him, and all Seryozha's words and actions seemed unexpected to him.

The boy stood there a little while more, thought about something vague and irrelevant, and set off for the parlor with a swaying gait. The student walked behind him and hoped the little brat wouldn't sass them any more. But everything worked out well.

When Seryozha entered the parlor, his mama, aunt, and cousin were all sitting and looking at him in silence, and his father, lanky and dressed all in gray, was standing by the fireplace, slightly smirking, indifferently and scornfully. Seryozha went up to his cousin, stopped in front of her, scraped his foot, and said in a flat voice, as if reciting a lesson learned by heart: "Forgive me, cousin, for sassing you."[5]

During this, his cheeks did not color at all. With cold eyes he looked into the affectedly benevolent face of his cousin, stood a little while more in front of her, then moved closer to her, bent, and kissed her hand with a movement that made it seem as if he were performing a ritual that was uninteresting to himself but done by convention. His cousin smiled sourly.

"I'm not angry," she said, "but it's bad for you if you get into the habit of behaving boorishly."

Seryozha again scraped his foot, and just as calmly turned to his mother and performed the same ritual with her that he had with his cousin. Mama said in a displeased voice: "If you hadn't been sassy, you wouldn't have to ask forgiveness."

Seryozha went up to his father. His father pretended to be stern and angry, but Seryozha knew that he didn't care, that he was a stranger.

"Well, little brat, so you've gotten into mischief again?" his father asked.

Seryozha frowned and realized that he didn't have to answer. His father thought for a moment and couldn't find any angry words, which made him angry, and he laughed with annoyance.

"Bedbug!" he said and pinched his son's cheek. "You'll end up getting what's coming to you, a real treat."

"Only not today, please," Seryozha said seriously, rubbing his cheek, on which a red spot had appeared.

"All right, go to your room," his father said gloomily.

Seryozha went out, but they kept the student back. Seryozha understood from this that they were going to talk about him again. He walked away a little bit, then quietly returned, hid behind the portière, and started listening.

"Did you see," Mama said in an exhausted, insincere voice, "how spitefully he asked forgiveness?"

"Who in your family does he take after in being so mean?" his cousin asked.

"It's nerves," his father growled angrily. "They treat the boy like a little girl, and he's become a nervous wreck."

"Oh, what do you mean 'nerves,'" his aunt suddenly said in a loud, coarse voice. "You've simply spoiled the boy. You should be stricter with him."

"Stricter how?" his father answered in a displeased voice. "Are we supposed to beat him?"

"Of course, it wouldn't hurt for you to give him a whipping every once in a while, it would be very good for him."

"That's impossible," his father said decisively and with annoyance, not because that was what he thought, but because he considered such a conversation with ladies to be unseemly, and he was ashamed of such coarse words in their presence.

"Why is it impossible?" his aunt rejoined with displeasure. "Don't worry, he won't get mussed up."

"Oh, I really don't understand this kind of talk," his father said irritably and immediately changed his tone and started talking about something else, in order to end this conversation that he didn't like. "Oh, I almost forgot, at Leonid Ivanovich's today I . . ."

Seryozha hurriedly walked away from the door, trying not to make any noise. He went into the garden. When he was walking past the kitchen, he heard Varvara laughing and telling the cook, "Well, our little squirt really gave the young lady what for!"

And Varvara told the cook what Seryozha had said, but added things and twisted it around, and they laughed resoundingly and coarsely. Seryozha walked on. He felt spiteful.

"They're laughing everywhere," he thought. "People can't help but laugh at each other."

He raised his eyes to the sky, but it was still covered by a whitish blueness. Seryozha sadly lowered his head and walked lazily along the garden paths.

At the very edge of the sandy path sat a small, unhealthy-looking frog. Seryozha found it disgusting.

Suddenly he had a naughty, mischievous idea. His dark eyes began to sparkle joyfully. He bent down and caught the frog in his hands. It was all slimy, and it was disgusting for Seryozha to hold it. This feeling of something slippery and repulsive crawled all over his body and tickled in his throat. Hurrying, and stumbling in his haste, he ran to the parlor. He father was no longer there, but the others were still sitting in the same places. All three of them looked at Seryozha with a contemptuous smirk. Seryozha went right up to his cousin.

"Look here," he said, "what a pretty thing I caught."

And he put the frog on his cousin's knees. His cousin squealed desperately and jumped up from her seat.

"A frog, a frog," she screamed, senselessly waving her arms.

Everyone panicked and jumped up from their seats, but Seryozha stood and looked at his cousin, who was screaming and sobbing hysterically. It seemed to Seryozha that she was faking, and he was ashamed for her.

"But it's harmless," he said, "it won't bite."

Seeing that no one was listening to him, he quietly turned and left the room. They didn't stop him, because the young lady had gone into hysterics, and Mama and his aunt were unlacing her corset and giving her water with medicinal drops in it.

Seryozha knew that now he would certainly be punished. But now he didn't care. He was a little dizzy and was being distracted by trifles. The portière under which he passed rippled, and its folds were dark, and it had certainly been hung solely in order to catch on his shorn head with its scratchy fabric. It was red and it remained behind him, and he went to his room.

In his room he sat down on the windowsill and looked into the garden with spiteful dark eyes. The trees were bright green with long twigs, sparrows were hopping, the sun was casting harsh spots onto the earth, and the yellow sand glittered harshly. Everything was coarse, and everything made Seryozha angry—and this made his heart ache, and he felt this just as distinctly as sometimes one clearly feels a pain in the hand or foot. Teasing and irritating his own spite, he started imagining what they were going to do to him: how they would scold him and shame him and how they would then start beating him. He was small and could fit on Varvara's lap; his head would hang down and his arms would be uncomfortable.

But it happened that they left Seryozha in peace for today. A rich, important landowner's wife came to visit Mama, and Mama was excessively happy about this. The lady was very gracious and sympathetic, so they told her about Seryozha, and she expressed a wish to see him. Seryozha scraped his foot before her in just the proper way, kissed her hand, and looked at her with attentive eyes. In Seryozha's eyes, she was big, coarse, and dark, wearing a showy, rustling dress; she smelled unpleasantly of perfume, with harsh scents that were somewhat unharmoniously mixed; and there was something extraneous on her face, powder or whitening. The lady wanted to smile at the boy, who was so short for his age, but his dark, attentive eyes and his pale, slightly swollen cheeks caused her to feel a vague unease, and she said to Seryozha's mother:

"Just leave him in peace—yes, leave him in peace. Let him play. He needs to grow up. It's all because he's too small for his age."

And they left Seryozha in peace, to the mercy of his muffled irritation, which tormented him without ceasing—as if last night's stars had poisoned him. He agonizingly awaited the evening, when again that luminous, heavy curtain with which the sun covers the stars would be removed.[6] And he got what he was waiting for.

IV.

They sent Seryozha to bed early. Today Mama was at home, and they didn't let Seryozha go into the garden in the evening, and because he had behaved badly, he wasn't allowed to stay with Mama. But he was happy when he was finally alone, undressed, in his bed. The day was over, the sun, that hot, coarse monster, was gone, and the night was quiet, and the stars were in the sky. He could admire them if he got up from his bed, ever so quietly went to the window, and moved the blind aside. He lolled in his bed, looked at the white blind, and quietly laughed, and his dark eyes burned joyfully.

The stars called to him with barely audible, delicate ringing. Seryozha threw back the blanket, lowered his feet to the floor, and listened. The rug under his feet was soft and warm. It felt nice to stand on it. Seryozha stretched, laughed quietly from joy, and ran up to the window—and the cold boards of the painted floor also made him happy. He moved the blind aside, knelt in front of the window, put his chin on the windowsill, and started looking at the clear stars with his twinkling dark eyes. In the uncertain light of the stars it seemed, because of the slight swelling of his pale cheeks, that there was a smile on his lips—but he was not smiling, although he was glad. He looked for a long time at the cold, clear stars, and through the windowpane he felt a breath of coldness and peace coming from them. His heart beat fast and joyfully in his chest, and he breathed gladly, hastily, as if something cold and joyful were being poured into his lungs. He wasn't thinking of anything—everything from the day left him like a dream.

The voices in the house and on the street fell silent. Seryozha got up, went over to the bed, and started getting dressed. He couldn't find his shoes; they had taken them away to be cleaned in the morning. But he knew that everyone was sleeping now and wouldn't see him. He went up to the window, got up onto the windowsill in order to open it, and climbed out into the garden, catching on the branches of the birch tree. Down below, on the earth, the moistness and cold of the July night enveloped him. He shuddered. But the stars were still looking at him. He raised to them his unattractive, pale face, joyfully laughed, and started running along the damp earth farther away from the house, to that same bench where he had looked at the stars the previous night. The branches of the bushes caught at him, and his feet felt damp and uncomfortable, and his heart was beating in his chest intensely, but he was hurrying. So much time had slipped by, and soon the sky would start to cloud over with a pale light, people would wake up, and the stars would grow sad.

He ran to the bench and lay down on it—and looking at the stars, he breathed heavily and didn't smile. He felt pain: his heart was pounding so hard in his chest that it echoed in his throat and temples with an unpleasant, harsh twitching. He peered at the stars and tried to calm down his heart this way. It started to quiet down from time to time, but then it would suddenly start thumping again, and he would feel pain. But when it quieted down and only lightly trembled in his chest, Seryozha felt an eerie, tremulous, happy feeling, and a pleasure he had never experienced before caused him to squeeze his lips firmly shut and stretched his lips into a pale, painful smile.

All these sensations kept him from devoting himself to the stars, and besides, a whole swarm of absurd, trivial recollections suddenly descended on him. They were tiresome. Seryozha tried to get rid of them but couldn't.

Here was his cousin in front of the mirror with a white powderpuff in her hands, sighing enviously. His father has a cigar in his mouth, and dark-blue smoke comes curling out of it. A street, dachas, red lights in the windows, droshkies are coming from the train station in an endless line, men in gray are riding in all the droshkies.[7] Seryozha is standing on a steamship pier and wants to tell people about the stars—but everyone is laughing at him.

A sharp pain in his chest penetrated the boy's whole body. Hazy, gray shadows ran past his eyes; something terrifying and faceless flashed from behind the bushes. Slowly, shivering all over, Seryozha got up from the bench. A delicate spiderweb touched his cheeks. The pale boy stood and peered with his dark eyes into the emptiness of the night.

Everything was quiet and peaceful. Seryozha turned toward the house. Its silent, attentive windows could be seen in the distance from behind the bushes, and Seryozha felt that it would be terrifying to go there, terrifying even to look there. He turned away from that house and lay down on the bench again.

He felt happy. His heart was calm, as if it wasn't even there in his chest. Seryozha listened to it. It was beating evenly, and there was only a slight tickle somewhere near it, but it was pleasant. Seryozha stopped thinking about his heart. All his recollections suddenly left and no longer kept the stars from moving closer.

And suddenly everything disappeared except the stars. It became utterly quiet, and the night got denser, moved closer to

Seryozha and listened along with him, but the stars were joyfully silent, and they shone, and they sparkled with shimmering fires. Their shining increased, and they circled sweetly and languorously, first slowly, then more and more rapidly. Seryozha looked down at their shining abyss from his height, and he wasn't frightened by the fact that now all these stars were gleaming and sparkling not up above, as before, but down below, under him. As they circled, they merged into clear arcs, their light blurred, as if a mild drowsiness had overtaken them. Someone spread a white canvas between them and Seryozha. Under the vaults of the canvas tent, a rosy-cheeked boy was saying something to Seryozha, and in Seryozha's hands was a prophetic, vivid bird.

"Look behind you!" the boy said.

Seryozha trustingly looked behind him. The boy grabbed the bird out of his hands and ran away. Seryozha felt that he was floating and rocking. The lilac branch above him started floating together with him. Again he felt eerie and joyful. The stars rang quietly and tenderly above him. Then their sounds became plaintive.

A chill passed over Seryozha's body, from head to foot.

"Escape! Come to us!" the stars whispered in alarm.

The bench on which Seryozha was lying pushed him and tried to throw him off. The wind blew—and suddenly terrifying sounds rose up everywhere in the trees.

Seryozha jumped to his feet. His heart was trembling as if it had grown wings. The earth swayed under his feet. Something disgusting and terrifying was coming close to him along the ground, something supple, with bright green eyes, and it screamed horribly and harshly. Behind Seryozha's back someone was laughing frantically in a coarse human voice. Above the chaos of the coarse, spiteful sounds that rose up all around Seryozha and deafened him, the stars rang joyfully and invitingly. Their voices were quiet, but Seryozha heard them distinctly. And in the air a sticky, delicate spiderweb floated and fell onto Seryozha's cheeks; amid the general tumult and noise it alone was silent, and this silence of the sticky spiderweb was the most terrifying thing of all.

Seryozha didn't know what he should do to escape this noise and this spiderweb. Anguish squeezed his heart. He started running, staggering, stumbling, and crying, not knowing himself where he should run. His legs got heavy, and his heart pounded in his chest with an excruciating rumbling, and everything around him was thundering and gnashing.

Seryozha ran into the dark trunk of a birch, leaned on it with his hands, jumped away, staggering backward, and stopped, swaying on his weakened legs and whispering in anguish: "What should I do? What should I do?"

His heart contracted with a terrifying pain that convulsed his entire body—and suddenly the pain and anguish disappeared. A quiet, tender joy nestled up to Seryozha. He felt that someone was breathing a cold breath onto him and leaning him with his back to the earth. Again beneath him, far below, the clear, quiet stars started to shine. Seryozha spread out his arms, pushed off from the earth with his palms, and with a loud, harsh cry, like the shrill voice of a night bird, he hastened joyfully from the dark earth to the clear stars. The stars started circling joyfully and ringing harmoniously and loudly, and they rushed to meet him, spreading open their golden wings. A huge, gentle angel put his white wing up to his chest, tenderly embraced him, and closed his eyes with a light hand. And in his embraces Seryozha forgot about everything forever.

Early in the morning they found him in the damp grass by the fence. He lay with his arms spread out, with his face turned to the sky. Near his mouth, on his pale cheek that seemed to be swollen with a smile, there was a dark trickle of dried blood. His eyes were closed, his face was unchildishly calm, he was all cold and dead.

1896

BEAUTY

I.

In the austere silence of the declining day, Elena was sitting alone, upright and motionless, her bare, slender hands on her knees. Without bending her head, she was weeping; large, slow tears rolled down her face, and her dark eyes glimmered faintly.

She had buried her tenderly beloved mother that day, and since people's noisy sorrow and coarse sympathy were disgusting to her, she had refrained from crying at the funeral, as well as before and after it, as she listened to words of consolation. She had now been left alone, in her white chamber, where everything was virginally pure and austere, and sad thoughts drew quiet tears from her eyes.

Elena's dress, austere and black, lay sadly on her, as if while clothing Elena on her day of woe her indifferent garments could not help but reflect her beclouded soul. Elena recalled her late mother, and knew that her previous peaceful, clear, and austere life had died forever. Before the new life was to begin, Elena was commemorating the past with cold tears and motionless melancholy.

Her mother was not yet old when she died. She was as lovely as a goddess of the ancient world. All her movements were slow and majestic. Her face seemed to be imbued with melancholy daydreams about something that had been lost forever or something desired and unattainable. A languid pallor, the sibyl of death, had spread over her face long ago. It seemed as if a great fatigue was inclining that lovely body toward its final rest. White hairs became more noticeable among the black hair on her head, and it was strange for Elena to think that her mother would soon be an old woman . . .

Elena got up, went to the window, and slowly moved the heavy curtain aside, so as to disperse the twilight, which she didn't like. But from there as well, from outside, the gray, dull half-light wearied her gaze, and Elena again sat down in her place, and patiently awaited the black night, and wept slow, cold tears.

Finally, night came on, a light was brought into the room, and Elena again went up to the window. Dense darkness enveloped the street. The poor, coarse objects of boring everyday life were hidden in the black covering of night, and there was something solemn in this sad blackness. Opposite the window where Elena was standing, one could dimly see on the other side of the street, by the light of the sparse streetlamps, the little red-brick house of the blacksmith. The streetlamps stood far from it, and it seemed black.

Suddenly a huge red spark slowly passed from the open smithy to the gates, and the gloom around it seemed to thicken: the blacksmith was carrying a piece of red-hot iron along the street. A sudden joy was ignited in Elena's soul and caused her to start laughing quietly. Her ringing, joyful laughter passed through the space of the silent chamber.

And when the blacksmith had gone by and the red spark was hidden in the gloom, Elena was amazed at her sudden joy and amazed that it was still playing in her soul, tenderly and tremblingly. Why does this joy arise, where does it come from, drawing laughter from the chest and igniting fires in the eyes that were just now weeping? Was it not beauty that caused this joy and excitement? And was not any appearance of beauty joyful?[1]

It passed in the gloom, momentary, born out of coarse materiality, and it was extinguished, just as beauty ought to appear and pass by, giving joy and not satiating the gaze with its bright, transient brilliance.

Elena went out into the darkened parlor where it smelled faintly of jasmine and vanilla, and opened the grand piano; solemn, simple melodies flowed from under her fingers, and her hands moved slowly over the white and black keys.

II.

Elena liked to be alone among the lovely objects in her rooms, where the color white predominated in the decor; light, faint fragrances wafted in the air; and it was so easy and joyful to daydream about beauty. Everything here wafted fragrances that could barely be distinguished: Elena's clothes smelled of roses and violets, the drapery smelled of white acacias; flowering hyacinths poured out their sweet, languorous smells.[2] There were a lot of books: Elena read a lot, but only carefully selected, austere creations.

It was oppressive for Elena to be with people. People tell untruths, flatter, get excited, express their feelings in an exaggerated, unpleasant way. There is a lot about people that is absurd and ludicrous: they conform to fashion, use foreign words for some reason, they have vain desires. Elena was reticent with people and could not love a single one of those that she met. There was only one person who was worthy of love—her mother, because she was calm, lovely, and truthful. Elena wanted all people to someday become that way, to understand that there is one goal in life—beauty—and to arrange a worthy, wise life for themselves.

The lamps were lit. Their light poured out, motionlessly clear and white. It smelled of roses and almonds. Elena was alone.

She locked the door, lit candles in front of the mirror, and slowly laid bare her lovely body.

All white and calm, she stood in front of the mirror and looked at her reflection. Flickers from the lamps and the candles ran over her skin and gave Elena joy. Tender as a just opened lily with soft, still crumpled little leaves, she stood, and a sinless scarlet spread over her virginal body. It seemed that the sweet-bitter almond smell wafting in the air was coming from her nude body. An ambrosial excitement made her languid, and not a single impure thought outraged her virginal imagination. And she daydreamed about tender, sinless kisses, quiet as the touch of a midday wind, and joyful as dreams of bliss.

The bared beauty of Elena's tender body was joyful for her. Elena laughed, and her quiet laughter rang out in the solemn silence of her imperturbable chamber.

Elena lay chest-down on the carpet and inhaled the faint smell of mignonette. Here, down below, from where it was strange to look at the lower parts of objects, she felt even more cheerful and joyful. Like a tiny little girl, she laughed, rolling around on the soft carpet.

III.

For many days in a row, every evening, Elena admired her own beauty in front of the mirror, and she never got tired of it. Everything was white in her upper room—and amid this whiteness, the scarlet and yellow tones of her body glimmered, recalling the tenderest shades of nacre and pearls.

Elena raised her arms over her head, raised herself up a little, and stretched, bent, and swayed on her taut legs. The tender suppleness of her body exhilarated her. She felt joyful as she saw how the strong muscles of her lovely legs tensed resiliently under the tender skin.

Nude, she moved about the room, she stood, she lay down; and all her positions, all her slow movements were lovely. She rejoiced in her beauty, and spent long hours bared, sometimes daydreaming and admiring herself, sometimes reading pages by lovely, austere poets . . .

A white, fragrant liquid lay in a hammered silver amphora: Elena had mixed perfumes and milk in the amphora. Elena slowly raised the bowl and tipped it over her high breasts. The white, redolent drops fell quietly on her scarlet skin, which flinched from their touch. The ambrosial smell of lilies of the valley and apples arose. The fragrances embraced Elena in a light, tender cloud . . .

Elena let down her long black hair and sprinkled it with red poppy flowers. Then a white rope of flowers embraced her supple figure and caressed her skin. And these fragrant flowers were lovely on the bared beauty of her fragrant body.

Then she took the flowers off and again gathered her hair into a high knot, clothed her body in fine raiment, and fastened the garment on her left shoulder with a golden clasp.

She had made this raiment for herself out of fine linen, so no one had ever seen it.

Elena lay down on a low couch, and ambrosial daydreams passed through her head: dreams about sinless caresses, about innocent kisses, about unashamed round-dances on meadows drenched in ambrosial dew, under clear skies where a gentle, blessed heavenly body shone.

She looked at her bared legs. The undulating lines of her shins and thighs came running softly out from under the folds of her short dress. The tender yellowish and scarlet tones on her skin next to the monotonously yellowish whiteness of the linen brought joy to her eyes. The prominent edges of the little bones in her knees and feet, and the dimples next to them—Elena examined it all lovingly and joyfully and felt it with her hands, and this gave her a new delight.

IV.

One evening, Elena forgot to lock the door before taking her clothes off. She was standing bared in front of the mirror, her arms raised above her head.

Suddenly the door opened a little bit. In the narrow opening, a head appeared. It was her maid Makrina looking in, a comely lass with an obliging and sly expression on her ruddy face. Elena caught sight of her in the mirror. This was so unexpected. Elena could not conceive what she should do or say, and she stood there motionless. Makrina immediately disappeared just as noiselessly as she had appeared. It was possible to imagine that she had not even come up to the door, that it was just an illusion.

Elena felt annoyed and ashamed. Although she had hardly had time to cast a glance at Makrina, it seemed to her that she had seen an impure smile flash across Makrina's face. Elena hurriedly went to the door and locked it. Then she lay down on the low, soft couch and pondered sad, vague thoughts . . .

Annoying suspicions unfolded within her . . .

What would Makrina say about her? Now, of course, she had gone to the servants' quarters and was telling the cook about it in a whisper, with a nasty laugh. A wave of shamefaced horror passed through Elena. She recalled the cook Malanya, a ruddy, cheerful young wench with a sly snicker . . .

What was Makrina saying now? It seemed that someone was whispering Makrina's words into Elena's ears: "And I see through the crack—the young mistress is standing in front of the mirror butt-naked—and she's all stretched up to the darn ceiling."

"You don't say!" Malanya exclaims.

"Swear to God!" Makrina says. "She's all naked, and she's showing it all off, just showing it off—and she turns this way and that . . ."

Makrina stamps in place, imitating her young mistress, and both women shout with laughter. The lewd, coarse words resounded with mercilessly vile clarity; these words and the coarse laughter of the maid and the cook caused Elena's face to be covered with the burning ruddiness of shame and insult.

She felt shame through her whole body. It flowed through her like a flame, like an illness that consumes the body. Elena lay motionless for a long time, in a kind of strange, dull perplexity. Then she began putting her clothes on slowly, knitting her brow, as if trying to solve some kind of difficult question, and attentively inspecting herself in the mirror.

V.

During the following days, Makrina behaved as if she hadn't seen anything that day and hadn't even passed by the door, and this pretending of hers irritated Elena. For this reason, everything about Makrina, which had been there before but Elena hadn't noticed, now became disgusting to her. It was unpleasant to get dressed and undressed in Makrina's presence, to accept her services, to listen to her sycophantic words, which before had been lost in the prattling sounds of the streams of water splashing over Elena's body, but now struck her hearing.

And for the very first time, when Makrina started talking the way she had before, Elena really listened to her words and gave free rein to her irritation.

In the morning, when Elena was getting into the bathtub, Makrina, supporting her by the elbow, said with a sycophantic smile: "Who wouldn't fall in love with a cutie like you! Maybe some guy who doesn't even have eyes, he's the only one who wouldn't notice you. What arms, what legs!"

Elena turned red.

"Please stop," she said sharply.

Makrina glanced at her with surprise, lowered her eyes, and then—or did it only seem so to Elena?—smirked slightly. And this smirk irritated Elena even more, but she regained control of herself and kept silence . . .

Obstinately, without her previous rejoicing, with evil thoughts and fears, Elena continued every day to lay bare her lovely body and look at herself in the mirror. She did it even more frequently than before, not only in the evening by the light of the lamps, but in the daytime, with the curtains drawn. Now she no longer forgot to lower the portiéres so that no one could peep at her or eavesdrop on her from outside, and as she did this, shame made all her movements awkward.

Now Elena's body did not seem as lovely to her as it had before. She found flaws in this body—she sought them out diligently. She imagined something disgusting about it, an evil that was corroding and dishonoring her beauty, a kind of incrustation, a spiderweb or slimy film, which was disgusting and impossible to shake off.

It often seemed to Elena that someone's alien, terrible gaze lay on her bared body. Although no one was looking at her, it seemed to her that the whole room was looking at her, and this made her feel ashamed and creepy.

If it was in the daytime, it would seem to Elena that the light was shameless, and it was peeping its sharp rays through a crack in the curtains and laughing. If it was evening, eyeless shadows were looking at her from the corners and moving unsteadily, and their movements, which were produced by the trembling light of the candles, seemed to Elena to be a soundless laughter at her. It was terrible to think about this soundless laughter, and Elena tried in vain to convince herself that these were ordinary, inanimate, insignificant shadows. Their shuddering hinted at an alien, unseemly, mocking life.

Sometimes there would suddenly arise in her imagination someone's face, flabby, fat, with rotten teeth, and this face was looking at her lustfully with small, disgusting eyes.

And on her own face Elena sometimes saw in the mirror something impure and disgusting and could not understand what it was.

She thought about this for a long time and felt that it didn't just seem that way, but that something nasty was being born in her, in the secret places of her saddened soul, at the same time as in her body, bared and white, a burning wave of trembling, passionate excitement rose up ever higher.

Horror and disgust tormented her.

And Elena understood that she could not live with all this darkness in her soul. She thought, "Is it possible to live when there are coarse, dirty thoughts? No matter if they are not mine, if they were not born in me—did not these thoughts become my own the moment I learned of them? And isn't everything on earth mine, and isn't everything bound together by unbreakable ties?"

VI.

In Elena's parlor sat Resnitsyn, a young man, fashionably dressed, a bit flaccid, but quite in love with himself and confident about his own merits. Today his compliments were having no success with

Elena, which was no different from before, by the way. But before, she would lend him her attention with that general, impersonal goodwill that is customary for people of so-called "good society." Now she was cold and silent.

Resnitsyn felt thrown off balance, and so he got angry and fiddled nervously with his monocle. He would have been quite willing to call Elena his fiancée, and her coldness seemed like rudeness to him. But Elena was more wearied than ever by his conversation, with its frivolous flitting from one subject to the next. She herself always spoke succinctly and precisely, and all human circumlocution oppressed her. But people were almost all like that—dissolute, disorderly.

Elena looked calmly and attentively at Resnitsyn, as if finding in him some kind of sad correspondence with her bitter thoughts. She surprised him by asking, "Do you love people?"

Resnitsyn smirked carelessly, with a look of intellectual superiority, and said, "I myself am a person."

"But do you love yourself?" Elena asked again.

He shrugged his narrow shoulders, smirked sarcastically, and said in an affectedly polite tone, "Have people failed to please you? In what regard, will you permit me to ask?"

It was obvious that he felt offended on behalf of people by the fact that Elena was admitting the possibility of not loving them.

"Is it really possible to love people?" Elena asked.

"Why is it impossible?" he asked in amazement.

"They don't love themselves," Elena said coldly, "and there's no reason to. They do not understand the one thing that is worthy of love—they do not understand beauty. They have vulgar thoughts about beauty, so vulgar that you become ashamed of having been born on this earth. You don't want to live here."

"But you do live here!" Resnitsyn said.

"Where else can I live!" Elena said coldly.

"Where are people any better?" Resnitsyn asked.

"They're the same everywhere," Elena answered, and a light, contemptuous smirk flashed on her lips.

Resnitsyn did not understand. This conversation embarrassed him, it seemed unseemly and strange. He hastened to make his good-byes and leave.

VII.

The day was declining. Elena was alone.

In the quiet air of her chamber, the vanilla smell of heliotrope did not blend in with the honeyed fragrance of bird-cherry and the sweet aromas of roses, and it tried to overcome them.

"To build life according to the ideals of goodness and beauty! With these people and this body!" Elena thought bitterly. "It's impossible! How can one lock oneself away from human vulgarity, how can one protect oneself from people! We all live together, and it is as though a single soul languishes in all the diverse forms of humanity. The whole world is in me. But it is terrifying that it is the way it is—and as soon as you understand, you see that it ought not exist, because it reposes in vice and evil. You have to condemn it to death, and yourself along with it."

Elena's yearning eyes rested on a shining object, a beautiful toy that had been thrown onto the table.

"How simple it is!" she thought. "Look, all you need is this knife."

A thin, gilt dagger, the kind that are sometimes used for cutting the pages of books, with a hilt decorated with skillful carving and a double-edged blade, lay on her desk. Elena picked it up and admired it for a long time. She had bought it not long ago, not because she needed it—no, her eye had been caught by the strange, intricate pattern of carving on the hilt.

"A lovely instrument of death," she thought and smiled. Her smile was calm and joyful, and the thoughts that passed through her head were clear and cold.

She stood up, and the dagger gleamed in her lowered, bared hand, on the folds of her greenish-yellow dress. She went to her bedchamber and lay the dagger on the pillows with its blade toward the head of the bed. Then she put on a white dress that smelled languidly and ambrosially of roses, took up the dagger again and lay down with it on the bed, on top of the white blanket. Her white shoes rested on the foot of the bed. She lay there for a few minutes motionlessly, with closed eyes, listening to the quiet voice of her thoughts. Everything in her was clear and calm, and only a dark contempt for the world and for earthly life tormented her.

And now—it was as if someone had peremptorily told her that her hour had come. Slowly and powerfully she plunged the dagger into her breast up to its hilt, right into her evenly beating heart— and quietly died. Her pale hand unclenched and fell onto her breast, next to the dagger's hilt.

1899

IN CAPTIVITY

I.

Paka was sitting in the tall garden pavilion by the fence of his dacha and looking into the field. It happened that he had been left alone. This did not happen often. Paka had a governess, he had a university student who taught him a few elementary subjects, and he had his mama, who although she wasn't constantly in his nursery—after all, she had a lot of those unbearable society obligations and relationships—nevertheless took very good care of Paka. She took care that he was cheerful, kind, courteous, didn't go near any dangers or strange bad little boys, and associated only with children of the families in their circle. And therefore, Paka was almost constantly under supervision. He had gotten used to this and didn't make any attempts to get free. Besides, he was so small: he was only seven years old.

Sometimes in the morning or the afternoon, when Mama was still sleeping or had already left the house, the governess and the student would suddenly discover some urgent matters they had to discuss privately. And it was at such moments that Paka was left alone. He was so quiet and obedient that they were not at all afraid to leave him alone: he would not go off anywhere and would surely not do anything he wasn't supposed to. He would sit and occupy himself with something or other. He was a very accommodating little boy.

Since he was not being distracted by his instructors, Paka became lost in thought and started comparing. The demon of comparison is a very petty demon, but one of the most dangerous.[1] He doesn't tie himself to strong people—he wouldn't have any luck with them—but he loves to tempt little ones. And his temptations for the small and the weak are irresistible.

Today, on a hot summer day, Paka felt an annoyance that was new for him. New desires were tormenting him. He knew that these desires were incapable of fulfillment. He felt unhappy and offended.

He wanted to go out of this sedate home into the broad, free field, and to play with other kids there. To be on the river, to go into the water.

Out there, down below, by the river, there were some boys. They were fishing and shouting something joyful. They truly had a better life than Paka. Why was his lot so different from the lot of these free and cheerful children? Did his darling mama really want him to pine and sorrow here? That could not be.

The burning sun sent a wave of heat over him and made his thoughts grow dim. Strange daydreams swarmed in Paka's head . . .

Darling Mama is far, far away, in another land. Paka is in captivity. He is a prince who has been deprived of his inheritance. An evil sorcerer has taken away his crown, acceded to the throne in his kingdom, and imprisoned Paka under the supervision of an enchantress. And the evil fairy has taken on the form of his darling mommy.

It was strange that Paka didn't guess earlier or understand that it was not Mama but an evil fairy. Was his darling mama really like that before, in the happy years, when they lived in the castle of their proud ancestors?

Far, far away!

Paka's sad eyes looked mournfully at the road.

The boys were walking by. There were three of them. The same ones who had been on the river just now. One was wearing a white smock, and the other two were wearing dark-blue sailor's shirts and short pants. Now he could see bows and quivers full of arrows slung over their shoulders.

Lucky boys! Paka thought. Strong and bold. Their feet were bare and tanned. They must be peasant boys. But they were lucky, nevertheless. After all, it's better to be a peasant boy in freedom than a prince in captivity.

But now Paka saw a *gimnazia* badge on the eldest boy's peaked cap, and he was surprised.[2]

The boys came up close. Paka said timidly, "Hello."

The boys raised their eyes to him and burst out laughing at something. The eldest, who had the badge and the white smock, said: "Hey there, little gnat, how're you doing?"

Paka smiled slightly and said, "I'm not a gnat."

"Well then, who are you?" the *gimnazia* student asked.

"I'm a captive prince," Paka confessed trustingly.

The kids stared at Paka in surprise.

"Why are you armed like that?" Paka asked.

"We are free hunters," the second boy said proudly.

"Red Indians?" Paka asked.[3]

"How did you find that out?" the smallest of the barefoot kids asked in surprise.

Paka smiled.

"Oh, I don't know," he said. "Is your father a Red Indian too?"

"No, our father is a captain," the eldest answered.

"Then you're bad Red Indians. What are your names?" Paka continued asking with the courteousness of a well-brought-up boy who is accustomed to keeping up his side of a conversation.

"I'm Levka," the *gimnazia* student said, "and these are my brothers Antoshka and Lyoshka."

"And I'm Paka," the captive said and extended his small white hand to the brothers down below.

They shook his hand and again burst out laughing.

"Why do you laugh all the time?" Paka asked.

"What do you want us to do, cry?" Antoshka answered him with a question.

"What does 'Paka' mean? What kind of name is that?" asked little Lyoshka.

"I am a prince," Paka repeated. "If I were a peasant boy, I'd be called Pavel."

"So that's how it is!" Lyoshka drawled.

The boys fell silent and looked at each other. Paka inspected them with curiosity and envy.

Levka was about twelve years old, with reddish, close-cropped hair, cheerful, kind eyes, and soft lips. His face was sprinkled with freckles. He had a rather broad, slightly upturned nose. He was a nice kid. Antoshka, about ten years old, and Lyoshka, about nine, were fairly close copies of their older brother, but they looked even more tender and kind. Antoshka smiled, squinted slightly, and looked very attentively at his conversation partner. Lyoshka's eyes were wide open, with a habitual expression of surprise and curiosity. They all tried to seem like brave lads, and for this reason they always went barefoot in the summer, fixed up a burrow in the woods, and cooked and roasted their food there.

Paka sighed slightly and said quietly: "You are lucky. You walk around in freedom. And I'm sitting here in captivity."

"How did you end up in captivity?" Lyoshka asked, looking at Paka with curious, wide-open eyes.

"Well, I myself don't really know," Paka answered. "Mama and I used to live in a castle. It was lots of fun. But an evil fairy, our distant relative, got angry at Mommy because Mommy didn't invite her to my christening, and then one night she carried me away on a flying carpet while I was asleep, and then she herself turned into Mommy. But she isn't Mommy. And I'm in captivity."

"You don't say! What an evil witch," Antoshka said. "Does she beat you?"

Paka turned red.

"Oh, no," he said, "how could she! And she's not a witch but an evil fairy. But she's a very well-brought-up fairy and never forgets herself. No, they don't beat me—how could they!" Paka repeated, his thin little shoulders shuddering at the thought that he could be beaten. "But they guard me, Mademoiselle and the student."

"Arguses?" Levka asked.

"Yes, Arguses," Paka repeated. "Two Arguses," he repeated once more, smiling, because he liked that word, and now he could use it to unite the two of them, Mademoiselle and the student.[4]

"And they never let you go into the field?" Lyoshka asked, looking at Paka with mournful sympathy.

"No, they don't let me go alone," Paka said.

"Well, you should escape and hightail it out of here," Antoshka advised.

"No," Paka said, "I can't hightail it out of here—the Arguses would immediately see me and bring me back."

"You're in a bad way," Levka pronounced, "but we'll free you."

"Oh!" Paka exclaimed with mistrust and rapture, clasping his hands prayerfully.

"Honest to God, we'll free you," Antoshka repeated.

"But for now, good-bye, we don't have any time," Levka said.

And the boys said good-bye to Paka and left. They started running ever so fast along the narrow path and disappeared into the bushes. Paka looked after them, and indistinct hopes excited him, and daydreams about his distant mommy, who was looking for Paka and couldn't find him, and who cried inconsolably because her darling Pakochka wasn't with her.

II.

As they left, the brothers talked about Paka.

"I'd like to get a look at that evil fairy," Lyoshka said, "and see what she looks like."

"Fairy! She's just a witch," Antoshka corrected him.

"Of course, she's a witch," Levka confirmed.

"But how can we free him?" Lyoshka asked.

The whole world appeared to little, curious Lyoshka from its interrogative side. Lyoshka was curious about everything, was always pestering everyone with questions, and believed every answer he got with simple-hearted faith. Antoshka loved to fantasize and devise more or less daring projects. And Levka, as the eldest, either approved or rejected these suppositions, and the brothers submitted to his decisions without question.

Antoshka said, "To combat a witch, you have to know a magic word."

"What word?" Lyoshka asked quickly.

The boys fell to thinking and walked along in silence for several minutes. Suddenly Antoshka shouted: "I know!"

"Well?" Levka asked, looking mistrustfully at Antoshka.

Somewhat embarrassed by the gazes fixed on him by both of his brothers, Antoshka said, "I think the peasants know this word. They have a lot of sorcerers in their villages. And all the village peasant men and women are always getting mad at each other, they put the evil eye on each other, and so that they themselves won't get the evil eye, they're always saying these incomprehensible words. They'll say something about their mother and then utter a word like that."

Levka thought for a moment and said, "Maybe you're right. Those are their winged words."[5]

III.

The next morning the three boys, while messing around by the river, kept looking at the fence of Paka's dacha. When Paka's blond head appeared above the fence, and it was evident that the boy was again alone in his tower, the kids picked up their fishing poles and started running up the path.

"Hi there, captive," Lyoshka said.

"Captive prince," Antoshka corrected him.

"Prince Paka, the little gawker," Levka said.

Paka, smiling guardedly, shook hands with them.

"Why don't you Red Indian hunters put on moccasins?" he asked.

The boys laughed. Antoshka said, "What's wrong with these fleet feet? They're made out of our own skin. At our dacha we have a rule that you're not allowed to get the sofas dirty with your boots, so we don't put our boots on."

"And I'm not allowed to walk barefoot on the sand," Paka said.

"Why should you!" Levka said. "Your shell is thinner than cigarette paper. But we've come to see you on business. We want to free you from the evil fairy. You know, un-enchant you. You let us know when it's most convenient for us to do it."

Paka smiled mistrustfully. Yesterday, after the first joy of hope, when Mademoiselle and the student came back to him, and then

Mama—the evil fairy—and the whole domestic way of life drew near with its adamantine order, the castle of the evil fairy seemed to the captive Paka to be so durable, so unshakable, that his heart contracted mournfully, and the darling, joyful hope turned pale and quietly melted away like the fog over a valley as day sets in. He said to the brothers: "You won't be able to do it."

"Yes, we will," Lyoshka answered ardently.

And Levka told him: "We learned the right words. We went to the village on purpose, we found the oldest sorcerer, we paid him to teach us, and we learned all the words you have to say, we learned them cold."

"What words are those?" Paka asked.

Levka whistled. Antoshka said, "You aren't allowed to know such words."

"You're still too little for that," Lyoshka said.

Levka said to Paka: "You tell us when your witch is going to be home—oh, you know, that fairy who has you in captivity," he corrected himself when he noticed a displeased grimace on Paka's face at the word "witch." "We'll go up under the window," Levka continued, and we'll say the winged words, and all the sorcery will disappear just like that, and you will be freed."

"And Mama will come back?" Paka asked.

"Well, we'll see what happens," Levka answered. "Of course, if all her sorcery disappears, that means you'll be back where you were when she took you."

Paka was silent for a moment and said, "We have dinner at seven o'clock."

And he suddenly felt eerie—both afraid and joyful.

"So we'll come at seven o'clock?" Lyoshka asked.

"No," Paka said, smiling slyly and bashfully, "better come a little later, about eight o'clock, after dessert, otherwise wherever Mama is they might have already eaten their dinner, and I won't get dessert."[6]

The barefoot kids burst out laughing.

"Oh, you Prince Pashka-Candyman," Antoshka said, "you do like your sweets."

"I do," Paka confessed.

The boys said good-bye and left.

IV.

At home—not at home at their dacha, but in their own dwelling in the forest, in a ravine, in a burrow under the roots of a tree that had been toppled by a storm—at home they held a consultation about how to carry out the enterprise they had planned. There was no sense in putting it off. They decided to do it this very day.

Antoshka had the idea that for greater strength they should not only say the words but also write them on arrows and shoot the arrows through the windows of the witch's dacha.

Levka assigned the roles: "We'll creep up under the windows and wait. When we see that Paka has eaten his dessert, we'll start shouting."

"All at once?" Lyoshka asked.

"No, of course not, they all have to be able to clearly make out the words. First I'll say them in the past tense, because I've already been the kind of little kid you are. Then, Antoshka, you'll shout in the present tense, because you're a little kid now, and then you, Lyoshka, shout in the future tense—you'll be as big as me some day. And each of us will write these same words on our own arrow."

"We should make black arrows," Antoshka said.

"That goes without saying," Levka agreed.

"We should write with our blood," Antoshka continued.

Levka approved of this as well.

"Well, of course," he said. "You don't write words like these in ink, after all."

V.

Paka was very excited. His whole fate was going to change on that day. He would return to Mommy. Which mommy? The evil fairy had taken on the guise of his mommy. So that means the same mommy. Only a really, really kind one, she'll play with her little boy all the time, and when her boy wants to go to the river, she'll let him go play with the other cheerful, tanned kids.

But Paka did have to admit that the evil fairy, although she was evil, was always gracious to him all the same. She kept him in captivity, but she apparently remembered that he was a prince. She even kissed him and caressed him sometimes. So she must have gotten used to him. When Paka got free from her, the evil fairy would be very angry. Or would she be sad? Maybe she would miss Paka? Would she cry?

Paka started feeling doleful. Couldn't the matter be settled peacefully? The evil fairy could make peace with Mommy, renounce her sorcery, and then she could even live with them. He needed to have a talk with the evil fairy and warn her. Maybe she would even repent all by herself.

When the student finished doing a problem with him and invited him to go into the garden, Paka announced that he needed to go see Mama. And he set off—to see the evil fairy.

The evil fairy was alone. She was expecting guests for dinner and was lying on a very beautiful, very soft couch and reading a little book with a yellow cover.[7] She was young and beautiful. Dark hair, languid movements. Dark eyes with a burning gaze. Plump, half-exposed, very beautiful arms. She was always dressed becomingly.

"Oh, my little one," she said, reluctantly tearing herself away from her book. "What can I do for you?"

Paka kissed her hand, looked at her indecisively, and said, "I need to have a discussion with you."

The evil fairy laughed.

"To have a discussion?" she asked. "Why so formal?"

Paka reddened. "Well, just to talk, Mommy. I really need it."

Laughing, squinting her shining eyes, and covering her laughing mouth with her book, the evil fairy said, "Sit down and have a talk, little one. What were you doing just now?"

"I was solving a problem with him," Paka answered.

"Oh, with him!"

The evil fairy wanted to say that this was impolite, that he should say the student's name, but she was already bored, and she said, "Well, Paka, tell me what you need."

Paka turned bright red and said, nervously wringing his hands, "I know everything."

The evil fairy started laughing cheerfully, irrepressibly, and resoundingly.

"Oh, really!" she exclaimed. "So young, and you know everything. You are a phenomenon, Paka, if this is true."

"No, Mama," Paka rejoined meekly, "I'm not a phenomenon, I'm just a prince who's been taken captive by you."

"Oh!" the evil fairy exclaimed, stopped laughing, and looked at Paka with surprise. "We're having fantasies!" she said in amazement.

Paka continued just as meekly: "I also know, darling fairy, that you are not Mama but an evil fairy. You are a very gracious personage, but please don't be angry, I know nevertheless that you are an evil fairy."

"My God!" the evil fairy exclaimed. "Who's been filling your head with these marvelous fairy tales? Come a little closer, my little one."

Paka approached fearfully, and the evil fairy felt his head and hands.

"Are you ill?" she asked.

"No, darling fairy," Paka said affectionately, kissing the evil fairy's small, white, tender hands, "but please let me go free."

"Go free?" the fairy asked.

"Yes," Paka continued, "I want to hightail it off to the river."

"Oh! To hightail it!" the fairy repeated in horror. "For the love of God, Paka, how can you use such words!"

But without listening, Paka continued: "To play with the boys. There are some great kids out there. But without the Arguses, please."

"Without the Arguses?" the evil fairy asked and laughed again. "Oh, you little dreamer! Somebody's given us too many fairy stories, little Paka, and everything's gotten all mixed up in our head. But Arguses—I like that one, truly. Tell your Arguses to come see me. We have to calm this down somehow."

Paka left.

"She's cunning!" he thought. "She doesn't get angry, but it's obvious she won't let me go free. They gave me too many fairy tales to read! She herself is constantly reading such long fairy tales in French in those yellow books! Apparently not everything in a fairy tale is a fairy tale, but some of it is true, if even adults like to read fairy tales."

VI.

Now it was already evening and starting to get dark. The cheerful lamps had been lit, dinner was coming to an end, to the most interesting part: they were serving dessert, meringue with wild strawberries and cream. There were guests, men and ladies, about ten people, but since they were all either relatives—Paka's uncle and his daughters and some other female cousins—or people who were planning to marry into the family, as well as close friends, the table was set family-style, and Paka was sitting with the adults, at the end of the table, opposite the evil fairy, between his Arguses.

The evil fairy told the guests about Pakochka's fantasy, and they were making fun of Paka and his Arguses. Paka smiled: he knew that he was right, and he liked this meringue. But the Arguses were very uncomfortable, and although they smiled and sometimes even laughed it off, Mademoiselle's ears were glowing, and there were some notes of annoyance in the student's voice. Before dinner, the evil fairy had spoken with them very sweetly and cheerfully about their lack of supervision: Paka's fantasies, the horrible expression "hightail it," where did that come from? the evil fairy wondered. She was very gracious, but somehow it turned out that the Arguses left her feeling they had gotten a severe rebuke.

Now, hardly had Paka managed to finish his dessert when a black wooden arrow with some faint reddish writing on it flew through the open window of the dining room with a slight rustling and whistling and fell onto the white tablecloth. And at the same time, outside the window, a child's voice shouted out a stream of foul language.

"It's started!" Paka thought.

He jumped up, trembling all over, and looked at the evil fairy with timorous impatience. The evil fairy, like the other ladies and young girls, was frightened by the unexpected event. The dinner guests could be heard exclaiming, but before anyone had the idea of going up to the window, a second arrow flew in and pierced a bouquet of flowers on the table, and another child's voice could be heard shouting nasty words. A third arrow landed on the student's uniform, a third voice resoundingly shouted hideous words, and then in the garden could be heard laughter, the rustle of steps receding into the distance, and the shouts of the servants—someone was running away, someone was trying to catch them.

And all this lasted less than a minute. When the men finally rushed to the windows, in the dim light of the sunset they saw three kids nimbly running away, already outside the garden fence.

"They won't catch them," Paka's uncle said. "Now there's a graphic explanation for you of the expression 'hightail it.'"

And everyone looked at Paka. He was standing, looking around, and marveling. Everything remained in place, the stupid boys had deceived him, they weren't able to free him from captivity.

"I told them they wouldn't be able to do it!" Paka exclaimed sorrowfully and burst into bitter tears.

They asked questions. They got excited. They laughed. It was noisy, a mixture of amusement and annoyance. The evil fairy exclaimed: "How opportune that we're leaving in a few days! What impossible little boys!"

"But they'll be punished!" Paka's uncle tried to calm her down.

"Oh, what do I care!" the evil fairy said and tried to pretend that she was crying. "Paka is so impressionable. My God, those two Arguses have really failed to supervise him."

She was crying and laughing. They laughed and consoled her. They took Paka away. Paka cried. The Arguses grumbled.

Yes, there were difficult moments in Paka's life. This was a boring, disgusting evening. It was good that now it was nighttime and he could go to sleep.

VII.

In the morning the barefoot boys had to explain themselves to their father. The captain looked frowningly at his sons. They were standing in a row, crying and repenting. Levka told him: "We believed him when he said he was a captive prince, and we wanted to free him from the evil fairy. We thought we had to say some magic words to do it."

"What words?" the captain asked frowningly.

He was forcing himself to frown in order not to laugh.

"Winged words," Levka said, piteously stretching out the ends of the words.

"What 'winged words'?" the captain asked again. "You know what they are, don't you?"

Levka nodded silently.

"Well, tell me what the words are," the captain ordered.

The boys repeated the words. The captain turned red with rage.

"I've raised a bunch of idiots," he growled angrily. "Don't you dare say that from now on! It's nastiness," he shouted at his sons. "Where did you learn that?"

Levka told him, sobbing: "We thought that the peasants know all kinds of winged words, the kind we needed. So we went to the village. We went to see the very oldest one. He was drinking vodka and pronouncing words. We gave him forty kopecks, that's all we had. So he taught us those words. We asked for some more. But he said, 'For forty kopecks you can't learn much.' But even so, he said no witch would be able to stand up against those words."

"You are fine fellows," the captain said. "And you went with words like that under strangers' windows. Oh, you scoundrels! What am I going to do with you now?"

VIII.

The kids knew that Paka was being taken away this morning. The evil fairy was going abroad and taking Paka and his Arguses with her. The boys came out onto the railway bed, where it ran close to their ravine, and waited. And now they could see the train coming quickly from the station.

Paka was looking out the window with beclouded eyes. They were taking him away, and the Arguses were with him again, and the evil fairy—gracious, affectionate, but still not Mama, but the evil fairy—and still the same captivity!

And suddenly Paka caught sight of the three barefoot boys. An insane, desperate hope flashed in his soul. Maybe they had learned new words? The real ones? And suddenly the joyful miracle would be accomplished?

And Paka leaned ecstatically out of the window and waved his handkerchief.

The kids started running joyfully along the railway slope, closer to the train. Paka's car was fast approaching. The face of the evil fairy appeared above Paka's face, the indifferently gracious face of a beautiful lady—and suddenly it was distorted by an expression of severe agitation.

And with joyful expectation the kids, one after the other, shouted new winged words that they had just learned by heart, and waved their caps in the air.

"Those horrible boys again!" the evil fairy exclaimed. "Paka, little one, don't look out the window just now."

But it didn't matter any more, the train had rushed past the kids—and they again remained powerless, disappointed in their passionate expectation of a joyful event.

"She took him away! The damned witch!" Antoshka shouted sorrowfully.

The kids tumbled onto the grass and cried bitterly.

And in the train-car that was quickly flying away, Paka cried, the evil fairy laughed, and the Arguses tried to distract Paka somehow.

Powerless, poor words! Indissoluble captivity! Children's bitter tears!

Pitiful, stupid ones—oh, if only they knew! The fairy who abducts sleeping children on a flying carpet, how durable, how indestructible is her dominion! And no one is granted the power to tear off her disguise. And the Arguses see nothing but will not let him outside the fence. And he cannot leave captivity. And the free hunters seek the wise and knowledgeable in vain.

Everything is in its place, everything is fettered, link to link, forever enchanted, in captivity, in captivity.

1905

THE TWO GOTIKS

I.

The deep calm of the summer night had set in. Both boys, Gotik and Lyutik, *gimnazia* students, were sleeping quietly.

All of a sudden, something woke Gotik up. It was a timid rustling behind the door. Gotik opened his eyes, roused himself—and his sleep had vanished.

It was almost completely light. Quiet, luminous, and strange. The white summer night, the northern night, was pouring through the curtainless window with a quiet, even light. Sleeping Lyutik was breathing quietly in his bed, turned to the wall, so that the smoothly cropped nape of his neck was visible.

Gotik stretched, got up on his knees in bed, and looked out the window.

Through the window the pale sky and the trees could be seen. A white, transparent vapor, barely visible beyond the trees, marked out the location of the river. The trees stood without moving at all and listened sensitively to the murmur of the swift and shallow river as it flowed over the rocks. And someone's soft steps could also be heard.

Gotik jumped out of bed. He was seized by a sprightly readiness to encounter something unusual, the nighttime daring to meet dangerous adventures, inherited from his immemorial ancestors. He ran up to the window.

His heart suddenly stood still for a brief, imperceptibly brief, instant and then started beating very fast. And in the garden, he saw himself, right there, under the window.

White smock, leather belt, peaked *gimnazia* cap in a white covering, his boots with the patch on the left one, his black trousers with the rip down below on the left that still hadn't been mended—Gotik's sharp eyes noticed and recognized all this in an instant.

The other Gotik quietly stole out of the garden. He is bent over, hiding behind the bushes . . . now he has darted past the wicket gate . . . he has disappeared behind the trees, on the path that descends steeply to the river.

Gotik looked out his bedroom door. The boys always left their clothes and shoes there so that the servant Nastya would clean them in the morning. Now all Lyutik's things were in their place, but Gotik's weren't there.

Gotik closed the door, looked at himself—and in the unconquerable enchantment of sleepiness he didn't recognize himself. His thoughts were clouded by drowsiness. His body felt calm and seemingly empty. He was lightly and weakly amazed.

"So where am I going?" he thought.

Suddenly sleep again overcame him. He couldn't even remember how he got under the blanket. He slept soundly until late morning, when playful Lyutik woke him up.

II.

In the morning, fragmentary memories tormented Gotik.

Something had happened at night. Not quite in a dream, not quite in waking life. Or it was a vision.

Noisy and playful, belonging too much to the daytime, Lyutik romped around, as always, bothered Gotik and pestered him, kept him from remembering, and joked—joked and laughed, laughed and joked endlessly.

But all the same Gotik gradually recollected where he, the second, nighttime Gotik, had gone and why he had gone, at the same time that the first, ordinary and usual Gotik, was lying in bed with his heavy, senselessly breathing body.

III.

In a quiet and magical castle, out there, in the distance, beyond an enchanted grove, dwells the tender princess Selenita, the light phantom of summer dreams.

The marvelous castle of Selenita is permeated by moonlight.

Along a foggy road, along a valley where midnight flowers see visions, Gotik passed quietly as a light shadow, barely audible, barely visible, hardly touching the grass. And he came to visit the marvelous princess, darling Selenita.

Quiet music, barely audible, came wafting from far away. The moonlight princess Selenita greeted Gotik with a tender smile.

Her voice rang like a stream in a brook.

Like a stream in a brook, like the tender ringing of a reed-pipe, the quiet voice of the princess Selenita resounded.

She was all tenderness, so airy and light that she seemed transparent.

The stars shone, not quite on her greenish-white clothing, not quite behind her, shining through her body.

And she smiled and enchanted. And she spoke in a tender reed-pipe voice, and fragrances streamed and were interwoven with the murmuring of her reed-pipe speech.

IV.

And Lyutik pestered Gotik with his jokes—endless, boring, obtrusive jokes.

"Lyutik keeps punning!" Gotik thought peevishly. "Why doesn't he get tired of it! It's no wonder Mama gets angry with him."

Indeed, it was horribly tiresome.

No matter what you said to him, he would immediately start turning words inside out and fitting them to each other.

But for some reason his father really liked this. Their father was a merry person himself. He would often say encouragingly to Lyutik: "Come on, now, Lyutie-patootie, get to work!"

And Lyutik would do his best and think something up.

It was silly.

And it was so obsessive that sometimes Gotik himself would start punning.

Then Lyutik would squeal with rapture, shout and jump: "He's become just like me, so you can't tell us apart. Are you Lyu, or am I you?"

And he'd just keep bothering Gotik: "Are you Lyu, or am I you," so that Gotik would get seriously angry.

Sometimes they'd come to blows. Little boys!

V.

Lyudmila Yakovlevna, Lyutik and Gotik's mother, had gotten up early this morning, which was unusual for her.

She got up at the same time as her husband. He was going to work in the city.

On other days she would get up after he had left, when the boys were getting up.

She went with her husband to the wicket gate, came into the kitchen, and saw that the stovetop was already heated up, which was not at all necessary this early, and Gotik's clothing was drying on a line by the window. It was all quite wet, and his boots were muddy.

Lyudmila Yakovlevna was alarmed.

"What's all this, Nastya?" she asked.

"Gotik managed to smush some kind of crap all over his boots and clothes," Nastya said with a laugh.

"But in the evening all his clothes were dry," Lyudmila Yakovlevna said anxiously.

"I have no idea how the little master got all smushed."

Nastya was laughing in a strange way, not quite slyly, not quite in embarrassment. This felt eerie to Lyudmila Yakovlevna.

"Do you know something?" she asked fearfully.

"No, my lady, indeed I don't. How am I supposed to know anything?" Nastya excused herself.

"Did Gotik go somewhere?"

"I don't know, my lady. Indeed, I don't."

VI.

When the boys were drinking their morning tea, Lyudmila Yakovlevna asked, "Gotik, where did you run off to in the night?"

Gotik turned red and said, "I didn't run off anywhere. I was asleep."

But he said it as if he were guilty—uncertainly, with hesitation.

"Your boots are wet," Lyudmila Yakovlevna said.

"I don't know, I was asleep," Gotik repeated.

"Gotik's talking in a funny accent today," Lyutik said. "He says, I was *a sleep*, but did he *sleep* and fall and that's why he was *a sleep*?"

"That's not at all witty," Lyudmila Yakovlevna said peevishly.

She didn't ask Gotik any more questions.

But she was severely anxious all day.

She waited for her husband to come home.

VII.

And Gotik daydreamed about the moonlight princess, the darling Selenitochka.

"Selenitochka."

"Sell 'n' eat okra," someone teased in Lyutik's voice.

And daydreams about bifurcation sweetly excited him all day.

He thought: "How good that there is another life, nighttime, marvelous, like a fairy tale, a different one from this daytime, coarse, sunny, boring life!

"How good that I can migrate into another body, divide my soul in two, have my own secret!

"To keep it secret from everyone.

"And no one will ever find out.

"At nighttime everything is different.

"The daytime ones are sleeping, they lie there with motionless bodies—and then the other ones, the inner ones come out, who we don't know in the daytime."

VIII.

Gotik was standing on the bank of a river, looking at the water, how it constantly runs and murmurs, and dreaming of Selenita, how she smiles and talks.

Lyutik came up to him.

"Gotik," he said, "you've forgotten your vocabulary."

"Get away from me," Gotik answered peevishly.

"It's true. Look, I'll prove it to you: Marya baked a pastry with blueberries. What is it?"

"A blueberry pie."

"Sasha baked a pastry with apples. What is it?"

"An apple pie."

"Ivan baked a pastry with black-and-white birds. What is it?"

"A magpie."

They both started laughing.

IX.

Their father was always merry and talkative; Lyutik resembled him. When their father returned from work, Lyudmila Yakovlevna walked down to meet him at the station, which she rarely did. On the way home she said with concern, "Can you imagine, Alexander Andreyevich, Gotik ran off somewhere last night, and he won't tell me where. He says he was asleep. Say what you want, Sasha . . ."

And she started crying.

Alexander Andreyevich gave a whistle and waved his hand.

"What silliness!" he said in a husky voice. "Where could he run off to? It's some silly fantasy. He just went to the river."

"It worries me so," Lyudmila Yakovlevna said in a crestfallen voice.

"Silliness!" Alexander Andreyevich repeated. "He won't say where he went?"

"He just won't say," Lyudmila Yakovlevna said mournfully.

"Well, I'll give him a good asking, and he'll tell me," the father said angrily.

It was hot, and he was annoyed that he had to get angry, which he didn't like to do.

X.

At dinner the conversation was restless and uneven. The father and mother both kept looking significantly and attentively at the boys. Lyudmila Yakovlevna started talking several times about dacha burglars. How Nastya would sometimes forget to lock the doors. That burglars could also easily climb in the window if it wasn't latched.

Gotik felt uncomfortable and depressed.

Only Lyutik was merry and joking as always.

"We have to always be sure to check that Nastya locks the doors," Alexander Andreyevich grumbled.

"Oh, that Nastya has a *nastya* habit of leaving the doors wide open," Lyutik said.

But to the surprise of both boys, their father said angrily: "Shut up. There's nothing funny about it."

Lyutik looked with amusement at his father and mother. "Why are they sulking?" he thought. "Did they have a fight on the way home?"

And he thought he should make a joke about something unrelated, not connected to home. Recalling a recent conversation with one of his innumerable friends, he snorted with laughter and said: "Gotik, there's a picture of a triangle with one eye inside it. Guess what it is."

"Who doesn't know that!" Gotik said. "The All-Seeing Eye of God."

"No, you didn't guess. Nikolai Alexeyevich told me that he saw a picture like that on the wall in a village church, and the caption said: The voice of one eye crying in the wilderness."[1]

They all laughed.

"Did you make that up yourself?" his father asked mistrustfully.

"You can ask Nikolai Alexeyevich yourself," Lyutik assured him.

His father suddenly frowned again.

"Well, we have to keep a close eye on you two," he said sternly.

They were silent for a little while.

Lyutik asked: "Gotik, what's the name of the leader of the modern Guelphs?"

Gotik thought for a moment.

"Oh, that's simple," he said.

"Then say it!"

"Togo."

"Attaboy!"

"Explain it," his father said gloomily.

"It's very simple," Gotik said. "If there are Guelphs, then there are Ghibellines. And of course, Lyutik derives the word Ghibelline from 'gimbal,' which keeps a ship's compass upright. The Russian sailors who steered their fleet to destruction at Tsushima, where they were destroyed by Admiral Togo, are the *Gimbal*-ines."[2]

"What nonsense," his father said. But he laughed.

"He spent a whole month making that one up," he said.

"Not at all," Lyutik said, turning red. "And after all, I never once said that Togo is a No-go. There were so many stupid rhymes based on that silliness."

"Yes, but you did think up something silly about General Nogi, didn't you," his father said, livening up.

"Well, that's simple. The Japanese have good noggins and a good Nogi, and they're going to Nog-in to Port Arthur."[3]

They laughed, and again their father said gloomily: "Some little noggins are running places they shouldn't."

The awkward silence was again broken by Lyutik.

"Gotik, did Nastya set your place with all the silver you need?"

"Yes, leave me be."

"Is there silverware?"

"Yes, leave me alone."

"There's silver-where, but is there silver here?"

"Stop playing the fool!" Gotik shouted.

"You keep thinking up nonsense," his father said angrily. "There's no connection in all your foolishness."

Unembarrassed, Lyutik answered: "That's exactly why it's fun, because there's no connection. It's not connected, it's free. Wherever there's a logical connection, I feel sick, sick to my stomach. I feel like a sick six-year-old sheep, dragging everything from cause to result. This is better, I can twist it around the way I want. When I reason in a sensible way, I feel like a sick six-year-old sheep, a sick sheep nobody wants."

"That's an old one, my boy," his father said. "Back when I was in school, we had a teacher who loved to assign tricky dictations. He had one like this: 'The sixth sick sheik shares six sick sheared sheep.'"

The boys laughed.

XI.

Finally, Alexander Andreyevich, gathering all the strength of his sternness, asked, "So, Georgi, where did you run off to last night?"

Gotik turned red. Tugging at his napkin, he said in a complaining voice, "Nowhere, Papa, really. Mama thinks I did for some reason, I don't know why. It's because my boots were damp. Well, after all, it was damp last night. Well, we walked by the river. Well, along the water."

"Don't you dare go out at night!" Alexander Andreyevich said sternly.

"Well, I won't," Gotik answered gloomily.

"And please stop saying 'well' all the time," his father said with irritation. "Idiotic habits. If you go running off, I'll thrash you with birch rods."

Gotik was offended and turned red, then said quietly: "That's out of the dark times of the savage Middle Ages."

His father laughed.

"Say one more word!" he threatened, half-jokingly, half-angrily.

Lyutik said merrily, "You can't thrash us, or we'll go on strike."

"We'll organize a walkout," Gotik kept it up.

"I'll thrash you both," their father teased.

"And we'll organize an obstruction," Lyutik shouted.

"We'll file a petition."

"Or you'll run to the police?"

"Well, no, I won't agree to that," Lyutik answered with animation, "you can flog us until we're chopped in two, but I won't go to the cops."[4]

Nastya removed the dishes for the next course. Distracted by listening to the conversation, she caught her elbow on a glass, and it rolled onto the floor. It didn't break; it fell in a lucky way.

"Nastya, you've tumbled the tumbler from the table," Lyutik said.

"You jokers!" Nastya shouted and ran off, laughing loudly.

Rice pudding was served.

"Gotik, you hick, are you really going to eat that cup of rice pudding?" Lyutik asked.

"Well, of course, I'm going to eat it," Gotik said with annoyance. "You think it's just for you?"

"Watch out," Lyutik said in a warning voice. "If a hick eats a cup of rice, he gets the hiccups."

"Leave me alone," Gotik shouted, both angry and laughing. "What an idiot you are! You keep thinking up silly stuff."

XII.

After dinner Alexander Andreyevich didn't go anywhere. He sat for a long time in the garden pavilion by the fence, looking at the river and smoking. Then he went to his wife's room.

"You know, Lyuba," he said quietly, "this is beginning to worry me."

Lyudmila Yakovlevna started crying.

"Now, now, don't cry, we'll find out what's going on," Alexander Andreyevich said, "but where could he have run off to?"

"It would be so easy for him to drown," Lyudmila Yakovlevna said, sobbing. "Every year somebody drowns."

XIII.

Over evening tea, they again talked about the need to lock the doors for the night. They reminded Nastya. The father and mother both repeated to the boys that they should not leave the windows open.

Two neighboring dachas had been burglarized a few days ago. They stole some freshly washed laundry and everything that was in the icebox.

Today they recalled that incident.

Lyutik said with annoyance, "Mama received an official notification that they're going to rob us tonight."

XIV.

In the evening after tea, when the boys had already gone to bed, Lyudmila Yakovlevna and Alexander Andreyevich began talking again in their bedroom about the nighttime adventure. They locked the door so the boys wouldn't come in. They were speaking quietly.

Lyudmila Yakovlevna was sitting on a chair by the bed and brushing out her hair for the night. Alexander Andreyevich was standing in front of her, scratching his shaven cheeks in indecision.

The candle was burning dimly.

"Hide his boots," Alexander Andreyevich advised.

"He'll put on Lyutik's," Lyudmila Yakovlevna answered plaintively.

"Well, then, hide Lyutik's boots too."

"Is that really going to restrain him," Lyudmila Yakovlevna said despondently. "He'll run away barefoot—what's it to him! If he's already gotten into the habit."

"So we'll have to catch him," Alexander Andreyevich said peevishly.

"Oh, yes, just try and catch him!"

"So we don't catch him, but we'll detect his tracks and follow his trail."

"Oh, how are you going to see tracks in the grass!" Lyudmila Yakovlevna said hopelessly.

"It's not all grass."

"I'll hide the boots in any case," Lyudmila Yakovlevna said.

She went into the entryway. Stealthily.

"You stay here," she whispered to her husband. "You'll make noise with your boots, but I'm in my slippers."

XV.

The boys had gone to bed. Tuned to a key of anxiety by the evening's conversations, they had locked themselves into their upper room.

Lyutik fell asleep as soon as he lay down.

Gotik settled into bed slowly. He was listening for something.

There was singing and music playing somewhere nearby. To the tender chime of the shimmering sounds, Gotik too started to fall asleep. He was embraced by the ambrosial anticipation of a darling dream.

Suddenly, hearing a light rustling outside his door, Gotik roused himself.

He lay for a moment, listening.

It was not quite joyful, not quite frightening. An eerie expectation.

He could hear someone stirring on the other side of the door, and someone's light movements outside the door seemed to echo in Gotik's heart, exciting his blood.

They touched the doorknob.

The door started shaking, slightly striking against the latch, but it didn't give way.

They went away quietly.

Gotik lay there and listened with keen sensitivity.

XVI.

Lyudmila Yakovlevna brought Lyutik's and Gotik's boots into the bedroom.

"They've locked the door," she whispered. "By every indication, he's planning to go out again. Today maybe they'll both go. Let them have a little stroll barefoot on the damp earth."

"What about their clothes?" the father asked.

"Their outfits are in place. But so what—those scamps will run off stark naked if they really want to."

"We have to wait. We'll see from the window. Or should we be in the garden?"

"But what if they run through the yard?"

They stayed in the bedroom to wait.

XVII.

Again, Gotik heard someone coming up to the door.

And again he heard a rustling, a long, careful rustling, as if someone were rummaging on the floor, looking for something.

They jostled the door. A peevish whispering. . . . Light steps going away . . .

A door creaked somewhere, the stairs started shaking.

Gotik kept lying there for a while. He listened. It was quiet.

Suddenly he jumped up. His heart was beating hard. He ran to the door, cracked it open, looked out; no one was there.

Gotik glanced at the chairs where their clothes were lying. Only Lyutik's clothes were there—Gotik's were gone. And there were no boots, either Gotik's or Lyutik's.

"They swiped them," Gotik thought. "Both the clothes and the boots."

He went into the room and ran up to the window.

Again a boy was making his way along the same path as yesterday, hiding in just the same way. Today he was barefoot.

Gotik was weakly amazed.

He thought bashfully: "But how can I go see darling Selenitochka barefoot?"

And again, suddenly an overwhelming sleepiness dragged him to his bed.

He fell asleep.

And again, he dreamed phantom dreams.

XVIII.

Gotik dreamed that he was going to see Selenita. His feet were damp, and he felt awkward about being barefoot. But he could not and did not want to stop. An unknown force was drawing him on.

Wondrous flowers in peaceful glades lightly waggled their darling, tender little heads, sprinkled with fragrant dew, and smiled at the moon with a smile that had never been seen on earth.

The moonlight spilled through the palace of darling Selenita, reflected in the mirrors on the marvelous walls, and inspired languor and enchantment.

And here was Selenita. Darling, like yesterday. Darling, darling. Her little feet were white, unshod, like Gotik's—so that Gotik wouldn't be ashamed.

Her greenish clothing quietly fluttered with her every movement. Her words resounded like music, and ambrosially tender was the rustling of her steps and her fluttering clothing.

And a joyful smile shone on her face—but that joy was dissolved in a marvelous sadness.

And that joy and that sadness made him dizzy, and made tears bubble up in his eyes.

Selenita snuggled up to Gotik and embraced him, and they started flying, lightly spinning, above the moonlit glades, hardly touching the tender grass with their feet. And it was joyful and languorous.

XIX.

They were whispering in the bedroom, trying to guess where Gotik might go.

Suddenly they heard a rustling. They fell silent and listened. A door creaked.

Lyudmila Yakovlevna went quietly out of the bedroom. Alexander Andreyevich followed her, carrying a candle. They stopped by the door of the room where the boys were sleeping.

"The clothes are gone!" Lyudmila Yakovlevna said in a frightened whisper. "He's run away!"

"It's good that he's alone," Alexander Andreyevich growled.

They went quickly into the garden.

Suddenly, before their eyes, a boy came running out of the bushes and nimbly darted through the wicket gate.

Alexander Andreyevich ran after him.

XX.

Lyudmila Yakovlevna was standing by the wicket gate and looking anxiously at the dew-covered bushes and the foggy river.

Soon Alexander Andreyevich returned, breathing heavily and unevenly.

"I couldn't catch him. He scampered away somewhere," he growled.

"What do we do now?" Lyudmila Yakovlevna asked.

"We have to wait. Let's sit for a while. He'll have to come back," the father muttered peevishly.

They went into the house. Lyudmila Yakovlevna said: "You could walk down to the mill."

"Where all do you want me to go!" Alexander Andreyevich answered angrily. "Go chasing after a kid! There are a lot of places here."

XXI.

Alexander Andreyevich curled up in an armchair in the parlor and soon fell asleep. He was sleeping away, snoring slightly.

Lyudmila Yakovlevna, annoyed at her husband, thought: "He doesn't care. His heart doesn't ache. He can sleep peacefully at such a moment. Another father would run all over the whole neighborhood. Anything might happen."

She went out onto the balcony. She sat down, hiding behind the balcony's calico curtain so that she couldn't be seen from the garden.

She fell into thought. About Gotik, about Lyutik. Her consciousness was veiled by a delicate drowsiness.

It was already getting light.

Suddenly something luminous flashed among the dark green foliage, out there beyond the bushes of the garden, on the road.

Lyudmila Yakovlevna jumped up as if something had given her a sudden push.

"It's Gotik running home," she thought.

She couldn't see clearly, but she was sure it was Gotik. And now it seemed to her that she could see his face clearly.

Lyudmila Yakovlevna started trembling and clutched at her chest. She became frightened. For some reason it didn't occur to her to run to meet Gotik.

She rushed to wake up her husband. She called to him in a whisper. Then she started shaking him.

She could hardly wake him. He had been sound asleep, and he was muttering something. Suddenly he woke up. He heard his wife's excited whisper: "Gotik, Gotik!"

He was frightened. It seemed to him that some misfortune had happened to Gotik. He jumped up.

"What's happened to him?" he asked in a trembling voice.

His wife shushed him: "Shhh! Quiet!"

She dragged him by the sleeve.

They both ran into the garden, both frightened.

They saw someone flash through the back door, the way into the kitchen. He evidently noticed that he was being chased and started taking off his clothes while running.

They both rushed after him. They didn't catch him.

In the entryway, Gotik's clothes were strewn about—on a chair, on the floor, just as they dropped.

They went to the boys' room.

Both Gotik and Lyutik were sleeping. Gotik's blanket had been kicked off and was bunched up at his feet.

"He's pretending," his father said angrily and loudly.

His fear had passed and been replaced by anger.

He was angry at Gotik because he had caused him to experience a moment of foolish fear, when his heart had throbbed and pounded so painfully and heavily.

"Come on, get up, traveler," he shouted angrily, smacking Gotik hard on the back.

Gotik jumped up. He woke up quickly, but his eyes were still heavy. Fear, confusion.

"Did they really find out?" the alarming thought flashed in his head. "But how could they have found out? And what will happen now?"

Lyutik woke up too. He yawned loudly and spoke in a piteous little voice: "What's going on! The big people aren't letting the little ones sleep."

Suddenly he guessed that something interesting had happened. He sat up on his bed, yawned, and stretched. He got up and wrapped himself in his blanket. He got ready to watch what would happen next.

"Why'd you wake us? Is it a tree problem? Wide yew ache us?" he muttered, out of habit.

The father and mother were both angry and excited, and this really put a scare into Gotik. They both asked Gotik at the same time, "Where were you just now?"

"Where did you run off to?"

"Where did you come from?"

"Tell us, why did you go out?"

Gotik sat up on his bed and started crying.

"I don't know anything," he said, quietly and sorrowfully.

His father seized Gotik by the shoulders and shook him angrily.

"No, answer us right now," he shouted. "Your tears won't help."

Gotik got up. He yawned spasmodically. He started wiping his eyes.

He didn't know what to do or what to say. It was painful and depressing.

His father kept interrogating him: "Tell us, where did you run off to?"

"I was asleep," Gotik said tearily.

"Oh, you were asleep! Well, fine, now we're going to see how asleep you were. Come on, my boy, let's go to the garden."

They dragged Gotik, undressed, into the garden. Lyutik went along too, wrapped up in his blanket.

"He was running right here, I saw him," Lyudmila Yakovlevna pointed. "Wait, here are his tracks on the path. Gotik, put your feet into the tracks."

"They're not my footprints at all," Gotik said. "Those are huge paws. I never had feet like that."

And in fact, the tracks did not fit.

The father and mother were confused.

"Did you dream it?" Alexander Andreyevich muttered angrily.

Lyutik laughed loudly and hopped around, getting tangled in the long folds of his blanket.

Gotik laughed joyfully.

"I didn't get caught! They didn't recognize me! They didn't grab me!" he thought joyfully.

"Whose tracks are they, then?" Alexander Andreyevich said in bewilderment. "That means somebody did pass by here."

They looked back at the house, making vague conjectures. Nastya peeped out of the kitchen.

"What is she doing here?" Alexander Andreyevich asked in a whisper.

"What are you doing, Nastya, you're already up?" Lyudmila Yakovlevna asked. "Could it be her doings?" she said quietly to her husband.

Alexander Andreyevich gave a whistle.

"Of course, it was her who was running. She organized a masquerade."

"Come over here," Lyudmila Yakovlevna called her. "Whose tracks are these? Who was running here a little while ago?"

Nastya burst out laughing.

"Well, what can I say, my lady," she said. "It seems there's no use trying to hide it. I was running in Gotik's little outfit."

"Why did you organize such a masquerade?"

"So that the neighbors wouldn't notice, and I was also hiding from you. Out there on the bridge we had balls, dances, lads, girls, it was a lot of fun."

"Well, we don't need such fun servants," Alexander Andreyevich decided. "You'll get your final pay in the morning, and then please leave."

XXII.

So it wasn't Gotik who went to see Selenita—it was Nastya running in his clothes. How silly!

How he regretted the loss of his nighttime, unrealizable dream!

His nighttime darling life, and Selenita, and everything that didn't exist!

The whole mystery had been explained in such a simple and vulgar way.

Gotik felt sad.

He started crying again.

His father picked him up in his arms and carried him to the bedroom, consoling him with the promise to buy him a bicycle.

But Lyutik found it all funny. He capered about, laughing loudly.

"Now sleep, children, sleep!" Alexander Andreyevich said.

And everyone was back in their bedrooms.

Sleep!

Farewell, that other, unknown, mysterious life. We have to live through our boring daytime experiences and, when night comes, sleep senselessly and heavily.

1906

THE YOUTH LINUS

Having carried out with great success the command to pacify the unsubmissive inhabitants of a rebellious village who had refused to offer sacrifices and perform pious worship of the image of the divine emperor, a detachment of Roman cavalry was returning to camp. Much blood had been spilled, many of the unrighteous had been exterminated, and the exhausted warriors impatiently awaited that gratifying hour when they would return to their tents and would enjoy there without hindrance the beautiful bodies of the women they had taken captive in the rebellious village, the wives and daughters of the impious madmen.

These women and maidens had already tasted the ambrosial but exhausting violence of hurried caresses on the outskirts of the destroyed and burned-out village, next to the mutilated corpses of their fathers and husbands, next to the tortured bodies of their mothers, bloodied by the blows of sticks and whips. These women and maidens were the more desirable for the soldiers the more unsubmissive they were themselves, and the more forced their embraces were. Now they lay firmly bound in the heavy carts that were being drawn by powerful horses along the high road straight to the camp.

The horsemen themselves had chosen a roundabout route, because the chief centurion had been informed that some of the rebels had managed to hide and were escaping in this direction. And although their swords were already nicked and covered with blood and their spears were blunted because of the doughty work of these warriors, zealous in the defense of the glory and dignity of the emperor—still, the sword of a Roman warrior is never sated with the bodies of prostrated enemies and eternally thirsts for yet more fresh, hot human blood.

It was a scorching day and the hottest hour of the day, soon after noon. The cloudless and mercilessly bright sky glittered. The fiery-hazy heavenly Dragon, trembling from the insane fury of the world, poured out streams of scorching anger from its fiery maw onto the silent and despondent plain. The dried-out grass pressed down to the earth, which thirsted for and awaited moisture in vain, and the grass anguished along with the earth, and agonized, and drooped, and choked on the dust.

From under the horses' hooves, gray, smoky dust billowed, standing and swaying in a barely mobile cloud in the immobile air. The dust settled on the armor of the exhausted horsemen, and the armor gleamed dully with a crimson tinge. And through the cloud of gray, motionless dust everything around them appeared to the gazes of the exhausted warriors to be ominous, dark, and sad.

Incinerated by the furious Dragon, the earth lay submissive and powerless under the heavy hooves shod in iron. Under the heavy, iron-shod hooves the desolate, dusty road hummed.

Only occasionally did they encounter poor villages with piti-ful hovels, but, wearied by the oppressive heat, the chief centurion forgot his intention of searching the whole road and, rhythmically rocking in his saddle, thought gloomily about the fact that this heat would end some time, and the long journey would come to an end, and they would lead away his warhorse, and they would take his helmet and shield, and under the broad canvas of his campaign tent there would be coolness and the quiet light of the night lamp, and again the naked slave girl would start to weep, she would weep in her reed-pipe voice, complaining and lamenting in a foreign, ridiculous tongue, and she would weep, but she would kiss him. And he would start to caress her, he would caress her to death—so that she would not weep, would not lament, would not complain, would not speak in her reed-pipe voice about the murdered ones, about those dear to her, about the prostrated enemies of the great Caesar.

A young warrior said to the centurion: "Over there, to the right, near the road, I see a crowd. Give us the order, Marcellus, and we will rush at those people and disperse them, and with the swift movement of our steeds we will awaken the wind that has been lulled to sleep by the oppressive heat, and it will blow the dusty lassitude away from you and from us."

The centurion looked attentively in the direction the young warrior was pointing. Sharp-sighted were the eyes of the old centurion.

"No, Lucilius," he said, smiling, "that crowd is a crowd of children who are playing by the road. It's not worth dispersing them. Let the urchins look at our powerful steeds and our intrepid horsemen and may this sight imprint worship in their hearts for the grandeur of the Roman army and the glory of our invincible and divine Caesar."

Young Lucilius did not dare to contradict the centurion. But his face darkened. Dissatisfied, he rode off to his place and quietly said to his friend, a young man like himself: "These children are perhaps the spawn of that same rebellious rabble, and I would happily hack them to pieces. In his old age our centurion has become too sensitive and has lost the stern decisiveness that is appropriate to a valiant warrior."

But even Lucilius's friend answered him with noticeable dissatisfaction: "Why should we fight with children? Where's the glory in that? We have enough battles with those who can defend themselves."

Then the young and quick-tempered Lucilius fell silent, turning red with annoyance.

The warriors approached the playing children. The children stopped by the road and looked at the warriors, marveling at their powerful steeds, their glittering armor, and their manly, tanned faces. They marveled, whispered, looked with eyes wide open.

Only one of the children, the beautiful youth Linus, looked at the warriors sullenly, and his dark eyes flashed with the fire of holy anger. And when the detachment of horsemen came even with the children, the youth Linus exclaimed loudly and angrily: "Murderers!"

And he raised his arms, stretched out threateningly to the centurion. The old centurion looked at him sullenly, not hearing what the boy was shouting, and rode past.

The frightened children surrounded Linus and forbade him to shout, and they whispered, "Let's run, right now, or they'll kill us all."

And the little girls were already weeping. But the beautiful youth Linus stepped fearlessly forward and shouted loudly: "Butchers! Torturers of the innocent!"

And again, the small, powerless hand of the youth Linus, clenched in a fist, was raised threateningly. Flashing his angry dark eyes, trembling all over, choking with anger, Linus shouted ever more loudly: "Butchers! Butchers! How will you wash from your hands the blood of those you have murdered!"

The little girls started howling, drowning out the shouts of the youth Linus, and the boys grabbed him by the arms and started dragging him away from the road. But Linus broke free, burning with holy anger, and shouted out curses to the warriors of the great emperor.

The horsemen stopped. The youngest of them exclaimed: "They're the spawn of the mutineers. Their hearts are infected with the rebellious spirit. We need to exterminate them all. There is no place under the sky for one who has dared to insult a Roman warrior."

And the older warriors said to the centurion: "The audacity of these scoundrels merits a cruel punishment. Marcellus, give us the order to chase them down and slaughter them all. We have to destroy the mutinous tribe before they grow up and have the strength to rebel and cause great harm to the divine Caesar and imperial Rome."

And the centurion said: "Chase them down, kill the ones who shouted, and punish the others in such a way that they will remember to the end of their days what it means to insult a Roman warrior."

And all the warriors turned off the dusty road and rushed after the escaping children.

Seeing the pursuit, the youth Linus shouted to his comrades: "Leave me. You can't save me, and if you run, you'll all perish under the swords of this impious and ruthless army. I will go to meet them—let them kill only me. I do not even want to live in this contemptible world, where such cruel deeds are committed."

Linus stopped, and his comrades, weakened by running and fright, could not drag him away any farther. They stood and wept loudly, and the horsemen swiftly surrounded them in a tight circle.

Their swords, drawn out of their sheaths, sparkled in the sun, and the unsteady smiles of the Dragon, ruthless and evil, played over the steely blades. The children trembled and pressed close to each other in a tight bunch, weeping loudly.

The Dragon, hastening the murder, inflaming the soldiers' hot blood, clouding their bloodshot eyes with the crimson smoke of fury, was already rejoicing from the heights at this evil earthly deed, was ready to kiss the innocent children's blood with the merciless rays of its snaky eyes and to pour the purulent heat of malice over the defenseless bodies, chopped to pieces by the cruel, broad swords. But the youth Linus boldly stepped out of the crowd and went up to the centurion. And he said loudly: "Old man, it was I who called you and your warriors murderers and butchers, it was I who cursed you and everyone with you, it was I who invoked the anger of the righteous deity down upon your impious heads. Look, there they are, those children, weeping and trembling from terror. They are afraid that your cursed warriors will follow your godless order and kill all of us, they will kill us and our fathers and mothers. Kill only me—because those others are submissive to you and the one who sent you. Kill only me, if you have not yet been sated by murders. But I do not fear you, I hate your fury, I despise your sword and your unjust power, I do not want to live on this earth, which is trampled by the steeds of your frenzied army. My arms are still weak, and I am still too short to reach your throat in order to strangle you—so kill me, kill me now."

The centurion listened to him with great amazement. And he said: "No, you little snake, you won't get your way—you're not going to die alone."

And he ordered his warriors: "Kill them all. We can't leave this snake's spawn alive—because the words of the audacious boy have sunk into their rebellious souls. Kill them all without mercy, large and small, even those who have hardly learned to prattle."

The warriors fell onto the children and hacked them up with their merciless swords. The gloomy valley and the dusty road shuddered from the wailing of the children, and the hazy distances moaned in answer, moaned in a tender, reed-pipe echo, and fell silent. And with hot, distended nostrils the steeds sniffed the smoking blood and slowly and heavily trampled the children's corpses with their iron-shod hooves.

Then the warriors returned to the road, laughing joyfully and cruelly. They were hurrying to get to their camp. They were talking cheerfully and rejoicing.

But the dusty, heavy path stretched on and on in the valley that languished under the angry, flaming eyes of the Dragon. The crimson Dragon began to decline, but there was no coolness anywhere around, and the wind slept, spellbound by silence and terror.

As it declined, the crimson visage of the scorching Dragon looked into the sharp-sighted eyes of the old centurion—and the heavenly Snake smiled a quiet and terrible smile. And because it was quiet, and scorching, and scarlet, and the step of the rhythmically ringing horses was heavily measured, the old centurion began to feel mournful and afraid.

And so rhythmic and so ringing was the heavy horses' pace, and so delicate and so gray was the immobile, hopeless dust, and it seemed that there would be no end to the lassitude and terror of the desolate path. And to every step of his tired steed the desolate distance responded with a hollow, reverberating hum.

And hollow moans were born in the desolate distance.

The earth hummed under the hooves.

Someone was running. Running to catch up with them.

A dark voice resembling the voice of the youth who had been killed by the warriors was shouting something.

The centurion looked around at his warriors. Their dust-covered faces were distorted by more than weariness. An indistinct terror was depicted on the coarse features of the soldiers' tanned faces.

The dry lips of young Lucilius trembled, whispering in alarm: "We should get back to camp as soon as we can."

The old centurion looked fixedly into the weary face of Lucilius and quietly asked the young warrior: "What's wrong with you, Lucilius?"

And Lucilius answered him just as quietly: "I'm afraid."

Ashamed of his terror and his weakness, he said more loudly: "It's very hot."

And again, unable to overcome his terror, he whispered quietly: "The damned boy is chasing us. He's been bewitched by the unclean spells of nocturnal sorceresses, and we were unable to hack him up so that he could not rise again."

The centurion looked attentively around the area. No one was visible either up close or far away. The centurion said to the young Lucilius: "Have you lost the amulet that the old priest of the overseas god gave you? They say that if one has such an amulet, the spells of the midnight and midday sorceresses are powerless against you."

Lucilius answered, trembling from terror: "I am wearing the amulet, but it is burning my chest. The subterranean gods have already drawn near to us, and I can hear their dark rumbling."

The valley moaned with a heavy hum. The old centurion, hoping to conquer his own terror with a pious speech, said to Lucilius: "The subterranean gods are thanking us. We did quite a good job for them today. Dark and inarticulate is the voice of the subterranean gods, and it is terrifying in the scorching silence of the wilderness, but does not the honor of a valiant warrior consist in overcoming terror!"

But again, the young Lucilius said: "I am afraid. I can hear the voice of the youth overtaking us."

Then in the scorching stillness of the valley a ringing reed-pipe voice proclaimed: "Curses, curses on the murderers!"

The warriors flinched, and the steeds bolted. An unknown voice, resembling the voice of the youth Linus, resounded so near, so clearly: "Murderers! Murderers of the innocent! There is neither forgiveness nor mercy for you."

And the steeds, urged on by the warriors, rushed swiftly. But anger was ignited in the heart of the old centurion. And he shouted, restraining the flight of his frightened steed and addressing the horsemen: "Are we not warriors of the great, divine emperor? Who are we running away from? The cursed boy, either not done to death by us or brought back to life by the unclean spells of evil sorcerers who collect blood for their nocturnal magic, continues to utter blasphemies against our invincible army. But it behooves Roman arms to defeat not only the enemy force but also dark spells."

The warriors were ashamed. They stopped their steeds. They listened carefully. Someone was trying to overtake them, proclaiming and crying out, and in the hazy silence of the valley as dark evening drew in, they could distinctly hear a child's shout: "Murderers!"

The horsemen turned their steeds in the direction from which the shouts were coming. And they saw the youth Linus running toward them in bloody, torn clothing. Blood was streaming down his face and along his arms, which were raised to the warriors in a threatening gesture, as if the youth wanted to grab each of them and cast them down to his own bloody, dusty feet.

The hearts of the warriors were filled with savage malice. Unsheathing their swords, infuriating their steeds with quick jabs of their sharpened stirrups, they rushed headlong at the youth, and hacked him with their swords, and trampled him, and satiated their fury over his remains, and then jumped down from their steeds, and tore the body of the youth into pieces, and swept it away, along the road and the surrounding area.

After wiping their swords with the grass by the roadside, the warriors got onto their steeds and rushed further along their way, hurrying to their camp. But again, a heavy moan resounded over the valley, dark in the rays of the declining Dragon—and again a sobbing, reed-pipe voice lifted up the same merciless words. And the howl rang repeatedly in the ears of the warriors: "Murderers!"

Then, exhausted by horror and malice, the warriors again turned their steeds—and again the youth Linus ran to them in his bloody clothes and stretched out toward them his threatening arms, awash in blood. And the warriors again hacked him up, trampled him, and cut his body into pieces with their swords, and scattered it about, and rushed off.

But again and again, the youth Linus overtook the warriors.

And the warriors had already forgotten in which direction their camp lay, and in the fury of endless murder, amid the howls of unceasing reproach, they rushed about the valley and circled around the place where the youth Linus and the other children had been killed.

Through the rest of the day, the Dragon, flaming with scarlet and hazily dying out, looked with a furious, merciless gaze at the horror and madness of eternal murder and unending reproach.

And the evening burned out, and it was night, and the stars twinkled, immaculate, innocent, and distant.

But in the valley where the evil deed had been accomplished, the warriors rushed around, and the youth Linus tormented them with an endless howling. And the warriors rushed around, and kept killing him, but could not kill him.

Before the rising of the sun, driven by horror, pursued by the eternal moans of the youth Linus, they came speeding to the seashore. And the waves foamed beneath the frantic flight of the steeds.

Thus perished all the horsemen and the centurion Marcellus along with them.

And there, in the distant field, by the road, where the youth Linus and the other children had been killed by the horsemen, their bodies lay, bloody and unburied. At night, cravenly and cautiously, wolves came to the prostrate bodies and sated themselves with the innocent and sweet bodies of the children.

1906

IN THE CROWD

I.

The ancient and glorious city of Mstislavl was celebrating the seven-hundredth anniversary of its founding.

It was a rich city, a center of industry and trade. In the city itself and on its outskirts, many large and small factories had been built, some of which were famous throughout Russia. The population was increasing rapidly, especially in recent years, and had reached an impressive figure. There were many troops stationed there. The population included many workers, traders, civil servants, students, and writers.

The members of the city council decided to mark the day of the city's founding with a first-rate celebration. They invited government authorities, they invited Paris and London and also Chukhloma and Medyn, and several other towns, but they were strictly selective.[1]

"You know, so that not just anybody can push their way in," explained the mayor, a young man of merchant origins and European education, known for the refined courtliness of his manners.

Then they somehow recalled that they needed to invite Moscow and Vienna as well. They sent invitations to those two cities, but only two weeks before the festival.

The writers and students reproached the mayor for such inappropriate forgetfulness. The mayor offered embarrassed excuses: "I was run off my feet. It went clean out of my head. You wouldn't believe all the things I have to do. I hardly ever spend the night at home: it's one committee meeting after another."

Moscow wasn't offended—it's a family affair, they said, we'll settle it ourselves—and they hastened to send a deputation with a congratulatory address.[2] Gay Vienna, on the other hand, contented itself with sending a greeting card. The card was artistically decorated: a naked boy wearing a top hat was sitting astride a barrel and holding a goblet of beer in his upraised hand. The beer was foaming luxuriantly, and the boy was smiling gaily and roguishly. He had a round, ruddy face, and the members of the city council found that his smile was quite seemly for the festivities, gay and kindly in the German fashion. They found the whole drawing very stylish. Only they couldn't quite agree about what the style was: some said "Art Nouveau," others said "Rococo."

In a city that was unpaved, dusty, dirty, and dark; in a city where there were many wretched street urchins and few schools; in a city where poor women sometimes gave birth in the streets; in a city where they broke up the old walls of a historically significant fortress in order to get bricks to build new houses; in a city where hooligans wreaked havoc on crowded streets at night, and in the outskirts the dwellings of the townspeople were burglarized without hindrance, accompanied by the loud sounds of the drowsy night watchmen's rattles; in this half-savage city they were organizing festivities and sumptuous feasts for honored guests and authorities who were gathering from all over, festivities that no one needed, and they were lavishly spending money on this empty and foolish undertaking, money that was lacking for schools and hospitals.

And for the common people (after all, you couldn't get along without them too) they were preparing entertainments on the city pasture, in a location called Opalikha for some reason. They were building show booths—one for folk drama, another for a fairy-tale pantomime, a third for a circus—they were setting up a roller coaster, swings, and poles that could be climbed to get a prize. They bought a new beard for the old man in the strolling players' troupe; it was made of tow but cost the city more than a silk one. After all, it was very artistically made.

They prepared gifts to be distributed to the people. They planned to give each person a mug with the city coat of arms and a bundle: gingerbread and nuts wrapped up in a kerchief with a view of Mstislavl. They prepared many thousands of these mugs and kerchiefs with gingerbread and nuts. They stored up the gifts well in advance—and so by the day of the festival the gingerbread was stale, and the nuts were rotten.

A week before the day appointed for the people's festival, they set up tables and beer kiosks on Opalikha field as well as two stages, one for the paying public and another for the honored invitees.

They left narrow passageways between the kiosks so that people would have to come up to the tables to get their gifts in line, one at a time. This was the mayor's idea, to make doubly sure there would be order. He was an intelligent and reasonable young man.

On the eve of the festival they brought in the gifts, piled them up in a shed, and locked it.

The people, hearing about the entertainments and gifts, came walking in crowds from all directions to the ancient and glorious city of Mstislavl, crossing themselves at the sight of the golden domes of its numerous churches in the distance. People were saying that gifts were one thing, but besides that, on Opalikha field there would be fountains of vodka and you would be able to drink as much vodka as you want. "Go ahead and drink yourself sick."

Many people came from afar. And in advance. By the eve of the festival, lots of visitors from far away were loafing around the streets of the city. Most of them were peasants, but there were also many factory workers. There were also lower-class townspeople from neighboring towns. They came walking, and some came by vehicle.

The celebration had already been going on for several days in the city. Flags were waving on the houses, and garlands of greenery were hung. Prayer services were held. There was a military parade. Then a review of the fire brigade. On the market square there was a bazaar, cheerful and noisy.

Many distinguished visitors arrived, both Russian and foreign, high-ranking officials and dignitaries and many curious tourists. The local inhabitants came out onto the streets in crowds and gaped at the out-of-town guests. The distinguished foreigners were the object of particular attention, but not very friendly attention. Some people also tried to make a profit: lodgings, food, goods—everything got more expensive.

The eve of the people's festival arrived. As it had throughout these days, the city shone with festive lights. A gala performance was scheduled in the city theater, and after it a great ball in the governor's home.

And the crowd was thronging onto Opalikha field. And there was no supervision over it. The distribution of the gifts was scheduled to begin at ten o'clock in the morning, and the city authorities were sure that no one would go to Opalikha before early morning. But before early morning there was night, and before that there was the evening. And starting in the evening a crowd began to gather on Opalikha field, so that by midnight in front of the sheds that separated the square for the people's amusements from the city pasture, it had become crowded, noisy, and anxious.

Word was that several hundred thousand people had gathered. Even half a million.

II.

On Nikolsky Square, on the edge of a cliff, stood the Udoyevs' little house. Above the cliff a garden had been laid out, and from it opened out a magnificent view of the lower parts of the city, of Zarechie and Market End, and of the outskirts.

From the heights, everything was purified and seemed small, beautiful, and festive. The shallow, dirty Safat River appeared from here as a narrow ribbon of changing color.[3] The houses and rows of market stalls looked like little toys, the carriages and people were moving peacefully, quietly, noiselessly, and aimlessly, a light, barely visible dust rose up, and the heavy rumbling of drays reached the heights as the barely audible music of the underworld.

Opposite the Udoyevs' house, across the square, was the Exchequer, a dismal two-story building painted with ochre. That is where the head of the family, State Councillor Matvei Fyodorovich Udoyev, worked.

The fence around the Udoyevs' house was sturdy and gray, the pavilion in the garden was so darling and cozy, the lilac exhaled sweet fragrance, the fruit trees and berry bushes promised something joyful and ambrosial: the family household of the old, venerable civil servant was well-husbanded and solid.

Udoyev's children, the fifteen-year-old *gimnazia* student Lyosha and his two sisters, Nadya and Katya, maidens of twenty and eighteen, were also planning to go to the festivities on Opalikha field. That is why they were so cheerful and so joyfully excited.

Lyosha was a white-skinned, easily amused, and studious boy. He had no particular, vivid features: the *gimnazia* teachers often confused him with another student, who was also white-faced and unassuming. The maidens were also unassuming, cheerful, and kind. The elder, Nadya, was a little livelier, restless and at times even mischievous. The younger, Katya, was quiet as a mouse, loved to pray, especially in the monastery, and moved very easily from laughter to tears and from weeping to laughter. It was easy to offend her and not hard to console her and make her laugh.

The boy and the maidens very much wanted to get a mug for each of them. They had begged permission from their parents in advance to go to Opalikha.

The permission was granted reluctantly. Their mother grumbled. Their father was silent. It was all the same to him. But he also didn't like it.

Matvei Fyodorovich Udoyev was a taciturn, tall, pockmarked, and indifferent person. He drank vodka but in moderate amounts, and he almost never quarreled with the people in his household. Domestic life passed him by. Like all of life . . .

It went past like clouds that fly by and melt in the sky, pierced by the sunlight. . . . Past, like a wanderer tirelessly striding past buildings he doesn't need. . . . Like the wind wafting from a far-off land. . . . Past, past, always past . . .

III.

Lyosha and his sisters were standing by the gate and looking at the passersby. It was noisy and crowded. People were walking by, all dressed up, and it was evident that they were strangers. They were mostly going in one direction, toward Opalikha. The hum of the crowd inspired a vague anxiety in the children.

Their neighbors, the Shutkins, came up to them: a young man, a boy, and two girls. They bandied some insignificant remarks back and forth, like people who see each other all the time and are used to each other.

"Are you going?" the elder Shutkin asked.

"We're going in the morning!" Lyosha answered.

Nadya and Katya smiled silently, joyfully, and a little bashfully. The Shutkins burst out laughing for some reason. They exchanged glances. They went home.

"They want to go earlier than us," Nadya guessed.

"Well, let them," Katya said, and became sad.

The Shutkins' house was next to the Udoyevs' property. It was distinguished by its messy and dilapidated appearance.

The young Shutkins were all brats and good-for-nothings. Sometimes they embarked on audacious pranks. Sometimes they got the Udoyev children involved in their pranks, and frequently the mischief was rather large-scale.

The Shutkins were swarthy and black-haired like gypsies. The elder brother worked as a clerk in the office of the justice of the peace. He played the balalaika with gusto. The sisters, Elena and Natalya, loved to sing and dance. They did it with great animation. The younger brother Kostya was a desperate mischief-maker. He was a student in the municipal school. He had been threatened more than once with expulsion. For the time being he was holding on somehow or other.

The Udoyevs returned home. They were in an uncomfortable and anxious mood. They couldn't sit still.

They had already decided to go early in the morning. But the gatherings had begun in the early evening. And the lower the tired sun declined, the stronger grew the worry and impatience of the children. They kept running out to the gate to look, to listen, to chat with their neighbors and with the passersby.

Nadya was the most worried of all. She was very afraid that they would be late. She said peevishly to her brother and sister: "You'll oversleep, you'll definitely oversleep, I have a premonition."

And she kept nervously wringing her slender, fragile fingers, which was always a sign that she was strongly agitated.

In answer Katya smiled calmly and said with assurance: "It's okay, we won't be late."

"We have to sleep, after all," Lyosha said lazily.

And suddenly he felt lazy, and he thought it would be unpleasant and useless to get up early, and he lost his desire to go. Nadya retorted quickly and hotly: "There he goes! Sleep. There's no need to sleep at all. I'm not going to sleep tonight."

"And you're not going to have supper?" Lyosha asked in a teasing voice.

And suddenly it seemed to them that as if on purpose it was taking a long time for supper to be served, and they got worried. They kept looking at the clock. They pestered their father.

Nadya grumbled: "Why is it that today, as if on purpose, our clock is slow. It was time to have supper a long time ago. No wonder we'll oversleep, if they don't serve supper until after midnight."

Their father said sullenly, "Why are you pestering me? Now one of you, now the other."

And he looked at his children with a gaze that didn't distinguish between them, as if he saw only that there were three of them. He indifferently pulled out his watch and showed them. It was still quite early. They never got ready for supper that early.

Meanwhile news was coming into the Udoyevs' home from all directions, telling them that people were already gathering on Opalikha field—they were coming in crowds—that there was already a crowd there: a whole encampment, with night lodgings and most likely even with tents.

And the children were starting to surmise that in the morning it would be too late to go to Opalikha. By then you wouldn't be able to get through. And this made the mood in the Udoyevs' house extraordinarily anxious.

People kept walking past the Udoyevs' house. More and more people kept walking by. There were some poorly dressed people in the crowd. There were a lot of rowdy boys. It was noisy, cheerful, and festive.

IV.

Several people stopped by the gate of the Udoyevs' house. Animated talk, argument, and laughter could be heard.

Lyosha and his sisters again ran out through the gate.

Several peasant men and women were standing in a small group. There were several of the local townspeople with them. They were talking in a loud, unfriendly tone, as if they were squabbling with each other.

A saucy, middle-aged townswoman with a sharp, crafty face, wearing a calico dress, bright with festive smartness and crackling with starched newness, with a pink kerchief on her oil-smeared hairdo, was saying to a tall, sedate peasant: "You should have stayed at an inn."

The old peasant answered in an unhurried and thoughtful way, as if seeking the precise words to express a significant and profound thought: "Your innkeepers are asking an arm and a leg. They're asking an arm and a leg, I tell you. You can't come to terms with them at all. They're kicking up their heels. There's no Christian cross on these people's gates. They're falling greedily upon their prey, I tell you. They're asking an arm and a leg. They all just want to get rich."

A good-natured lad, with a white face and fair hair, with gentle, clear light-blue eyes and a constant smile on his plump lips, said, "There are some good people who let you stay for free."

Everyone looked at him mockingly. They said, "Yes, there are, but not here."

"Go find some and then tell us about it."

They laughed, with malicious glee for some reason, although there was apparently no reason at all for such glee. The lad grinned, looked around with innocent eyes and assured them: "They let me stay. I swear. One lady let me stay."

"You're a real smooth one," said a red-haired, rough peasant.

The two Shutkin sisters, Elena and Natalya, who looked just like each other, so that it was strange to see that one of them had red hair and the other black, approached along with their elder brother. They listened and smiled slyly, and for some reason it seemed today that their smiles were nasty and they themselves were unclean.

Winking at the Udoyev sisters, the elder Shutkin said, "Are you going to get up early tomorrow?"

"Yes," Lyosha answered with animation, "we're going to get up before dawn, we'll get there before everybody."

And suddenly he remembered that it was quite impossible to get there before everybody, and he felt annoyed.

"Oh, sure, you'll get up, good luck with that!" Shutkin said.

His sisters laughed insolently and slyly. It was unclear what they were laughing at and why. Shutkin said: "What good does it do to go early! It'll be like last year when we went to matins at the monastery."

"That was a lot of fun!" Elena shouted, laughing loudly.

And it was evident that it was all the same to both her and her red-haired sister what they were laughing at, and it didn't seem at all strange or unseemly to them to make fun of themselves.

Shutkin told the story: "It was back last year. We went to bed early, before the lamps were lit. We got a good sleep and then we got up. We didn't have a clock at that time, it was lying around in the pawnshop for the simple reason that we had had a surplus of expenditures over income and there was the necessity to resort to a bond issue of an external twelve-percent loan. So we set off. We walk and walk, and we get there. We see everything is still locked up. We think maybe we came too early. We sit down on a bench by the gate of the holy cloister. The watchman comes up to us and asks us with downright natural amazement, 'What are you all doing sitting here? Did you get bored at home?' And we say to him in a really free-and-easy way, we say, 'we've come for matins; your monks,' we say, 'must have overslept today.' And he says to us, 'What brings you here at the crack of dawn! It just struck eleven a little while ago. Are you really,' he says, 'going to wait that long? You,' he says, 'should go home.' So we listened to his sensible advice and went on home. It was so funny."

The Shutkins and the Udoyevs laughed.

Just then the younger Shutkin boy, Kostya, came running up, panting and sweaty. He shouted joyfully: "I've already been to Opalikha and back."

"Well? What's going on?" both his siblings and the Udoyevs asked him.

Kostya said with a joyful guffaw: "A big mess of peasants has come swarming in, a whole slew of them. The whole field's been dammed up real good."

"What nutcases!" Lyosha said with a peevish laugh. "They aren't even going to start giving out the presents until ten o'clock in the morning, and they've gone there in the evening."

The elder Shutkin burst out laughing and winked at his sisters.

"Who told you that?" he shouted. "They're going to start at two o'clock so that the foreign guests can see. They aren't used to going to bed early. And they get up late."

"No, that's not true, it starts at ten," Lyosha retorted hotly.

"No, it's at two, at two," all the Shutkins shouted at the top of their voices.

By their insolent laughter and the looks they exchanged it was immediately clear that they were lying.

"Well, I'll go find out for sure right now," Lyosha said.

He ran over to the secretary of the city council. His house was not far away. He returned exultant. He shouted from a distance: "At ten."

The Shutkins chuckled and didn't argue any more.

"You thought that up on purpose," Lyosha said, "so that you could go earlier, without us. "You're fine ones!"

The *gimnazia* student Pakhomov, a slim and fidgety boy, ran briskly by. He greeted the Udoyevs hurriedly. The Shutkins looked at him in an unfriendly way.

"What do you say, are you going?" he asked, and without waiting for an answer, he said, "We're going in the evening. A lot of people are going in the evening."

He said good-bye hastily. He glanced at the Shutkins, wanted to nod to them, but he thought better of it and ran on. The Shutkins watched him leave spitefully. They laughed. Their laughter seemed unpleasant and strange to the Udoyevs. What was the point of it?

"Mr. Clean!" Kostya said contemptuously.

Elena said loudly and spitefully: "He's a nasty little show-off. Who needs him! He's a fibber."

The evening was so quiet and beautiful that the pointless and coarse words of the Shutkins produced a particularly abrasive dissonance.

The sun had just gone down. The fiery gleam of its farewell, its scarlet-dead rays were still reflected in the clouds.

Such a beautiful, such a peaceful evening it was. . . . But the burning poison of the dead Serpent was still flowing above the earth.

V.

The Udoyevs returned home. It felt eerie and uncomfortable, and they didn't know what to do with themselves. Quarrels and arguments flared up over every trifle. They were all overcome by restlessness.

And Lyosha suddenly became worried and anxious, like Nadya.

"We won't get there until the whole thing's over," he said loudly and peevishly.

As often happens, these insignificant words decided the matter. Nadya said, "So let's go in the evening."

And everyone agreed with her and immediately cheered up.

Suddenly red-faced, Lyosha shouted, "Of course, if we're going to go, we should go now." All three of them ran to their father to ask permission.

"We changed our minds—we want to go this evening!" Nadya shouted, fidgeting in front of her father.

Their father was sullenly silent.

"There's no harm in not sleeping for one night," Lyosha said, as if he were trying to convince his father of something.

But their father remained silent, and his face was as immobile and sullen as before.

The children left him. They ran to their mother. Their mother started grumbling.

"Papa said we could," Lyosha shouted.

And the sisters laughed and chattered gaily and resoundingly.

With joyful squealing all three of them ran around the house and garden. They tried to hurry the serving of supper.

They remembered the Shutkins. For some reason this memory was annoying. Lyosha said to his sisters, "Not a word to the Shutkins."

The sisters agreed.

"That goes without saying," Nadya said. "The heck with them!"

Katya frowned and drawled out, "They're so disgusting!"

And they immediately started laughing again with joy.

At supper the children ate hastily, and they weren't hungry, and they were annoyed that the old people were dawdling, as if nothing special were happening.

When they were finishing supper, their father suddenly fixed his gaze on the children and looked at them for a long time, so long that they grew quiet under his sullenly indifferent look, and finally he said, "To get shoved around by a lot of drunks—what a great pleasure."

Nadya quickly turned red and started assuring him: "There aren't any drunks. There are no drunks anywhere. Really, it's even strange, but all day today around our house there were no drunks to be seen at all. It was even surprising."

Katya laughed gaily and said, "They're just thinking about the gifts and they don't want to drink. That's not what they're interested in."

Finally supper was over.

They ran off to get dressed. The maidens wanted to dress up in holiday clothes. But their mother vehemently objected.

"Where are you going? Why? To get shoved around by a lot of peasants?" she said angrily.

And it was evident in her entire figure, suddenly on guard, and in her gray, insignificant face, that she was not going to allow holiday clothing to be spoiled for any reason whatsoever.

So the maidens had to put on more ordinary clothes.

Finally, they made their way out of the house. They started running along the steep slope to the river. Hardly had they started the descent when they suddenly saw the Shutkins.

They had to go together. It was annoying.

The Shutkins were annoyed too. Neither the Udoyevs nor the Shutkins would get there first. They had lost their chance to brag and tease.

The Shutkins thought up various ways of making fun of the Udoyevs. They almost had a falling-out several times along the way.

The evening was like daytime, animated and noisy.

Above the city the stars twinkled quietly, as always, so distant, so unnoticed by the distracted gaze and so close, when you peered into their light-blue surroundings.

The clear, pale sky quickly turned dark, and it was joyful to look at the mystery that was being immutably accomplished in it, of the night that was uncovering distant worlds.

There were bells ringing in the monastery; they were holding an all-night vigil. The luminous, sad sounds slowly poured out over the earth. Listening to them, you wanted to sing, and weep, and go somewhere.

And the sky listened spellbound, listened to the bright brass lamentation—the tender, touched sky. And the quiet little clouds listened spellbound as they melted, they listened to the hollow brass lamentation—the quiet, light little clouds.

And the air flowed, made tender and warm as if from a multitude of joyful breaths.

The touched tenderness of the lofty sky and the quietly melting clouds pressed close to the children. And suddenly everything around—the lamentation of the bells, and the sky, and the people—for an instant began to smolder and became music.

Everything became music for an instant—but the instant burned out, and again there stood the objects and deceptions of the material world.

The children were hurrying out of the city, there, to the valley of Opalikha.

In the city it was crowded and noisy, and everyone seemed to be cheerful. Flags waved over the houses. Festive lights burned on the streets, and here and there they smelled of disgusting tallow.

Crowds were walking along the streets, down the slopes, along the embankment of the Safat River. Laughing children darted in and out among the crowd. And everything was resounding and gay, as it is in a fairy tale and as it never happens in life, so ordinary and gray. Because of this, muffled throughout by the general hum, people's speech seemed resonant and like something that could suddenly come true.

Carriages bearing honored guests passed by, and the gracious faces of the important ladies and gentlemen smiled at the crowd.

One could hear quiet, indistinct, foreign talk and light laughter coming from the carriages.

The Shutkins looked with hostile eyes at the rich gentlemen as they passed by. And evil, stupid thoughts were born in their minds.

When they were already leaving the city, the elder Shutkin, grinning stupidly, said, "It would be neat to set fire to the town right now. That kind of thing can be enjoyable, let me tell you."

His sisters and Kostya laughed loudly.

Katya flinched, twitched her little shoulders, and exclaimed anxiously: "What are you talking about, how can you! What terrible things you say!"

"That would really raise a fuss," Kostya said with delight, hopping and squealing.

"But your place would be burned up too," Nadya said in amazement. "What is there for you to be happy about?"

"Well, now," Natalya retorted, "what do we have to burn? We wouldn't miss it."

Nadya looked at her. In the weak gleam of the smoky festival lampions, her freckled face and red hair seemed to be flaming, and her quivering nostrils made it seem as if fire was running over her face.

VI.

They quickly arrived at Opalikha at a run, urged on by feverish, joyful excitement.

Already from afar they could hear the vague and menacing hum of the human multitudes. It inspired an eerie and sweet terror. They ran in the darkness that was setting in along with bursts of night wind. Together with them, now overtaking them, now lagging behind, the people hurried. Big and small. Men, women, children, and old people. Mostly the young. And they all were just as agitated, and their voices resounded unevenly, and their laughter would rise up and suddenly fall silent.

Around a bend in the road the whole valley of Opalikha was revealed all at once, dark, eerily noisy, anxious.

Here and there bonfires were burning, on the outskirts of Opalikha, and because of this the field seemed even darker.

They could see the lights of bonfires even further in. But one could see them, one after another, dying out smokily in the distance of the smoky, noisy field. The crowd must have been putting them out with their feet, trampling the fires' sudden, flaming-aspiring souls with their coarse boots.

And an ever eerier and sweeter terror seized the Udoyevs, trembling behind their twitching shoulders. But they put on a brave face.

The Shutkins were overjoyed that there would be shoving, disorder, and turmoil, and that later they would be able to tell long stories about the curious and significant details of various events.

The elder Shutkin looked at the noisy, dark field, smirked stupidly, and said with inexplicable joy: "They're going to crush some of the weaker ones for sure. You'll see."

But the Udoyevs didn't dare to believe in the nearness of misfortune and death. This field, where there was a noisy multitude—and death. It wasn't possible.

"No two ways about it, they'll crush somebody," one of the Shutkin sisters said in a strangely unfamiliar voice.

And someone laughed a dark laugh, coarsely and mirthlessly, in the darkness.

"Oh, sure!" Katya said indifferently.

It got boring for a moment. Because it was dark. Because of the fleeting and uncertain illumination of the bonfires. And they started to look and listen, and they walked forward, with no fixed destination.

The faces illuminated by the bonfires, for the most part very young faces, and the carefree voices and laughter made it seem as if everyone was having fun.

Noisy multitudes of people were walking, standing, and sitting all over the field.

Getting drawn in more and more to this troubled throng, the Udoyevs were again infected by the cheerfulness and liveliness of the crowd, who had left their accustomed human roofs and walls.

It became cheerful. Too cheerful.

The Shutkins went off somewhere and they didn't see them again. But then the Udoyevs met a lot of other people they knew. They saw a lot of people. They exchanged glad remarks. They came together and again dispersed in the crowd.

They walked forward, or maybe to the side, and the field seemed endless. And it seemed so entertaining that different faces kept coming into view.

"It's so much fun here. You won't even notice the night passing," Nadya said, nervously yawning and shrugging her slender shoulders.

And they walked for a long time, stopping now and then, walked again, got lost among the bonfires, listened in on strangers' conversations, and themselves had conversations with quite strange people.

At first it seemed as if they were walking toward some kind of goal, getting ever closer to it, and everything was defined and connected, although it was also sinking into the sweet eeriness of the throng.

Then suddenly everything became fragmentary and lost connection, and scraps of unnecessary and strange impressions started swarming all around . . .

VII.

Everything became fragmentary and unconnected, and it seemed that absurd and unnecessary objects were emerging out of nothingness. Out of the stupid and hostile darkness something absurd would unexpectedly emerge.

In the middle of the field a ditch had once been dug out for some reason. It remained there to this day, unnecessary, hideous, overgrown with prickly grass that was black in the darkness, and for some reason it seemed terrifying and strangely significant.

The children went up to the edge of the ditch. Two telegraph clerks were sitting with their legs hanging down into the ditch and conversing. They were recalling young ladies they knew and for some reason they were uttering unprintable words with great enjoyment.

The Udoyevs started walking along the edge of the ditch. They saw a plank bridge across it with crooked railings. They walked onto the bridge. The railings seemed flimsy and unsteady.

Lyosha said fearfully, "If they pushed you down here, you'd break your legs."

"Well, we'll walk away a little further," Nadya said.

In the darkness her voice sounded uncertain and timid. It was strange that you couldn't see her lips move as she spoke.

And again they walked on, amid the echoing multitude, passing from circles illuminated by bonfires to pitch darkness—and again the field seemed endless.

"Where the heck are you going?" one tipsy tramp said to another in a persuasive voice. "They'll crush you like a bedbug."

"Let them crush me," his comrade answered. "Do you think I'd miss my life? If they crush me, there won't be anybody to cry for me."

They caught sight of a well. It was covered with half-rotten boards. For some reason they were weakly amazed.

A tipsy peasant, shaking his long, disheveled head, looked into the well and drawled: "Eech."

He ran away from the well, shouting: "Malanya!"

And again he returned to the decrepit structure with the short, sagging steps of a drunk person.

They looked. They laughed. They passed on. His drunken shouts could be heard for a long time.

"I've brought a knife along," a lanky, scrawny ragamuffin said in a hoarse voice.

His comrade, just as ragged and almost as lanky, answered in a sweet tenor voice: "Me too."

"Just in case," the first man's hoarse voice could be heard again.

And they could hear the other one titter.

In the rippling darkness, in the nervously trembling illumination of the bonfires, inhaling the sweetish smoke of damp wood, the children kept walking somewhere, Lyosha in front, his two sisters behind him.

They pretended that they weren't terrified.

Again the field seemed endless, again the bonfires confused them, and the tiredness in their legs made them think that they had been walking for a long time.

"We keep going around in circles," Lyosha said.

And these words expressed their common thoughts. Katya became sad, and Nadya said with feigned cheerfulness: "It's all right, we'll get to where we need to be."

Suddenly Lyosha fell. His feet flashed up above, his head was invisible. The sisters rushed to him. They helped him get out. It turned out that he had fallen with his head and arms into an unexpected hole.

"We need to get away from this place, it's dangerous here," Nadya said.

But later they stumbled time and again on the uneven ground.

VIII.

"So the lords of the manor are here too," a vile tenor voice could be heard saying near the Udoyevs.

They couldn't see who was talking and who was laughing in sympathy with the evil words.

And the children understood that the whole crowd here was hostile and alien through and through—incomprehensible and uncomprehending. And where the bonfires were burning, they could see faces that frowned angrily as they looked at the *gimnazia* student and his sisters.

These hostile gazes perplexed the children. They couldn't understand what this hostility was for. What gave rise to it?

Some strange people were looking in a gloomy and forbidding way at the children as they walked past.

At times they could hear lewd jokes. And since this was in the middle of a huge crowd and no one even thought of standing up for them, the children became afraid.

A drunk workman got up from a bonfire and approached the children.

"Mam'selle!" he exclaimed. "I have the honor of congratulating you on our rendezvous. Pleased to meet you. We can afford you all kinds of pleasure. We wish to give you a kiss."

He swayed. He took off his cap. He grabbed Katya with his paws. He kissed her right on the lips.

A roar of laughter resounded in the crowd. Katya burst into tears.

Lyosha shouted something, rushed at the drunk and pushed him away.

The drunk growled ferociously: "What right do you have? You push me? And what if I wish to kiss her? Where's the displeasure in that?"

The sisters grabbed Lyosha by the arms. They quickly led him away into the darkness.

They were very frightened. The insult burned agonizingly.

They wanted to leave this dark and unclean place. But they could not find the way. Again the lights of the bonfires confused them, blinded their eyes, manifested a dark that was blacker than dark and made everything incomprehensible and torn.

Soon the bonfires started to go out. And it became evenly dark in the air, and the black night pressed down to the echoing field and became heavy above its noises and voices. The fact that people were not sleeping and were in a crowd made it seem that this night was significant, unique, and the last.

IX.

They hadn't been there long, and already it was disgusting, nauseating, terrifying.

In the darkness, for some reason, an unnecessary, incongruous, and therefore vile life was being created. Shelterless people, far from the coziness of home, became drunk on the savage air of the dark, hellish night.

They had brought with them nasty vodka and strong beer, and they drank all night, and they yelled in hoarse, drunken voices. They ate stinking food. They sang indecent songs. They danced shamelessly. They guffawed. Here and there one could hear absurd fussing. A vile harmonica squealed.

It smelled awful everywhere, and everything was disgusting, dark, and terrifying.

And tipsy, hoarse voices resounded everywhere.

Here and there men and women were necking. From under one bush two pairs of feet stuck out, and one could hear the fitful, disgusting squealing of passion being satisfied.

Here and there in the few open spots, circles gathered. Something was being done in the middle of the circles.

Some disgusting, dirty boys were dancing a wild Cossack dance.

In another circle, a drunken, noseless peasant woman was dancing frantically and waving her dirty, torn skirt shamelessly.[4] Then she started singing in a repulsive nasal voice. The words of her song were just as shameless as her horrible face, as her awful dance.

"Why do you have a knife?" a policeman asked someone sternly.

"I'm a working man," an insolent voice replied. "I grabbed my tool for any eventuality. I can also use it to stab."

A guffaw rang out.

And it was in that disgusting crowd, cast into a vile orgy at the wrong time of their awakened life, that the children walked and were lost in the throng. The field seemed endless because they were walking in circles in a small space.

It got more and more difficult to pass through; it became more cramped everywhere.

It seemed that more and more people were appearing all around from out of nowhere.

And suddenly the crowd contracted around the Udoyevs. It became cramped. And suddenly it seemed that a heavy stuffiness was spreading over the earth and creeping up to their faces.

But a dark, strange coolness was flowing from the dark sky. They wanted to look up, at the bottomless sky, at the cool stars.

Lyosha leaned on Nadya's shoulder. An instantaneous sleep had overcome him . . .

. . . He's flying in the dark-blue sky, light as a free bird . . .

Someone shoved him. Lyosha woke up. He said in a sleepy voice: "I almost fell asleep. I even dreamed something."

"Don't go to sleep, Nadya said worriedly. "We'll get lost in the crowd."

"I'd love to sleep," Katya said quietly and plaintively.

"We really shouldn't get lost," Nadya said.

She tried to gather her courage. She said with animation, "Let's put Lyosha in the middle."

"Oh, yes," Lyosha said sluggishly.

He was pale and strangely dull.

But the sisters put him between them. They were distracted by protecting him from the shoving. For the time being the crowd did not disturb their arrangement as it restively shoved them in all directions.

"We're here, so they should give out the gifts now," a strangely cheerful and indifferent voice could be heard.

And someone answered: "Just wait. In the morning the gentlemen who are assigned to the distribution will arrive."

X.

It was cramped and stuffy, they wanted to make their way out of the crowd, into the open space, to breathe with their whole chests.

But they could not make their way out. They were entangled in the dark, faceless crowd, like a canoe entangled in the reeds.

They could no longer choose their route, turn at will in one direction or the other. They had to be dragged along with the crowd, and the movements of the crowd were heavy and slow.

The Udoyevs slowly moved somewhere. They thought they were walking forward because everyone was walking in the same direction. But then suddenly the crowd would move backward, heavily and slowly. Or it would be dragged slowly to the side. And then it became quite incomprehensible where one should go, where was the goal and where the way out.

They caught sight of dark walls nearby, a little to the side. For some reason they wanted to make their way out to the walls. They imagined something familiar and homey in them.

They didn't say anything to each other but started pushing their way through to those dark walls.

And soon they were standing next to one of the folk theaters.

It seemed that next to the walls there was something familiar, protective—a kind of coziness—and hence it wasn't so terrifying.

The dark top of the wall rose up and covered half of the sky, and that made them lose the eerie impression of the elemental, boundless crowd.

The children stood pressed up to the wall. They looked timidly at the gray, dim images of people, which flickered so close by. And it was hot from the breathing of the nearby throng.

From the sky a chilly coolness came pressing down in bursts, and it seemed that the stuffy earthly air was struggling with the heavenly coolness.

"We should go home," Katya said plaintively. "We won't be able to push through, no matter what."

"It's okay, let's wait," Lyosha answered, trying to seem lively and cheerful.

At that moment a heavy movement passed through the crowd, as if someone was pushing through to the wall, right at the children. They were pressed to the wall, and it became quite stuffy and hard to breathe.

Then with an effort the crowd gave way, and it seemed that the wall was shaking and wobbling, and out of the crowd two very pale students emerged carrying a burden.

They were carrying a little girl, and she seemed to be lifeless. Her pale arms hung down like those of a dead person, and on her face with its tightly compressed lips and closed eyes there lay a dim blueness.

In the crowd there was grumbling talk: "She's weak, but she pushed her way in here."

"What are the parents thinking of—to let a kid like that come here!"

In the confused crosstalk of the crowd could be heard the desire to justify something that should not have happened—and it seemed that for an instant these people understood that they should not be here pressing each other.

XI.

Again the crowd started moving coarsely and heavily. The heavy shoves agonizingly reverberated in their bodies. Coarse boots stepped on the children's lightly shod feet.

They couldn't keep standing by the wall. They were pushed away, driven away. They were squeezed in a cramped ring. Again it became terrifying in the stuffy throng.

The children had difficulty raising their heads, and their lips greedily tried to catch the intermittent streams of heavenly coolness, while their chests suffocated in the dense and incomprehensible crush.

They were not quite moving somewhere, not quite standing. And they had no idea how much time had passed.

The children were worn out by an agonizing thirst for space.

And by thirst.

It had come creeping up slowly for a long time now. Suddenly it was expressed in piteous words.

"I'm thirsty," Lyosha said.

And as he said it, he felt that his lips had long been dried out and that his mouth felt uncomfortable and worn out from dryness.

"Me too," Katya said, moving her parched, pale lips with difficulty.

Nadya was silent. But from her pale and suddenly hollow-cheeked face and her dryly burning eyes it was evident that she too was being tormented by thirst.

To drink. If only a little swallow of water. Water—holy, dear, cool, fresh water.

But there was nowhere to get water.

And the coolness from the distant sky became ever more fleeting, rippling, uncertain. It would puff into their greedily opened mouths and then burn out.

Nadya was hiccuping. She flinched slightly. She hiccuped again and again and again.

She couldn't restrain it. Such agonizing hiccuping in the crowdedness and stuffiness!

Lyosha looked at Nadya in fright. How pale she was!

"Lord," Nadya said, hiccuping. "What torture! What made us want to come here?"

Katya started quietly weeping. Swift, tiny tears ran down one after another, and she could not stop the tears or wipe them away. She couldn't lift her arms, they were crushing her so.

"Why are you pushing!" a thin little voice squeaked somewhere nearby. "You're crushing me."

A hoarse, drunken bass voice answered maliciously: "What? I'm crushing you? You don't like such a ceremony? Well, so you crush me. Everyone's equal here, goddamnit."

"Ow, ow, they're crushing me," the same thin little voice squealed again.

"Stop squealing, you snotnose," the ferocious bass voice rasped. "Just wait till you get home, or they drag you there. They'll have your guts, you brat."

After a brief moment a thin, harsh squeal shot out, without words, plaintive and piteous. And in answer to it a ferocious shout: "Stop squealing."

Then a thin, crushed howl.

Someone screamed: "They've crushed a little child! His little bones are crunching. Holy Queen of Heaven!"

"His little bones crunched, his bones!" a peasant woman squealed.

Her voice could be heard nearby, but they couldn't see her in the crowd.

And then it seemed that she was screaming somewhere very far away. Had she been pushed away from this place? Or had she suffocated?

The children were so crushed by the crowd that it was hard to breathe. They talked to each other in a hoarse whisper. They couldn't turn around. They had difficulty looking at each other.

And it was terrifying to look at each other, at the dear faces clouded by leaden terror in the dim pre-dawn twilight.

Nadya continued to hiccup, and Katya also hiccuped.

All around, in all this crowd that was so terribly and so absurdly pressed together, could be felt a single desire, tormenting and thus not yet recognized, and thus even more tormenting: to be liberated from this terrible vise.

But there was no way out—and a frenzy began to simmer in the insane crowd, absurdly compressed by their own will, in this spacious field, under this spacious sky.

The people turned into beasts and looked with beastly malice at the children.

They could hear hoarse, terrible talk. A person nearby, indifferent and so strangely calm, said that there were already people who had been crushed to death.

"The poor little corpsie is standing just as they squeezed him," a piteous whisper could be heard nearby. "He's all blue, so horrible, and his head keeps waggling."

"Did you hear, Nadya?" Katya asked in a whisper. "They say a dead person is standing over there, crushed."

"They must be talking nonsense," Nadya whispered. "He just fainted."

"But maybe it's true?" Lyosha said.

And terror could be heard in his hoarse voice.

"It can't be true," Nadya argued. "A dead person would fall down."

"But there's nowhere to fall," Lyosha answered.

Nadya fell silent. Again the hiccuping started to torment her.

A gray-haired, shaggy old woman, waving her arms over her head as if she were swimming, came crawling out of the crowd straight at the Udoyevs. Howling frantically, she pushed her way by them, and it was so cramped and heavy that it seemed she was passing right through them like a nail.

Her frantic wailing, her agonizing appearance in the pale, turbid pre-dawn haze was like a phantom from a bad dream. And from that moment everything in the consciousness of the suffocating children was lassitude and delirium.

XII.

Finally, after the exhausting and terrible night, the light quickly set in.

Quick, joyful, childishly cheerful, the dawn blazed up and began to laugh with the laughter of its little pink clouds. Golden spangles flared up in the hazy distance. And while the earth was still dark and stern, the sky was already blazing with joy, the worldwide joy of eternal triumph. And people—oh, people! They're still only people!

Between the dark earth, so sinful, so burdened, and the blessed sky, illuminated anew, there spread a dense vapor from the breaths of a great multitude of people.

The night's coolness, rolling up into the sky's golden dreams, burned away in the light clouds, in the rays of dawn.

And the crowd, so strangely and unexpectedly illuminated from above by the serene laughter of dawn—that huge earthly crowd was penetrated through and through by malice and terror.

The crowd moved with difficulty, straining forward . . . and again, those coming from the city dull-wittedly and maliciously crowded forward those standing in front, toward the sheds in which the gifts were stored.

Under the eternal gold of the dawn, the dull tin of the wretched gift mugs dragged the people into turmoil and congestion.

In lassitude and delirium, grievous, slow thoughts crowded into the consciousness of the children, into their dark consciousness as they suffocated, and each thought was terror and anguish. A cruel doom was drawing near. Their own doom. The doom of their dear ones. And which was more painful?

As if waking up from time to time, they began to shout, and complain, and beg.

Their hoarse voices flew weakly up, like a wounded bird with a broken wing, and piteously fell, and they drowned in the hollow hum of the dull-witted crowd.

The dull, stern gazes of sullen people were their answer.

Anguish cramped their breathing and whispered evil, hopeless words.

And there was no longer any hope of leaving. People were evil. Both evil and weak. They could not save them and they could not save themselves.

Begging could be heard all around, howls, moans—vain begging.

Whom could you beg here, in this crowd?

They no longer seemed to be people. It seemed to the suffocating children that ferocious demons were looking at them sullenly and laughing soundlessly from under human masks that were slipping down and rotting away.

And the devilish masquerade kept on going, agonizingly. And it seemed that there would be no end to it, no end to the boiling of this satanic cauldron.

XIII.

The sun rose rapidly, the joyfully energized, evil Dragon. It smelled of the hot breath of the Serpent. Incinerating the last streams of coolness, the evil Dragon rose up.

The crowd started heaving to and fro.

The hum of voices swept past above the crowd.

Everything around became so distinct. As if pulled off by an invisible hand, the worn-out masks fell away.

Demonic malice boiled all around, in lassitude and delirium.

Ferocious, satanic muzzles could be seen everywhere. The dark mouths on the dull faces vomited out coarse words.

Lyosha started moaning.

A red-haired devil, flashing his dry eyes, roared at him: "You got yourself here, so just put up with it. Get a grip on yourself, you scum made of sugar. We didn't invite you. We'll squeeze the guts clean out of you."

The raging Serpent enraged the people.

It seemed that the sun had risen rapidly and immediately become high and merciless.

And it became so hot and stuffy, and such thirst was wearing everyone out.

Someone was sobbing.

Someone prayed piteously: "If only a little bit of water from the sky!"

Katya was hiccuping.

Sometimes some strangely, terribly familiar faces would appear. Like all the faces in this beastly crowd, they too had hardened in their horrible transformation.

It was even more terrible to look at them than at the strangers, because a familiar face that had turned beastly was even more pain- fully perceived.

Lyosha felt that someone was pressing on his shoulders. They were pressing him so heavily into the earth. Into the dark, cruel earth.

Someone was trying to climb up.

There were several sharply agonizing minutes. Then for a brief moment there was relief. Then the person who was climbing up stepped on Lyosha's head with his boot. Lyosha could hear Nadya's quiet scream.

Someone dark and heavyset started walking over the top of the crowd to the side, along people's shoulders and heads, and was swaying strangely in the air.

Lyosha raised his head in order to breathe in the air of the high open spaces. But it was hot in the heights.

The sky shone, clear, triumphant, unattainably high, tenderly strewn with the mother-of-pearl of fleecy clouds in the west.

A sea of triumphant light was pouring forth from the just-risen sun. And the sun was new, bright, majestic, and ferociously indifferent. Indifferent forever and ever. And all its splendor sparkled over the hum of languor and delirium.

Someone stomped heavily on Lyosha's feet.

Katya was hiccuping painfully and agonizingly.

"Just stop!" Lyosha shouted hoarsely.

Katya started laughing loudly. Laughter mixed with hiccups was strange and pitiful.

And now, all over the spaciousness of the field, drifted a heavy, unceasing hum of shouts, moans, and squeals.

And then came minutes of reciprocal, senseless malice.

People beat each other, as much as the congestion allowed. They kicked each other. They bit each other. They grabbed each other by the throat and tried to strangle each other.

They shoved the weaker ones to the earth and stood on them.

Shouts and moans, begging and cursing—everything Lyosha heard, he repeated in a lifeless, suffocated voice, and like two more puppets, his sisters prattled it all after him.

XIV.

The begging and moaning suddenly became quiet and drowsy.

There set in brief and strange half-hours of lull, languor, weariness without end, quiet, eerie delirium.

The hum of delirium was floating above the crowd, a quiet hum, so crushed, so eerie.

And now this hum was poured out in everything, and all three of them saw, glimmering through the smoke of delirium, the terrible consciousness of doom.

The two sisters were painfully hiccuping.

"God's little angel!" someone squealed nearby.

The morning drowsiness of the people half-crushed in the crowd was occasionally interrupted by savage howls of despair.

And again it would become quiet, and an eerie hum would drift over the crowd, not rising up to the exultant open spaces, to the immobile, evil Serpent of the heights.

Someone was agonizingly hiccuping. It seemed that it was someone dying in agony.

Lyosha listened and understood that it was Nadya hiccuping. With an effort, Lyosha turned his head toward her. Nadya's blue lips were opening and closing with a strange, mechanical movement. Her eyes were not looking anywhere, and her face had taken on a dull, deathly hue.

XV.

The languid period of calm lasted only briefly. And suddenly a storm of absurd hums and howls began wailing over the turbulent crowd. Savage exclamations scourged the air.

It was evident from the faces distorted by malice that there were no longer any people here. The devils had torn off their momentary masks and were exulting painfully.

Several people in the crowd suddenly went mad in these moments. They howled, and bellowed, and shouted something absurd and horrible.

From under the feet of the people there often burst forth savage, dying howls. There on the earth, thrown down, people who had been knocked off their feet could no longer get up.

And these howls shook the souls of those few who had remained human in the terrible crowd of devils in human form.

A ragged hooligan and his debauched and drunken girlfriend were standing next to each other. They looked at each other and said malicious words. The hooligan moved his shoulder strangely.

He freed his arm with an effort of frenzied malice. A knife flashed in his hand. The swift steel trembled with such sharp laughter in the bright rays of the sun.

The knife pierced the body of the harlot. She squealed: "Goddamn you!"

She choked on her squeal. She died.

The hooligan cried out. He bent over her. He gnawed at her fat red neck.

"They've completely crushed us, we're going to die now," Katya said in a hoarse voice.

Lyosha looked at her out of the corner of his eye, laughed senselessly and said loudly and distinctly: "They've crushed Nadya. She's cold."

And big tears rolled down his face, but his pale lips were smiling senselessly.

Katya was silent. Her face started to turn blue, and the light went out of her eyes.

Lyosha was suffocating.

His feet stepped on something soft. An acrid stench rose up from the earth. Something was tossing around down below, wheezing heavily.

"It stinks!" a strangely indifferent voice said from behind Lyosha. "They knocked a woman down and squeezed out her belly."

Katya's blue face drooped strangely, lifelessly.

Lyosha became cold all of a sudden.

XVI.

"It's six o'clock," someone said.

By his voice it could be heard that it was a hefty, calm person who wasn't terrified to be in the crowd.

"We have to wait another four hours," a timid, suffocating whisper answered him.

"Wait for what?" someone barked maliciously in an echoing voice.

"We're all just going to croak," a woman's deep voice answered calmly and quietly.

Someone cried out desperately in a breaking, half-childish shout: "Brothers, are we really going to have to keep getting squashed for all that time!"

An agitated hum dashed around the field, like a noisy flock of skittish, black-winged birds. It dashed, it howled, it swayed. And the crowd dashed to meet it.

"It's time, brothers!" someone's shrill voice screamed. "Look sharp, or those damn devils will grab it all for themselves."

"Go, go," buzzed all around.

The whole crowd now started moving rapidly and heavily.

And the bent, immobile faces of Lyosha's sisters looked at him, his sisters who were cold and heavy on his shoulders.

The undone hair of his dear ones tickled Lyosha's pale cheeks.

His feet could not take a step. The crowd carried all three of them, Lyosha and his sisters.

"They're handing them out!" someone shouted.

One could see some multicolored little bundles flying in the air, seemingly not far away.

"Grab what you can!" a haggard, scrawny peasant wheezed sullenly.

"Why did you stop, get going!" those in the back shouted frantically to those in front.

"They're not letting our bunch through, those anathemas are pushing to the front, and we're just—stop and wait!" someone screamed ferociously.

And frenzied shouts flew from all directions: "Brothers, shove on through!"

"Why are you staring at that damn devil—grab him by the throat and push him to the ground!"

"Shove on through, why are you staring!"

"If they don't give it to us, we'll take it ourselves!"

"Ow, ow, they've crushed me!"

"God in heaven, my guts are slipping out!"

"Choke on your guts, you goddamned scum!"

"Slash her, that Astrakhan bitch!"

"Give it to us, don't hold it up!" a ferocious voice roared up in front.

XVII.

All around, ferocious, desperate faces threatened.

A heavy stream. And always the same malice . . .

A knife cut clothing. And a body.

She howled. She died.

So terrifying.

The strangely blue faces of his dear ones look at him lifelessly . . .

Someone is laughing loudly. About what?

The end is near. Here are the walls of the sheds already . . .

In the upraised hand of a hefty lad a mug shone dully in the golden sunlight. And his hand was raised to the sky strangely and unnaturally, like a living gesture.

Someone dashed upwards. They knocked the mug out of his hand—so weakly was his hand, blue with strain, holding it.

The mug fell slowly, heavily, describing an arc. It slipped along somebody's back.

The hefty lad cursed foully.

He was red and sweaty, and the whites of his eyes, bulging out from the strain, seemed large.

He bent over with great difficulty to get the mug. You could see how his elbows were moving.

Suddenly he collapsed with a muffled cry.

Someone had toppled onto his bent back. He toppled and started shouting. Floundering, he began crawling forward over the back of the fallen man. Someone else toppled onto both of them, stomach first. All three of them sagged down. One could hear muffled howls. The topmost one got up and seemed very tall. The crowd merged over the fallen ones, and by its heavy settling you could see how the two crushed men sank to the ground.

A hefty peasant with a face reddened to a crimson blueness, moving his elbows and shoulders, freed his right arm and stretched it forward. They squeezed him. His hand waggled strangely on someone else's shoulder, its redness next to a red kerchief.

The woman in the red kerchief turned and dug her teeth into the hand of the hefty peasant. Her malice was incomprehensible.

Ferociously screaming, the peasant pulled his hand away. He worked his elbows desperately. It seemed as if he was growing.

He was pushed upwards. He fell onto some people's heads, and malicious voices buzzed beneath him. He got up onto someone's shoulders with his knees. He fell again.

Falling, getting up, again falling, getting onto his hands and knees, he made his way forward, and the crowd below him was a continuous, uneven pavement, a heavily moving glacier.

And now many people were pushing upwards by using their elbows.

Several people could be seen awkwardly running over shoulders and heads to the roofs of the kiosks.

And now many had clambered up onto the roofs.

XVIII.

Two women grabbed each other. Silently, sullenly. One stuck her fingers into the mouth of the other and tore her mouth. Blood could be seen. A desperate squeal was heard.

They slashed out with knives in order to make a path for themselves, and they shoved the people they had killed under their feet. Sometimes the murderer would fall on the person he had killed, and both of them would droop under the feet of the multitude of ferocious devils.

Many fell into the ravine. Others toppled onto them. In a short time, the ravine was filled with grievously howling people, dying in agony. And the devils trampled them with their feet, shod in heavy boots.

A red-haired lad in front of Lyosha had long been climbing upwards, desperately working his elbows, leaning on the shoulders of his neighbors. He was shouting something indistinct and laughing hoarsely.

At first it was impossible to understand what he wanted and what was happening to him. Suddenly he began to rise up quickly, and for a short time he blocked everything that was up ahead from Lyosha's eyes.

His absurd shouts fell into the dull-witted crowd from above like sharp, whistling scourges, and it was strange to hear the vile voice seemingly descending from the sky. And then his words became clear.

And his words were—sacrilege, and blasphemy, and foul profanity.

Then he suddenly collapsed headfirst and hit Lyosha in the forehead with his heel.

But he immediately started to rise up again. He got up onto his hands and feet. He grabbed the light-brown braid of a half-crushed young girl. He got up onto someone's shoulders.

Red-faced and red-haired, he guffawed as he walked forward unevenly, stepping with his heavy boots on shoulders and heads indiscriminately.

Resembling a devil, he walked slowly over the compressed, heavily roaring crowd, and disappeared into the distance.

And again it seemed to Lyosha through his terrible languor, and nausea, and the crimson fog in his eyes, that someone enormous, with his head as high as the sky—and even higher—a person, or a devil, or a person-devil, was walking along the heads of the dying and suffocating crowd of people and hurling terrible blasphemies at them.

Up in front, the crowd was pressing through the narrow passageways between the wooden cabins. Howls, squeals, and moans could be heard from there. Caps and scraps of clothing flashed, flying upwards for some reason.

Someone's light-brown head knocked several times against the sharp corner of the show booth, drooped, was carried with a burst forward, and suddenly disappeared.

It seemed that people who became taller and taller were crowding between the show booths. It was strange to see heads on a level with the roof of the booth. They were walking on the bodies of the fallen.

From behind the show booths one could hear the triumphant roar of the victors. Some multicolored rags flashed; something was being tossed back and forth through the air.

And now Lyosha and his sisters were pushed into one of the passageways between the booths.

Here it was unbearably cramped—it seemed to Lyosha that all his bones had been broken. And the broken bodies of his sisters weighed terribly on his shoulders.

But the narrow passageway ended.

Beyond the show booth it was spacious, light, joyful.

"I'm going to die now," Lyosha thought and laughed happily.

For an instant Lyosha saw someone's red, joyful face and a person shaking a bundle over his head.

And he fell.

His two sisters had collapsed onto him. They covered half of him with their crumpled bodies.

Lyosha could still hear people running over him, stepping in a staccato along his back. The ferocious blows of the devilish feet reverberated heavily in his whole body.

Someone's heel stepped on the back of his head.

There was a momentary sensation of nausea.

Death.

1907

DEATH BY ADVERTISEMENT

Rezanov felt so weak, tired, and faded. His thoughts inclined more and more often to the eternal quietus. It seemed that there was no sweeter rest than on the couch made of boards, in the pinewood casket.

And suddenly he desired an entertainment that was not on the established program.

He was sitting alone in his quiet room.

He was reading the advertisements in *New Times* very attentively. He was looking for something. He was comparing and selecting.

His pale face, which was beginning to fade, showed signs of confusion and indecisiveness. Deep in thought, he took up a pencil. He put the pencil point on the lampshade.

His hand was trembling. The pencil point rattled. He grinned. He thought: "I'm getting old."

Again he lowered his eyes, which had once been eternally merry, but now were weary and indifferent, and bent his attentive, calm gaze to the newspaper pages.

Finally, he chose a certain advertisement.

A cultured young lady, beautiful and well educated, finding herself in extreme want, was asking kind people to lend her fifty rubles; she would agree to any conditions. She asked that they write to Post Office No. 17, *poste restante*, to the bearer of Receipt No. 205824.

From a little box Rezanov took a sheet of yellowish, rough paper with uneven edges, with the watermark Margaret Mill.[1]

Grinning mirthlessly, he wrote:

Dear Madam,

I will give you the money you are asking for, but not as a debt and not for nothing, but for work, about which I will now write you. By necessity, I will write in brief; there is much one cannot say in a letter. But since, according to you, you are a cultured lady, you will perhaps understand what exactly is being required of you. You must appear to me in the form of my death—the more appealing the death, the better—and you must conduct yourself consistently with this. If you find a way to enliven this merry game, to diversify it to a sufficient degree, your wages henceforth may suffice for your living expenses even into the future. Do you agree? Are you not afraid? Do you understand what is being required of you? If you agree, and you are not afraid, and you understand, then write me when and where I can meet you for the first time. For me the most convenient time is after five o'clock in the evening. Write to the Main Post Office to the bearer of a three-ruble note numbered 384384. I will pick up the letter on Thursday.

The fresh new three-ruble note, in the tastelessly beautiful 1905 design, crackled unpleasantly, like the starched dress of a scatterbrained woman taking Communion. The numbers 384 were repeated twice. This coincidence seemed strange and momentous.

He thought, "And if?"

He gave a pallid smile.

"Well, let it be so."

He didn't sign it. He sealed it. He took it himself and threw it into the mailbox, so that it wouldn't be forgotten until morning, so that it would arrive more quickly.

Then he went home and thought about what form she would come in.

Scrawny, ugly, with a face turned brownish from poverty and suffering, with yellow teeth, with sparse, reddish hair hanging in disheveled locks under a hat well-worn by rain and wind, with a feather and a ribbon fluttering on it pitifully and ludicrously?

Or young, shy, quiet, with the slender fingers of a seamstress, pricked all over by her needle, with a pale, seemingly waxen little face, with a big, sweet mouth?

Or would she come as a drunken prostitute, painted, saucy, with a shrill voice and coarse gestures?

Or a vulgar provincial lady in an unbelievable outfit, with impossible manners, with an unwashed neck, abandoned by her husband and unable to find a job?

What will she be like, my death? My death!

Or will she meet me in a dark passageway, and will I not see her, but just drop my poor gold into her cold hand?

On Thursday he went to the post office. The summer day in the capital city was dusty, hot, and noisy. Here and there the pavement was being repaired, houses were being painted, and it smelled so unpleasant. But all the same it was cheerful and habitual, and the signboards of familiar restaurants looked festive and elegant.

He didn't hurry. He drank beer at Leiner's restaurant.[2] He didn't meet any people he knew. And who would he meet now? Unless maybe by chance.

It was almost four when he passed through the narrow open doors into the new glass-roofed hall of the post office. He recalled the old, spittle-flecked nook where they used to hand out *poste restante* letters. These days even government officials worry about having things look pretty.

He stopped by a booth selling paper and envelopes. The revolving display window showed him all kinds of saccharine vulgarity on greeting cards, one worse than the other.

"Do people buy these?" he asked the saleswoman.

The comely maiden with a bored face twitched her fat shoulders petulantly.

"What do you need?" she asked in a hostile tone. "Envelopes, letters, postcards."

He looked fixedly at her. He noted the crimped curls on her forehead, her porcelain skin, her dark-blue pupils. He said, "I need nothing at all."

And he walked on.

Right opposite the entrance, behind a central double window in a large square partition, sat three maidens sorting letters. The recipients were standing outside. A fat lady with a wart on her nose was asking for a letter addressed to Ruslan-Zvonaryova.

"Is your last name Zvonaryova?" asked the young lady postal employee with a face the color of a wheaten bun, and she went into the depths of the room to the cabinet that held the letters.

"Ruslan-Zvonaryova," the lady with the wart said to the retreating girl in a frightened half-whisper.

And when the wheaten postal maiden returned to the window with a packet of letters, the lady with the wart repeated: "I have a hyphenated last name, Ruslan-Zvonaryova."

Next to her stood a red-haired gentleman with a bowler hat in his hand who was looking with anxious eyes at the letters that a second postal maiden was sorting through; she was the most beautiful of the three and very proud of it. The gentleman, by all indications, was awaiting a "sensitive and frivolous" letter, and he was excited, and he was homely and pitiful.

The third maiden, plump and ruddy, with a broad, short face, with a broad curtain of thick chestnut hair lowered onto her forehead, was laughing at some private joke. She kept turning to the two other girls—they were smiling too—and she kept laughing and saying fragmented words about something amusing.

Rezanov extended his three-ruble note to her silently. He was looking at the maidens and thinking that they were young, healthy, and comely. The post office authorities had selected them for this reason, in their worry about the decorous look of their establishments.

He recalled a recent newspaper polemic between the postal director and a woman applicant who had been denied a position at the post office because she was scrawny, homely, listless from timidity, poverty, and malnutrition, and old—a whole thirty-two years old.

He closed his eyes. Someone's pale, emaciated, frightened face with eyes wide open, with lips twitching nervously and timidly, rose up before him. Someone whispered, so clearly and quietly: "I have nothing to live on."

Someone answered, quietly and calmly: "Then don't live."

Rezanov opened his eyes. He looked with a gaze of hatred at the plump-faced maiden who was looking for a letter filed under his number, tossing postcards and letters out of the packet onto the table one after the other. She kept laughing. So disgustingly, so tiresomely.

Finally, she held out a letter in a narrow, stamped envelope. She riffled through the other letters.

"There aren't any others."

"I don't need any others," Rezanov said peevishly.

He went off to the side and sat on a bench by a column. He tore open the envelope. He was hurrying, but he was calm.

Large, narrow letters, fine lines, an even and calm handwriting, unexpectedly beautiful.

Dear Sir,

I agree. I am not afraid. I understand. Thursday, after five o'clock. Mikhailovsky Garden, the avenue of trees to the right of the entrance. White dress. In my right hand your letter in an envelope.

Signed, Your Death.

The watchman rang a bell. The hall emptied. Rezanov went to the "Vienna" restaurant. He had dinner. He drank beer. He was in a hurry.

He got to the garden at five thirty.

She was standing not far from the entrance, at the edge of the avenue, under a tree. Her dress showed white against the dark green of the quiet garden.

Slender, pale, very quiet and calm. She looked at him attentively as he approached her. Gray, calm eyes. They gave nothing away. But they were attentive. On the quite plain face there was an expression of clarity and submissiveness. The lips of the large mouth smiled in a sweet, sad way.

"Darling death," he said quietly.

He stood before her. Strangely excited, he extended his hand to her.

She was silent. She put his letter into her left hand. She pressed his hand with her slender, cold, quiet hand.

"Have you been waiting for me long?" he said in an intimate tone.[3]

She answered just as intimately, slowly pronouncing the words one after the other, in a clear, lifelessly flat, deathly calm voice: "You weren't expecting me. You thought you would meet someone else."

And it seemed that coldness was wafting from her. And so quiet, so motionless were the folds of her white dress. Her simple straw hat with a white ribbon, placed high on her head, cast a yellow shadow on her serene face. Standing in front of Rezanov, she bent slightly and drew a thin line on the sand with the tip of her light umbrella, from left to right, between him and her.

He asked: "Is it true that you have agreed to be my death?"

And this was the quiet reply: "I am your death."

He asked again, feeling coldness in his body: "Are you really not afraid to perform such a dismal role?"

She said: "Death is afraid of the living and does not show herself to them so directly. You are perhaps the first who has seen my face, the earthly, human face of your death."

He said: "You are assuming your role very quickly and too conscientiously. Tell me, what is your name?"

She smiled sadly and gently. She said: "I am your death, white, quiet, and placid. Hasten to breathe earthly air—your hours are numbered."

He frowned. He said: "You are a cultured lady, you find yourself in a straitened situation, and you're asking for money. What brought you to such an extremity that you would agree to any conditions? And even to play such a terrible game?"

She answered: "I am hungry, ill, tired, and sad."

He burst out laughing. He said: "First of all, take a rest. Why are you standing? Sit down on a bench."

They walked a few steps. They sat down. She was drawing an intricate pattern on the sand.

He said: "You are hungry. If you like, we can go somewhere, and I'll feed you. I'll give you money, as much as you want. Tell me, is there anything else you want from me?"

She said: "I will take from you everything that you can give—your gold and your soul."

He flinched. He laughed. He said: "You are playing your role well."

She answered: "I have arrived. My hour will come soon. I am waiting."

He pulled out a little purse.

In a small middle compartment behind a steel fastener lay five gold coins that had been prepared in advance. He took them out.

She silently extended her pale, narrow hand—so quiet and calm—with the open palm turned upwards. Faint lines drew a clear and simple pattern on her white, motionlessly opened palm.

The five gold coins, quietly jingling against each other with a resonant ring, fell onto the cold, unwavering palm. The hand closed unhurriedly, the slender fingers, long and white, clenched, and the hand with the money sank deliberately into a slit hidden in the side of her white skirt.

And he thought: "My poor gold . . . my last gift . . . the meager wages of the day-laborer . . . a small payment for a boundless labor—to you, my darling."

Did he only think it? Did he say it aloud? These words resounded so clearly! Such sadness constricted his chest!

And she sadly looked at him sideways with her attentive gray eyes and smiled. Then she bent over, and the tip of her umbrella rustled quietly on the sand.

And she whispered: "I have taken your gold—I will take your soul. You have given up your gold to me—you will give up your soul to me."

He said quietly: "You have taken my gold, because I gave it to you. But how will you take my soul? And in what place are you going to take it?"

And she said: "I will come to you at my hour and I will take your soul. And you will give up your soul to me. You will give it up because I am your death, and you will not be able to get away from me."

He was wearied by anguish. He said in a harsh voice, conquering his anguish and terror: "You live in a rented room, you are looking for a position or work, your name is Marya or Anna. What is your name?"

And he shouted with savage malice: "Tell me what your name is!"

She repeated impassively: "I am your death."

Those were the hopeless and merciless words that fell. He flinched. He drooped. He asked in a crestfallen voice: "You need my gold because you are hungry and tired. But my soul, why do you need my soul?"

She answered: "With your gold I will buy bread and wine, and I will eat and drink, and I will feed my hungry little deathlings. And then I will pull out your soul and take it carefully, put it on my shoulders, and descend with it into the dark palace where your and my invisible lord dwells, and I will give your soul up to him. And he will squeeze the juice of your soul into a deep chalice, where my quiet tears will also sink. And he will splash the juice of your soul, mixed with my quiet tears, onto the midnight stars."

Quietly, unhurriedly, word after word, the strange speech resounded, like the formula for a dark spell.

And who was walking by, and what kind of voices were resounding all around, and what carriages were flying by, thundering over the pavement outside the park fence, and whether there was swift, fleet-footed running, and children's laughter and prattle—everything was hidden behind the magic shroud of her slow speech. And as if behind the melting smoke of incense, the resounding, multicolored day lurked and was hidden, as it cheerfully turned to evening.

And there was anguish, and weariness, and indifference. He quietly said: "If the trembling of my soul rises even up to the stars and ignites an unquenchable thirst and ecstasy of existence in the distant worlds, what is that to me? As I rot, I will rot away here, in the terrible grave, where indifferent people will bury me for some reason. What use then is the eloquence of your promises to me? What use is it to me? Tell me."

Smiling gently, she said: "Eternal rest in blessed repose."

He repeated quietly: "Eternal rest. And is that supposed to be a consolation?"

"I console in the way that I can," she said, smiling the same immobile, gentle smile.

Then he got up and went to the exit from the garden. He could hear her light steps behind him.

He walked for a long time through the city streets—and she walked after him. Sometimes he would hasten his steps in order to get away from her—and she would walk faster, hurry, run, raising the edge of her white dress with her slender fingers. When he would stop, she would stand at a distance, inspecting the objects displayed in shop windows. Sometimes he would turn peevishly and walk right at her. Then she would hurriedly run to the other side of the street or hide in entrances or under portals.

And she watched him with her gray, calm, attentive eyes. She watched him unrelentingly.

"I'll get into a cab," he thought.

He was amazed that such a simple idea had not come to him before.

But hardly did he begin talking to the cabby than she came near. She stood quite close and wafted coldness and sadness onto him. And smiled.

He thought peevishly: "She'll get in with me. I can't get away from her by foot or vehicle."

The cabby asked sixty kopecks.

"Thirty," Rezanov said and quickly walked away.

The cabby cursed at him.

Rezanov went up to the third floor. He stopped at the door of his apartment. He rang. The whole time, he could hear the rustling of quiet steps coming up the stairs. He rang impatiently a second time. The coldness of terror passed down his spine. He wanted to go into the apartment before she came up, before she saw what door he went into—there were four doors on the landing.

But she was already coming up. The white of her dress was already visible nearby, in the half-light of the stairway. And her gray eyes were looking into his frightened eyes attentively and nearby when he glanced at the stairway for the last time as he went into the apartment, closing the door behind him hastily.

He locked the door himself. The lock clinked so harshly. Then he stopped in the half-dark anteroom. He looked at the door with melancholy eyes. He felt, as if he could see it through a door suddenly become transparent, how she was standing on the other side of the door, quiet, with a gentle smile on her darling lips, and how she raised her clear, pale face to read and memorize the number of the apartment.

Then he could hear quiet steps going down the stairway.

Rezanov went into his study.

"She has gone away," it seemed someone said in a clear voice.

And another voice seemed to be heard in answer, a hopelessly calm voice: "She will come again."

He waited. It got darker and darker. He was wearied by anguish. His thoughts were unclear and confused. He was dizzy. Chills and feverish heat passed over his body.

He thought: "What is she doing? She's bought food, she's come home, she is feeding her hungry little deathlings. That's what she called them—deathlings. How many of them are there? What are they like? Just as quiet as her, my darling death? Skinny from malnutrition, white, fearful. And homely, and with the same attentive eyes, the same darling eyes as her, my darling, my white death.

"She is feeding her deathlings. Then she will put them to bed. Then she will come here. What for?"

And suddenly curiosity was kindled in him.

She would come again, of course. Otherwise, why follow him to his home? But what would she come for? How did she understand her task, that terrifying lady, who was ready to agree to any conditions in exchange for money, and even to walk among deaths?

Or maybe she was not even a woman, but actually death? And she would come, and she would take his soul out of this sinful, weak body?

He lay down on the sofa. He covered himself with a blanket. He was shaking all over with paroxysms of a cruel, sweet fever.

What strange thoughts come into one's head! She is intelligent and conscientious. She took the money and she wants to earn it, and she is playing the role that was suggested to her very well.

But why is she so cold?

Well, because she is poor, hungry, tired, ill.

She is tired from work. She has so much work to do.

I've been scything all day long,
I am tired, I am ill.[4]

She walks, she seeks, she's hungry and ill. Her poor little death-lings are waiting, their hungry little mouths open wide.

And he recalled her face—the earthly, human face of my death. Such a familiar face. Familial features.

In his memory, feature after feature, her face arose ever more clearly—familiar, familial, darling features.

But who is she, my white death? Is she not my sister?

I feel weary—I am ill.
Darling brother, help me now.

And if she is my eternal Sister, my white death—what do I care that here, in this incarnation, she came to me in the form of a woman placing an advertisement, who lives in a rented room?

I put my poor gold, my meager gift into her hand—ringing gold, into her hand that was growing cold. And she took my gold with her cooling hand, and she will take my soul. She will carry me away under the dark vaults—and the visage of the Lord will be revealed—My eternal visage, and the Lord is I. I summoned my soul to life, and I ordered my death to come to me, to come to get me.

And he waited.

It was night. The doorbell jingled quietly. No one heard. Rezanov hastily threw off the blanket. He went into the anteroom, trying not to make noise.

The lock clinked so harshly. The door opened. She was standing on the threshold.

He stepped back, into the darkness of the anteroom. He asked, as if amazed: "Is it you?"

And she said: "I have come. It is my hour. It is time."

He locked the door after her and went to his own room through the unlit rooms. He could hear the light rustling of her feet behind him.

And in the darkness of his chamber she nestled up to him and kissed him with a tender, innocent kiss.

"But who are you?" he asked.

She said: "You called me, and I have come. I am not afraid, and don't you be afraid. I will give you the last delight of life—the kiss of death—*'and light your death will be and sweeter than a poison.'"*[5]

He asked: "And you?"

She answered: "I told you that I would descend with your soul by the only path that lies before us."

"And your deathlings?"

"I sent them on ahead, so that they would go before us and open the doors to us."

"But how can you take out my soul?" he asked again.

And she tenderly pressed herself to him and whispered: "*'The sharp stiletto wounds with sweetness.'"*[6]

And she nestled up to him, and kissed him, and caressed him. And it was as if she stung him—she pricked him in the nape of the neck with a poisoned stiletto. A sweet fire rushed through his veins like a whirlwind—and he lay, already dead, in her embrace.

And with a second prick of the poisoned blade she killed herself and fell dead onto his corpse.

1907

THE WHITE DOG

She had gotten so sick of everything in this small dress factory in a backwater provincial town—these patterns, and the clatter of the sewing machines, and the whims of the female customers—in this factory where Alexandra Ivanovna had first been an apprentice and had worked for so many years now as a cutter. Everything irritated Alexandra Ivanovna, she found fault with everyone, berated the meek apprentices, and she also attacked Tanechka, the youngest of the seamstresses, a girl who had just recently been an apprentice here. At first Tanechka kept silence, then in a polite little voice, so calmly that everyone but Alexandra Ivanovna burst out laughing, said: "Alexandra Ivanovna, you are a real dog."

Alexandra Ivanovna was offended.

"You're a dog yourself!" she screamed at Tanechka.

Tanechka was sitting and sewing. She would stop work from time to time and say calmly and unhurriedly: "You're barking everlastingly. . . . And you really are a dog. . . . You even have a dog's snout. . . . And dog's ears. . . . And a scutched tail. . . . The proprietress is going to kick you out soon, because you are the most downright vicious dog, just a mangy cur."[1]

Tanechka was a young, rosy, plump girl with an innocent, pretty, slightly crafty little face. She looked like such a quiet little thing, she was dressed like a little apprentice girl, she was sitting there barefoot, and her little eyes were so clear, and her eyebrows played in cheerful, high arcs on her evenly curved white forehead under her smoothly combed dark-chestnut hair, which seemed black from a distance. Tanechka's little voice was ringing, flat, sweet, and insinuating, and if you only listened to the sounds and didn't pay attention to the words, it would seem that she was paying compliments to Alexandra Ivanovna.

The other seamstresses were guffawing, the apprentices were snorting, covering their faces with their black aprons and casting fearful glances at Alexandra Ivanovna, and Alexandra Ivanovna was sitting there, crimson with fury.

"You trash," she screamed, "I'll throw you out by the ears! I'll pull out all your hair!"

Tanechka answered in a tender voice: "Your forelegs are too short. . . . The cur is barking and biting. . . . We have to buy a little muzzle."

Alexandra Ivanovna rushed at Tanechka. But before Tanechka had time to put down her sewing and stand up, the proprietress came in, heavyset and broad, rustling the folds of her lilac dress. She said sternly: "Alexandra Ivanovna, what are you brawling about!"

Alexandra Ivanovna said in an agitated voice: "Irina Petrovna, what on earth is going on! Forbid her to call me a dog!"

Tanechka complained, "She just yapped at me for no reason at all. She's always finding fault with me and barking at me over nothing."

But the proprietress looked at her sternly and said, "Tanechka, I can see right through you. Isn't it you who starts it? Don't you get the idea that just because you're a seamstress you're also an adult. Watch out, or I'll invite your mommy in, for old times' sake."

Tanechka flushed crimson, but she preserved her innocent and affectionate appearance. She said submissively to the proprietress: "Forgive me, Irina Petrovna, I won't do it again. As it is, I try not to get on her bad side. But she's so awfully strict, you don't even say a word to her, and she's always going, 'I'm gonna pull you by the ears.' She's a seamstress just like me, and I've graduated from being a little girl."

"Did that happen a long time ago, Tanechka?" the proprietress asked commandingly, went up to Tanechka—and two resounding slaps could be heard in the silent factory, as well as Tanechka's feeble cry: "Oh! Oh!"

Almost ill from fury, Alexandra Ivanovna returned home. Tanechka had guessed her sore spot.

"Well, so maybe I'm a dog," Alexandra Ivanovna thought, "what business is it of hers? I don't go trying to find out who she is, a snake or maybe a fox, and I don't try to spy or track down who she is. She's Tatyana, and that's that. You could find out about everybody, but why make it into a term of abuse? How is a dog worse than anyone else?"

The luminous summer night languished and sighed, wafting lassitude and coolness from the nearby fields onto the peaceful streets of the little town. The moon rose, clear and full, just the same as then, just the same as out there, over the broad, desolate steppe, the homeland of the wild ones who freely range and howl out of ancient earthly anguish. Just the same as then, as out there.

And just the same as then, anguishing eyes burned, and a wild heart, which in the towns had not forgotten the wide-open spaces of the steppe, contracted with longing, and a throat contracted with the agonizing desire for a wild howl.

She was about to start undressing, but why? She wasn't going to fall asleep anyway.

She went out of her room. In the entryway, the shaky boards of the littered floor creaked, and chips of wood and grains of sand cheerfully and amusingly tickled the skin of her feet.

She went out onto the porch. Granny Stepanida was sitting there, black in a black kerchief, dried-up and wrinkled. The old woman was bent over, and it seemed that she was warming herself in the cold rays of the moon.

Alexandra Ivanovna sat down next to her on the steps of the porch. She looked sideways at the old woman. The old woman's large bent nose seemed to be the beak of an old bird.

"A crow?" Alexandra Ivanovna thought.

She smiled, forgetting her anguish and terror. Her eyes, intelligent like a dog's, lit up with the joy of her guess. In the pale green light of the moon, the smoothed-out wrinkles of her withered face had suddenly become invisible, and she had again become young, cheerful, and light, like ten years ago, when the moon did not yet summon her to bark and howl at night by the windows of the dark bathhouse.

She moved closer to the old woman and said affectionately: "Granny Stepanida, there's something I keep wanting to ask you."

The old woman turned her dark face with its deep wrinkles to her and asked in a harsh old-woman's voice, as if she were cawing an evil prophecy: "Well, what is it, my beauty? Ask your question."[2]

Alexandra Ivanovna laughed quietly, twitched her slender shoulders because of a chill that suddenly passed along her spine, and said very quietly: "Granny Stepanida, it seems to me . . . is it true or isn't it? . . . I don't know how to say it . . . now, granny, don't be offended . . . I don't mean anything by it . . ."

"Well, come on, don't be afraid, dearie," the old woman said.

She looked at Alexandra Ivanovna with her bright, sharp-sighted eyes. She waited. And again Alexandra Ivanovna said, "It seems to me, granny . . . now don't be offended . . . that maybe you, granny, are maybe a crow."

The old woman turned away and was silent, shaking her head. It seemed that she was recalling something. Her head with its sharply outlined nose bent and swayed, and at times it seemed to Alexandra Ivanovna that the old woman was drowsing. She was drowsing and whispering something to herself under her breath. She was shaking her head and whispering ancient, primordial words. Words of sorcery . . .

It was quiet outside, neither luminous nor dark, and everything around seemed to be spellbound by the soundless whispering of the ancient, prophetic words. Everything languished and luxuriated, and the moon shone, and anguish again contracted the heart, and all around was neither sleep nor waking. Thousands of smells that were unnoticeable in the daytime could be sensitively distinguished, and they recalled something ancient and primitive, forgotten over the long centuries.

The old woman was muttering barely audibly: "A crow for sure. Only I have no wings. And I caw, and I caw, but they don't pay me no mind. But I've been granted the gift of foresight, and I simply have to caw, my beauty, but those pitiful people don't want to listen to me. But as soon as I see a doomed one, I just want to caw, I want to so much."

The old woman suddenly flapped her arms and shouted twice in a harsh voice: "Caw, caw!"

Alexandra Ivanovna flinched. She asked, "Granny, who are you cawing at?"

The old woman answered, "At you, my beauty, at you."

It felt creepy to sit with the old woman. Alexandra Ivanovna went to her own room. She sat down under the open window. She listened—two people were sitting outside the gates and talking.

"She keeps howling and howling," a low, angry voice could be heard.

"Did you see her, uncle?" a sweet, thin tenor asked.

Hearing this tenor voice, Alexandra Ivanovna immediately pictured a freckled lad with curly red hair, a local boy from the same courtyard.

A minute of dull silence passed. And suddenly a hoarse and angry voice could be heard: "I saw her. She's big. She's white. She lies by the bathhouse and howls at the moon."

Again, hearing this voice, she pictured the black spade beard, the low, goffered forehead, the piggish little eyes, the fat straddled legs.

"Why is she howling, uncle?" the sweet voice asked.

And again the hoarse voice took its time to answer: "It's a bad omen. . . . And where she came from, I don't know."

"And uncle, what if she's a shape-shifter?" the sweet voice asked.[3]

"Well, don't shift around," the hoarse voice answered.

It wasn't clear what these words meant, but she didn't want to think about them. And she no longer wanted to listen to them. What, after all, was the sound and meaning of human words to her?

The moon looked right into her face, and summoned her insistently, and tormented her. And her heart contracted with a dull anguish, and she couldn't sit still in one place.

Alexandra Ivanovna undressed hastily. Nude, white, she went quietly out into the entryway, cracked open the outer door. There was no one on the porch or in the courtyard. She ran through the courtyard and the garden and reached the bathhouse. The harsh sensation of cold in her body and of the cold earth under her feet made her cheerful. But soon her body warmed up.

She lay down on the grass, on her stomach. She propped herself up on her elbows, raised her face to the pale, deathly anguishing moon, and uttered a long, drawn-out howl.

"Listen, uncle, she's started howling," the curly-haired lad said by the gates.

His sweet little tenor voice was trembling cravenly.

"She's started howling, the damned one," the hoarse, angry voice responded unhurriedly.

They got up from the bench. The latch of the wicket gate clicked.

The two men walked quietly through the courtyard and the garden. The elder went in front, hefty, black-bearded, with a gun in his hands. The curly-haired one pressed behind him cravenly. He looked out from behind the other man's shoulder.

Beyond the bathhouse a large white dog was lying in the grass and howling. Her head, black on top, was raised to the moon, which was telling fortunes in the cold sky; her hind legs were strangely stretched out behind her; and her forelegs were resting straight and resiliently on the earth. In the pale-green, uncertain illumination of the moon, she seemed to be enormous—more enormous than dogs ever are in life—fat and corpulent. The black spot that began on her head and stretched in uneven coils down her whole back seemed like a woman's undone plait. Her tail was not visible—it must have been tucked up under her. The fur on her body was so short that from a distance the dog seemed to be quite naked, and her skin shone without luster in the moonlight, and it looked as if a naked woman was lying and howling like a dog.

The black-bearded man took aim. The curly-haired lad crossed himself and muttered something.

The crack of the gunshot resounded with an echo. The dog squealed, jumped up on her hind legs, toppled over in the form of a naked woman, and bleeding profusely, she ran around squealing, howling, and shrieking.

The black-bearded man and the curly-headed man collapsed onto the grass and began howling in wild horror.

1908

THE SADDENED FIANCÉE

What better time for strange things to happen than in our days? Ferocious and sad days, when the diversity of possibilities that can be embodied in life seems inexhaustible.

In our days, several young girls formed a club to which admission was rather difficult and the purpose of which could of course be called strange.

When a young man in the city died without yet having a fiancée, one of the members of the club would dress in deep mourning and go to the funeral as his fiancée.

The family members would be quite surprised, the friends less so, but both the family and the friends would believe that there was a beautiful, sad secret near the fresh grave.

The members of the club included Nina Alexeyevna Bessonova, a young girl who was bored for some reason, not very beautiful but reasonably comely. She had even had people fall in love with her—what else do adolescent *gimnazia* students have to do with themselves!—but all the same she was bored.

And now, after one of her friends, it was Nina's turn to see off an unknown fiancé into the grave.

"The next one is yours," they told her.

The ones whose turn had not yet come envied her. The friends who had already carried out their sad, beautiful assignment looked at Nina with sympathetic sadness.

That day Nina returned home strangely excited.

Long, languorous days of idly yearning sadness stretched before her.

She was tormented by painful premonitions, and at every step, omens of loss, tears, and the doom of the one close to her heart lay in wait for her.

How painful to know that an unknown period of time would pass and someone she did not yet know but who was already beloved and dear would die! And along with him would perish the possibility of happiness.

And who would he be? And why was he fated not to meet her before the limits of the tomb? Perhaps she could have saved him, protected him, implored from cruel fate some hours and days of sweet oblivion of sadness.

I don't know who he will be, but how sorry I am for him! What anguish!

So young, and implacable death is already following him, lying in wait for him, and will inflict a horrible blow from which nothing will save him, nothing will protect him!

Sometimes Nina almost envied her friends in the club who had already performed the sweetly sad ritual and now had only to wear their light, beautiful mourning dress for the rest of the prescribed period. Mourning dress that was so becoming to their sweet faces that passersby on the streets would stop to look at them.

It was impossible to know in advance whether this event would happen soon. You had to be prepared to go at the first summons and not be late. For this reason, Nina ordered a whole set of mourning dress for herself. On the sly from her family. Although it was annoying that she had to hide and keep secrets from them.

Nina didn't have to worry about the money for the mourning dress: this was an expense that was covered by the funds of the club. The club had a rather orderly organization. They collected monthly member dues, and as with other organizations, they also had various incidental sources of income.

But although she didn't have to worry about obtaining a lot of money right away for the mourning dress, although she could hide the already made and purchased clothing somewhere in the house, all the same, at some point she would have to put it on. And of course, it would be better to say something about it well in advance. But for some reason Nina was embarrassed to speak about it with her mother.

And what could she say about it! She had to explain what and why, but the rules of the club did not permit her to speak about its purpose and activities to anyone who was not a member. She would have to invent something and lie, and this was disgusting for Nina. She put it off from one day to the next, and then decided to leave it all up to chance.

"It'll work out somehow," she thought.

They brought the clothing—Nina chose a time when her mother wasn't home—and she hid it in her room.

In the evenings she would lay the mourning clothes out on her bed and on the chairs. In her room everything was white and pink; transparent, light curtains fluttered in the windows, wildflowers smelled tender and caressing in beautiful vases, and outside the window, over the distant, steel-blue sea, the fading sunset would blaze with a maidenly blush. And because of all this background of virginal purity and luminosity, the black clothes seemed particularly terrifying, and frightened her heart, and wrung quick streams of tears from her yearning eyes.

She would look at the black color and weep. She would weep for a long time.

Sometimes she would try on the mourning clothes and look at herself in the mirror. The black color, and the modest cut of the dress, and the austere style of the hat, all this was so becoming to her, and because of that her heart would become sadder, and she would have an even more irrepressible urge to weep.

In the mornings, as she woke up, she would open her eyes with a secret terror: had the expected sorrow perhaps arrived? The sun was already high, the garden was aglow, flooded with the molten splendor of the dragon's fierce malice, and through the light, pinkish, transparent film of the elegant curtains, the frantic day would rush into her eyes. And as a greeting to the day and the tumult of impetuous life, Nina would hurl an evil word, the poison of a yearning premonition: "And he, my darling one, will die soon!"

She would come out into the dining room looking hazy and foggy, the turmoil on her sweet face strangely conflicting with the light, luminous clothing of a young lady at her dacha.

Her mother would look at her in bewilderment and ask, "Why are you so dull, Ninochka? What are you worrying about? What's wrong with you?"

Nina would keep silence, smiling enigmatically and sadly, and sit at her place at the table, quiet, gentle, beautiful, dressed becomingly, with a becoming hairstyle, looking just like the heroine of a novel, the dénouement of which did not promise a happy ending.

And her mother could not get to the truth of what was wrong with Nina.

But one day, at a moment of sudden candor, touched by sadness and spellbound by the quiet of the northern white night, excited by the beautiful flights of nearby fireworks for some stranger's name-day party right across from the veranda of their dacha, where the two of them were sitting after evening tea, Nina trustingly nestled up to her mother, suddenly started weeping, and said very quietly, so tender and white in the twilight, marked out against her mother's dark gray dress as a beautiful, pacified spot: "How painful my heart feels! I have a premonition that something will happen . . . something terrible . . . some kind of sorrow."

Her mother became anxious. She embraced Nina. She spoke caressingly, consoling her as if she were a little child: "What's wrong with you, Ninochka, God bless you, what could happen? What's going to happen? Dear child, don't believe in premonitions, you're not an old woman. Who believes that kind of thing in our days?"

Nina wiped away her tears; in an affectedly calm voice she said, smiling affectedly: "It's true, Mama, I know myself that it's very stupid, but all the same it seems to me that he is threatened by a misfortune."

"Who, Nina?" her mother asked.

She moved away a little bit so as to look at her daughter, squinting her gray, slightly nearsighted eyes. Nina said, almost weeping: "My darling one, my fiancé."

"What are you saying, Ninochka!" her mother said in surprise. "What darling one? Do you really have a fiancé?"

"I have no fiancé," Nina said dolefully, "I don't, but what does that matter? I have this premonition that I'm going to fall in love with him, and he will be more beloved to me than all the earth and dearer than life—and all of a sudden he'll die."

And Nina again began weeping inconsolably, and her surprised mother caressed her and tried to calm her. She gave her some medicinal drops. Nina peered into her frightened, ludicrously anxious face, and burst out laughing.

That evening she did not spend time admiring her mourning clothes, and she fell asleep peacefully. But in the morning, hardly had she opened her eyes, hardly had she caught the sound of the cheerful birdlike laughter and voices of Minka and Tinka, arguing about something, when her anguish again set in.

The two *gimnazia* students, her little brothers Minka and Tinka, were laughing at her mysterious sadness. They were mocking her.

And she was so sad that she didn't even get angry at the boys, so tiresome, noisy, and stupid—the little sillies.

The day was declining toward evening, but it was still hot and bright on the festive summertime earth, and the breadth and silence of the high dome seemed solemn. Nina was standing on the broad beach and peering at the open spaces of the water and the heavens.

Birds were rushing by, small and swift, fussy and preoccupied, and their prolonged, feeble cheeping darted in the air above Nina.

The firm, fine-grained sand, compacted by the waves, imparted its warm fragility and moisture to her soles. It slightly tickled the skin of her tender feet, not yet coarsened by frequent contact with the dear sand of earthly seashores.

The waves splashed as they rolled in—the windless, broad waves of the nearby, dear sea, where people drown as they do in the distant sea—the waves splashed as they rolled in, kissing her shapely, already tanned legs. And under her light clothing her chest breathed cheerfully and freely, raising two dusky waves.

She stood, she looked into the dark-blue distance, she day-dreamed languorously, sweetly, sadly.

Who will he be, my darling, whom will I see off into the grave, for whom will I weep? And the eyes that will never look at me, and the lips that will never smile at me.

He will not say a word, he will not embrace me, he will not say: "My darling, I love you! My darling, you are dearer to me than life."

Her heart languished with a dark premonition of sadness, and she wanted to weep, but she didn't yet have anything to weep about.

But how delightful it would be to fall onto the sand and sob in boundless despair, confiding the sadness of her beclouded soul to the winds and waves!

She recalled the conversation she had had the day before with one of her friends about the impending duel between Prince Ordyn-Ulusov and the husband of a woman who loved him. What a pity that Nina would not be able to walk behind the coffin of the handsome young Ulusov! After all, he loved another, and everyone in town knew the story of this love, so beautiful, touching, and mad: love, if there is truth in it, verily despises all the conventions of life and dares even to the point of death.

Granted, it could happen that neither of the rivals would kill the other, and everything would end happily this time. Let him live, what did she care!

The impatience of her premonitions kept increasing, tormenting her unbearably.

The flaming sky of sunset blazed, poisoning the quiet sadness of her soul with bright passion, spreading scarlet despair over the earth in streams of multicolored, burning blood under the exhausted desert of the cold zenith.

Nina set off for home. The sand seemed damp and unpleasant. And she became annoyed at having left her shoes at home and having to walk barefoot.

No, that wasn't what was annoying her—it was just a pointless languor, a vague anguish. A burden she had to carry.

Near her dacha Nina caught sight of a familiar figure. She looked more closely; it was Natasha Leshchinskaya.

And Nina was overjoyed, and also somehow frightened. Was she perhaps coming with the horrible, expected tidings?

She was coming like fate to torture Nina's yearning heart with sadness, to cover it with wounds.

Even from a distance it was evident, from the haste and awkwardness of her movements, that Natasha was excited about something. And that of course she was bringing some significant news.

Nina's hands began to tremble from excitement and her knees turned cold. She wanted to run to her friend, but suddenly her heart started beating so hard that she had to stop.

She turned red. She stood, smiling and holding her arms crossed on her chest, in an awkward, strange pose. Her smile was so embarrassed and uncertain.

"Natashechka, is it you?" she said awkwardly. "I'm so glad to see you!"

And she fell silent, confused by the uncertainty of her own intonations.

"Well, Ninochka," Natasha said, approaching her, slightly out of breath from walking fast.

She also had an anxious face, and her black hair, curled up on hairpins and now coming loose from under her little yellow straw hat with its yellow ostrich feather, lent her dusky face a kind of boyishly sprightly and excessively self-confident air.

"Yes? He has died? Mine?" Nina asked incoherently and fearfully.

Natasha said with animation: "He has died. And can you imagine, he shot himself! Isn't that interesting? You're so lucky."

Nina burst into tears. She seemed so pitiful, lost, and sweet amid this space permeated with pink and sky-blue light, in her simple dark-blue suit with white edging, with her tanned, shapely, slender, quiet legs, next to this elegant, dusky-rosy, perky guest dressed in monotone yellow, breathing heavily from her fast walking along the sand on her high heels.

Weeping, Nina asked quietly, "Who?"

The sound of her voice was thin and timid, like the voice of a crying child.

Natasha affectionately pressed her hand.

"It's true, it's a great pity," she said. "He was very young. The university student Ikonnikov."

"Was he alone?" Nina asked.

"Yes, he was alone when he shot himself. His family was living at their dacha. He came in the daytime to the empty apartment, wrote letters, put them in the mailbox himself, spent the night alone. In the morning he shot himself. No one in the building even knew, until his parents came—he sent them a letter to the dacha. Apparently, they were living in Pavlovsk."

Nina was silent. When they were already in the garden of her dacha, she looked inquiringly at Natasha. Answering that look, Natasha said, "They'll bury him the day after tomorrow. In Petersburg."

They came home.

"Why are you crying, Nina?" her mother asked.

"He has died," Nina answered shortly, in a dry, seemingly hostile tone.

"Who has died?"

As almost always happens with aging women, the sudden mention of someone's death flooded Nina's mother with a chill of terror, as if someone had said in a distinct, dark voice: "You too will die!"

"Oh, Mama," Nina answered with unaccustomed peevishness. "You don't know him anyway."

"And I myself don't know him," Nina thought.

And because this thought was intertwined by a ludicrous thread into the sad fabric of what she was living through, she felt even more pain.

Her mother turned to their guest: "Natasha, could *you* at least please tell me who has died."

Natasha, taking off her hat in front of a mirror, said unhurriedly, trying to be calm, but herself excited for some reason, "A student we know shot himself. Ikonnikov. In the city. No one knows why. So young. You know, there are so many suicides in our days, and it's such a pity. So young, and no one knows the reason. A wound in his temple—a little dark-blue spot, like a bruise. And his face was quite calm."

"I'm going to the funeral service," Nina said decisively.

"Nina!"

Her mother sat down in an armchair, looked at her daughter, and didn't know what to say.

"I absolutely have to! For God's sake, don't try to stop me!" Nina exclaimed.

Natasha sat down next to Alexandra Pavlovna and said quietly, "Please don't worry. I will go with her and we'll be together the whole time."

Nina went to her room.

"What's wrong with her? Do you know, Natasha?" Alexandra Pavlovna asked. "She's been so depressed recently. What's going on? Who is this Ikonnikov?"

"She is so impressionable," Natasha said. "I don't know Ikonnikov very well. I really don't know. In our days there is so much that oppresses us. I really don't know what their relationship was."

Nina soon emerged, all dressed in mourning and wearing gloves and a hat with the veil let down, and again her mother looked at her in bewilderment.

"Nina, where did you get mourning clothes?"

"Oh, Mama!"

"Nina, that is not an answer. I want to know. You must tell me."

"Mama, don't torture me. It's so hard even without that. I told you that I had a premonition of misfortune. My fiancé has died. I'm going right now."

She said this almost calmly now.

"Wait a little bit, at least have some tea. What train are you going to be able to get now," her mother said with bewilderment, terror, and annoyance.

And the boring hour of waiting dragged slowly by. The unnecessary beverage, the disgusting food, the light of the lamp, mixed with the scarlet dying of the wounded sunset, the clinking of the spoons that made her flinch, and the giggling of Minka and Tinka, and the bewildered interrogations of her mother—and she had to say something!

Nina was very sad. Several times she set herself to weeping. Natasha whispered anxiously, "You're starting too soon. You'll get tired. You won't be in the right frame of mind at the decisive moments."

"Leave me alone, Natasha. You don't understand anything," Nina whispered peevishly.

But now she was in the train car with Natasha.

The car was half empty. Two or three random fellow passengers looked at Nina with sympathetic curiosity.

Natasha asked, "Nina, you never met him, did you?"

"Of course not."

"Then why are you crying?"

"You think it's easy to bury your fiancé?"

Suddenly Nina burst out laughing.

"I'm not crying at all. I'm laughing."

"With tears?"

"It's so funny it makes me cry."

She wept.

Natasha tried to turn Nina's thoughts to something cheerful, pleasant, and funny. She failed.

"Oh, what a crybaby you are," Natasha said. "Please pull yourself together. You're going to go into hysterics. Then how am I going to deal with you in a train car?"

It was already dark when they were riding through the streets of the summer city, and everything all around seemed to Nina like the delirium of a nightmare that was being materialized.

The pale moon was shining between two clouds, and its rippling reflection flowed in the water of the canal. And bitter was the poison in its boundless, quiet shimmer, above the coarse rumble of the evil, dirty streets.

A pleasure garden sparkled with multicolored garlands of red, yellow, and blue lights above the white boredom of a fence and the insolence of gaudy posters on a gray wall.

People dressed up in gaudy clothes, with heavily painted faces, came driving up and walking up, and someone's invisible but long-familiar index finger pointed to the frank, pitiful words "cheap debauchery."

There was merriment in the crowd that was going to make merry, a poor, laborious merriment, cost what it may.

An insulting merriment, when there was such sadness in one's soul. Cruel people! How could they make merry when he, so young and beautiful, was lying with his head shot through!

Nina spent the night at Natasha's place. It was easier there than at home. Natasha said quietly, "Her fiancé has died."

And no one pestered her. They pitied her tenderly and with admiration. She had affectionate, sad, and somewhat frightening— or rather eerie—dreams.

The sun, indifferent to earthly sadness, bright and evil, quietly and as if furtively cast into the room its molten flickering, its fire that was life-giving to the point of death, and its scorching, liquid gold poured out ever more broadly and brightly from behind the dark curtain onto the green carpet.

It was the morning of a day that promised sadness, and labors, and hopeless prayers.

And on a strange bed, above the green carpet flooded with evil gold, Nina woke up, and there were tears in her eyes, and weakness in her body, and she could hear the distinct words: "He has died."

It was not said by anybody—and her heart, bound by sadness, shivered and sank.

And the tears . . .

She thought, "And now, my whole life through, whenever I wake up, I will remember that he, my darling, has died."

As she got dressed, she noticed that the mourning clothes became her. She smiled joyfully. She hurried Natasha, so that they could drive to the house where he, her darling, had lived. But she carefully placed the folds of the black veil over the tanned pallor of her sweet face . . .

The flowers and carpets on the stairway by his apartment, the orange and green glass leaves in copper moldings on the windows, the bronze railings and the marble columns—so her sadness would remain thoroughly beautiful and would not be offended by an untidy stairway, smelling of cats, leading from a courtyard.

On the landing of the third floor, by the doors of the apartment, there was a white coffin-lid. . . . And the stone walls swayed . . .

Natasha's hand was under her elbow. Her quiet voice: "It's here. Nina, darling!"

Nina went in, covered by the long black veil, silent, crushed by sorrow. Not seeing anyone, she went right into the hall where, on a high black bier, in a white coffin, her darling one was lying.

Someone was walking around, handing out candles for the service, and from out of a side door curled a puff of smoke from lighted incense. There were not many people in the hall—and Nina's appearance was very noticeable. No one knew her, and they were all surprised by the deep mourning and tears of this girl who had come out of nowhere.

Nina went up close, stood for a moment next to the coffin, and quietly went up the steps of the bier. The pall, the flowers, the yellow face. She bent over and peered closely at the quiet smile of the deceased man.

How terribly, how coldly the dead lips smile! How cold his dead lips are to the yearning lips of his fiancée! The sepulchral, cold, dead lips, ardently kissed, will not tremble with a hot kiss!

Stung by the coldness of the dead lips, Nina feebly cried out. Someone took her by the arm and helped her come down from the bier onto the austere yellow gloss of the parquet floor. And they carefully placed the weeping girl on her knees when the service began in the dark-blue smoke of the incense.

The family members whispered to each other: "Who is it?"

"That girl?"

"Do you know?"

"It seems no one knows."

Natasha was standing by the door.

Someone asked her, "Do you know who that young lady in mourning is, who's crying so hard?"

Natasha answered just as quietly, "She's the fiancée of the deceased."

"But none of his family members know her," the person whispered with surprise.

"Yes. It's a sad story."

They started passing it on to one another: "She's the fiancée of the deceased."

The family were bewildered. But they all believed it. How could they not believe it!

For all these people, family members and non-family members, all disposed in various ways, some sad, some indifferent, Nina, whom nobody knew, weeping, sweet, and pitiful in her mourning dress, was verily the fiancée of this student who had shot himself for some unknown reason, who was quiet and beautiful in his beautiful white coffin. No one knew what secret connected this coffin and this weeping girl, and whether she might have been the cause of his death, but everyone was touched as they looked at her. Next to the despair of the old, gray-haired mother and the dull sorrow of the old father, which was expressed so strongly and had such an unattractive external appearance, with their reddened eyes, their tearful snuffling, their disheveled gray hair, the mute woe of this girl in mourning, praying on her knees, seemed lofty and splendid. And although everyone knew the parents, and no one knew her, they all felt much sorrier for her, so sweet and pitiful with her touchingly bent knees, so elegantly enchanting under the folds of her half-transparent crepe veil. And even the thought some of them had, that the saddened and weeping fiancée might have been the cause of the death of this splendid young man, bestrewn in the coffin with flowers that exhaled a fragrance he had no need of—even this cruel, stern thought did not conquer their pity for her, born in the quiet streams of her luminous tears. And her deep sadness, and her tear-drenched face, bent down to the cold parquet floor, and her entire mournful figure—oh, if there was in this sorrow the implacable aura of evil remorse, what of that, did that not make one pity her even more? People who love each other quarrel and part temporarily for all sorts of reasons—and after all, it was obvious that she loved him; people do not weep this way or put on mourning clothes for those they do not love—all sorts of things might happen between sweethearts, but he was cruel and killed himself, he couldn't bear a slight sadness, he plunged her heart into the horror and anguish of a terrible memory forever!

And she, the weeping and praying fiancée of a bridegroom she did not know, she, who had surrendered submissively to the outbursts of her created sadness—what was she feeling?[1]

No matter how glad she was to surrender her heart to the languors of sadness, no matter how prepared she was for this anguish of her realized premonitions, all the same, what presented itself to her exceeded her expectations.

The enchantment of this young face, so mortally calm, to which she had pressed down for a kiss of affected woe, this enchantment had taken possession of her in one brief moment, and she felt that to the end of her days she would not be able to throw off this sweet and burning enchantment. Something more beautiful than beauty, and more powerful than the power of a love that despised the cold of the grave and the darkness of the funerary crypt, something inexplicable and incapable of being expressed by any human words, a fascination known only to death had pressed close to her, and she already knew that the man lying in the white coffin, bestrewn with scarlet roses, fanned by the flaming incense being waved in the air, surrounded by rippling waves of dark-blue, fragrant smoke into which the dark incense had been dissolved, that he was verily her desired, beloved bridegroom.

And when she was descending the steps of the black bier and cast her anguish-filled eyes around the expanse of the cold chamber, seeking a place to hide her tears, her heart was already permeated by unbearable torment. She took two or three steps and felt dizzy. She turned her face to the coffin; her trembling knees were increasingly weak. She no longer tried to choose a place and just sank down where she had to, almost falling down next to the coffin. Next to her his gray-haired mother was weeping, sobbing quietly and tearfully. The priest's black cassock moved slowly, close to her face. She wept with her face pressed down to her hands that were cast down to the floor, and over her the rings of the censer chain quietly jingled, the lector's low, assured voice floated by, and the singing of the service flowed out sadly, beautifully, and resoundingly—the touching, significant words, more weighty than poor human faith, so wise, so consoling—and so unconsoling. Covering her face with her hands, barely hearing the words and the singing, barely inhaling the incense of grief, she clearly saw before her the face of the deceased, a face that was suddenly dear to her. She saw him alive—his eyes were laughing, and his lips, half-covered by his black mustache, were moving, and his words were wise and truthful, and his words were about what was abidingly close and dear to the heart. She looked closely, and the features of his face, which had been grasped at the moment of kissing by the tenacious memory of the girl who had instantly fallen in love, now came to life before her, and his dear image appeared to her more and more clearly. And each feature of that face spoke in truth about something that was endlessly dear and close.

The service ended. People started leaving. Intimate friends stood around the parents of the deceased. They were offering consolation, whispering something.

Nina was standing alone. It seemed to her that she was surrounded by an alien and hostile atmosphere.

She was quite alone . . .

Did she really have to leave? To abandon her darling one?

She began weeping. She left the room, quiet, grieving, sweet, pitiful, accompanied by the moist glances of his family and friends.

On the stairway, on the landing of the lower floor, she stopped, weeping. And suddenly she heard light steps running down from above. Nina looked up the stairway. Some vague premonition told her that it was someone coming for her.

A freckled girl with light-brown hair, in a calico mourning dress, with a crepe bonnet on her head, with gray eyes turned red with tears—chambermaids weep this way for good masters—was quickly running down the stairs. She stopped in front of Nina.

"Oh, miss," she said quietly, stammering slightly, as if embarrassed, "our mistress, the master's mommy, asks you to be so good as to come see them for just a second."

"Why?" Nina asked timidly.

"I have no idea, miss," the chambermaid answered, but it was evident from her tone that she knew and wanted to say. "But they beg you to come," she continued. "It seems they have a letter. But I really don't know. Only they beg you to come."

Nina went up the stairs, and a vague dread tormented her, plunging her into external apprehensions, so petty in comparison with the depth of her sadness. She thought: "Are they really going to ask me not to come any more? But why? Or are they going to blame me for the death of my darling?"

And her tears gushed in torrents. She staggered. The chambermaid supported her by the elbow, looking into her face sympathetically.

"Let them blame me," Nina thought, "I won't argue. Let me be to blame. How do I know? What do I know?"

The chambermaid led her into the parlor.

It was evident that the whole family had been living at the dacha and had come here only for the funeral. The furniture was in slipcovers and was arranged haphazardly, not quite the way it would be in the winter. A mirror on the wall between the windows had been hastily and unevenly covered by something white—this was because there was a deceased person in the house.

Nina moved the crepe veil away from her face, which had turned pale under its summer tan and had even seemed to grow gaunt from sadness, and looked with sad, timid eyes at the thin, gray-haired, rather tall woman who had risen from the sofa to meet her.

"His mother," Nina thought.

She made a kind of mechanical inventory. "Gray hair. Slim. Light-blue luminous eyes. She looks like her son."

It seemed for some reason that only a few days ago this woman with the tear-stained eyes and desperate face had not had gray hair. She used to arrange her hair carefully, and perhaps she even colored it, but now suddenly she had let herself go all at once and had forgotten about her appearance and the gray, disheveled locks on her head.

They invited Nina to sit down. In the same room, by the window, the father was standing, a tall, upright old man. He was standing half-turned to the window, as if he wanted both to look at their guest and also to hide from her the expression of sadness on his proud old face.

"Now," the old woman said, "I'm looking at you, and you're the only person here we don't know. So I'm thinking that Seryozha's letter must be for you. Is it?"

"I don't know," Nina said. "How can I know?"

She was trying not to cry, but the tears again gushed from her eyes. The mother also started crying.

"This is so unexpected for us," she said. "We were waiting for Seryozha to come home by dinnertime . . . he'd gone to the city for a day . . . and suddenly. . . . Oh, yes, I was talking about the letter. You see . . ."

The old woman took a letter in a narrow grayish-green envelope out of an album that was lying on the table and said: "We simply cannot guess who Seryozhenka is writing about. But this letter—he left a letter for me, and this letter was enclosed—he asked that we give it to a young lady who had never been at our house, to give it to her if she came to the funeral service or the bearing-out of the coffin. And, he writes, you will know her by the fact that she's wearing mourning clothes and will perhaps weep a little bit. Give it to her, he writes. If she doesn't come, then burn it, he writes, without reading it. So I was wondering if the letter is for you."

Without hesitating a moment, Nina said, "Yes, it's for me."

She turned pale. Filled with terror, she extended her hand for the letter. Would her darling one hurl heavy reproaches at her from beyond the mysterious boundary? Or words of tender love and consolation?

She thought: "But what if she comes, the other one?"

The envelope rustled in her trembling fingers. And already the edge of the envelope had been torn by her impatient hand. Swift thoughts came one after another as she drew the letter out of the dungeon of the envelope: "If she comes, I'll give it to her. But she won't come. The evil woman, she abandoned him, she forgot him, in the last terrible hours before his death she was not tormented by the anguish of premonition. Like me. It is my letter. But if she comes, and puts on mourning clothes, and weeps—I will give it to her."

The father and mother were both standing in front of her and looking at her face as she read. As if they wished to learn some terrible secret from her face.

She read:

My darling, my dear, I am writing to you in the strange, perhaps unrealizable hope that after all you will come to my coffin, will weep over my grave, will wear mourning for me for at least a short time. Why do I need this? I know that it is horrible nonsense, but all the same I am consoled by the dream that you will come. And if you come, they will give you this letter. And if you don't come, they'll burn it. That's what I asked Mama, and she's so nice, she won't deceive me, she'll do what I ask. I know you won't distress her with a single unnecessary word. As you see, I am dying. It was just one thing on top of another. Don't blame yourself, darling. I myself am to blame for our parting, I alone. And I have no one to reproach, it was just as if someone pulled a connecting thread out of the fabric of my life, and everything started to fall to pieces. I continued to look just the same, and I walked in solidarity with my comrades, on the whole I kept my chin up. I even took on a task that in days gone by I might have accomplished with enthusiasm. But now it has crushed me once and for all. . . . It is always difficult to kill, but I know that. . . . What's the

*use of talking about it! I took it on, and I can't. I prefer
to kill myself. Not because of old copybook moralizing,
something about the sanctity of human life—well, maybe
because of that too. It's just that it's terrifying and dark. I'm
completely exhausted. I am a finished man (by the way, I
swiped that phrase from somebody, but it's okay, it'll do).
I would like to say something very bright and calm to you.
Perhaps you will smile through tears, but so be it—all
the same, Pussycat, I love you very much. Be happy, don't
remember me too often and remember me without distress.
And if you did return—but anyway, why do you, the living,
need behests from beyond the grave? It's nonsense, isn't it?
Nevertheless, my dear, my darling, the person who has seen
the light and turned away from it is nothing but trash.*

Farewell.

Your Sergey.

Nina put the letter into the envelope. She wanted to go away, to be alone, to reread it, think, and cry. And she already wanted to leave. But someone's imploring glances held her back.

"What does Seryozha write you?" the mother asked.

Nina was silent. She didn't know what to say. And the old woman continued.

"Please understand the horror of our situation. We have absolutely no idea for what reason Seryozha, for what reason—why, it's horrible! If we at least knew something, at least something!"

Nina thought, "What can I possibly say? And if she comes? And if I have to give her the letter? It would be better if she told them."

She smiled and wept. She said decisively: "Forgive me, I understand perfectly, but right now I must be silent. I cannot tell you, I cannot do anything."

"Madam," the father, who had been silent up until then, began, and the sound of his voice was strangely harsh and rasping. "After all, we did not have to give you the letter. In such a situation. . . . We would have had the right to unseal it ourselves. And you are concealing . . ."

He didn't finish. He sobbed strangely. He turned away.

Nina looked down and said quietly, "Yes, you had the opportunity to read this letter—but you did not."

"No, of course," the mother said, "who's even saying that! Of course, we would not read someone else's letter. But our . . . our sorrow. . . . I implore you, have pity on an old woman."

"For the love of God," Nina cried out, "wait, wait until tomorrow. I swear to you I can't right now. I will tell you tomorrow. Tomorrow, when he . . . when Seryozha is . . . for the love of God."

They both wept, embracing each other. And suddenly the mother pushed Nina away.

"God will not give you happiness, if he did it because of you!" she cried out feebly in a weeping howl, and she rushed out of the room sobbing.

The father went quickly after her. Nina remained alone.

The day passed dully and listlessly, in a tumult of thoughts and dreams. She reread the letter from her darling. She thought fearfully: "And what if she, the other woman, the evil one, comes?"

It was bitter to think that she would have to give her the dear little pages, covered with the small, hurried, precise handwriting. And consoling herself, she would think again, "No, she won't come."

She awaited the evening with impatience—to go again to the service, to put a white rose into her darling's coffin, to leave the white wreath of the saddened fiancée by his coffin. And to find out whether her evil rival had come.

The tiresome, superfluous, flaming minutes of the Serpent-sun day dragged by.

After dinner, Nina said to Natasha, "The final delight is to receive a letter from your darling one. I received mine."

Natasha looked at the narrow green envelope in amazement. For the first time, Nina noticed the inscription on the envelope. She read: "To my saddened fiancée."

The other woman did not come. She was not at the evening service, where a white wreath lay on the steps of the black bier, and a white rose, the gift of his fiancée, fell next to the darling one's black hair. She was not at the bearing-out of the coffin, or at the burial service.

And the beauty of his fiancée's sadness was not disturbed by anything.

Along the scorching morning streets of the indifferently noisy city, behind the coffin, along the dusty pavement, Nina walked with the parents of her fiancé. One of his family members, an elegantly dressed, handsome gentleman with a graying mustache and the upright figure of a retired officer, led Nina with her arm in his.

The beauty of her sadness dragged along the hideously dusty, scorching streets, under the frantic blazing of the ancient Serpent, amid the passersby, who were momentarily moved and crossed themselves—the fatal beauty of her sadness dragged along in the gray, evil apathy of Aisa.[2]

She was tired, but she didn't want to get into a carriage. She was mortally tired. The tiredness crowned the beauty of her sadness, and the sweet languor of her face was even more touching to these alien people.

The mournful ritual was long, because they did not spare any expense, and in the beautiful church an excellent choir sang very well. The ritual that consoles the weak—but what consolation could it give to Nina, the poor fiancée of a bridegroom who only from beyond the grave had said words of love to her, but also words of reproach? And she thought, "Where must I return in order to console him? In order not to remain, according to his frank, dear words, nothing but trash, which has turned away from the light in cowardice?"

And it seemed to her that she knew where to go and how to console him.

The grave. The last handfuls of earth have been thrown in.

The mother and the fiancée were sobbing—the homely old woman, his kinswoman with the reddened nose, was bending over, with her hat knocked sideways—and the young, pale, tear-stained girl, a stranger to him in life and now the only one who was close to him.

And they stayed alone over the fresh grave. One had not been able to protect her son, and his heart was dark to her, and his thoughts were incomprehensible and alien to her. And the other: his dear eyes had never once looked at her, but his heart had been opened to her, his weak, earthly heart, exhausted from a burden beyond his strength, the heart of a person who had wanted to perform a great feat and was unable to do so.

"Darling," she whispered, "I know the path I have to walk in order to be with you, in order to console you. You could not do it, you became weak from sadness, it's dark and cold for you in the grave, but it's all right, don't be afraid, I will do everything that was your task. And if there are sufferings along your path, they will be mine."

One woman looked at the other. Nina thought, "What can I tell her? How can I console her?"

She said quietly to her: "You said yesterday that God would not give me happiness if he died because of me. God knows that I am not at all to blame for this. But what use is happiness to me if he, my darling, is in the grave? I did not know how to be with him when he was alive, but believe me, I will always be true to his memory. And I will carry out what he left me as a behest—and his love will be my love, his friends will be my friends, his hatred will be my hatred, and I will undergo that for which he perished."[3]

1908

THE SIXTY-SEVENTH DAY

A Novella

I rina was youthful, pure in body, and beautiful, and more than anything in the world she loved herself, loved her shapely, lithe, virginally fresh body, a body that had ripened for ambrosial embraces, that had been poured into perfect forms for torrid joys.[1]

Long had her girlfriends with their depraved thoughts opened up to Irina the secrets of external love, the fatal temptations of coarse life. But childish, premature lustfulness had not long tormented her—that poison full of early premonitions was soon expended in the languid caresses and immodest embraces of her fellow girls, in the eerie, dark minutes of shy solitude.

But when her youthful breast grew strong, elastically pressing the perfection of pure forms out from her tender flesh, and a pair of milky buds was filled with carmine, buds that were widely separated from each other by the elastic tension of her skin, above the gentle slopes to that enchanting valley on whose floor there pulsates a fiery fount, when the swaying of these marvelous slopes came to resemble the rising and ebbing tide of enchanting waves—when the runes of dark, spellbinding powers, of lust and shame, were clearly outlined by the dark-blue heat lightning of her eyes and the crimson dawn of her cheeks, Irina began to feel disgusted by the terrible thought that a coarse barbarian would take possession of her and crumple the captivating blossom, worthy of a Hellene. And he would barbarically plunder the lofty possession, the perfect and blessed world.

The perfect and blessed world!

Irina felt in those days that the whole world was confined within her tender, radiantly pearly, joyfully restless skin. All of life along with the ecstasies of the flaming world was hidden in that body penetrated by currents of youthful passion, and all horizons interlocked on the fine outlines of her little pink toes, which captivated her gaze. And there was no other life, and there was not and could not be any other times.

Zenith and nadir, the two poles and the equator, everything was on her delectable body, on that marvelous flesh so joyfully reflected in the mirrors of glass, water, dim steel, and bright imaginings, from the lush ocean of her black hair that flowed down along her enchanting curves, down to the dear surface that trod boards and the earth and tremulously shrank from caresses and kisses. And what is the sun! The bright, priceless diamond on the turquoise of her crown. And what is the moon! The light, silver *kokoshnik* on the dark-blue sea of her velvet headscarf.[2] And what are the stars! The golden buzzing bees on the dewy rustling of her veil.

How fortunate will be that bold seeker who with the fiery knife of audacious desire will cleave the girdle above the pearly nakedness of her loins!

But will he really bestow only coarse consummations upon her? Where then are the exquisitely ambrosial delectations, the alternation of piercing and tender sensations, the polyphonic, brightly colored symphonies of desires, languors, passions, enjoyments, and moaning caresses?

He will come, he will say the decorous things, they will perform the usual rituals, they will put on the golden ring, they will convey her, languid, modest, without any rosiness in her face, to the wedding crown, and then will begin an endless rigmarole!

May there not be the disgrace of boring embraces, of authorized coupling!

If I am verily I, a boundless and blessed universe that brings out of myself the swarms of golden-winged stars with their spellbinding twinkling, and the moon dreaming with its clear cold, and the fiery Dragon of the azure heights hurling its arrows, if the life in me is mine, my singular one, which rejoices in me to me for me, then what are law, power, limits to me? A phantasmal web cast over me by a phantasmal enemy!

A phantasmal web—and I struggle in its sticky loops. Why? I will tear, I will tear apart the suffocating captivity!

Baring her innocent body in her austere cell, Irina daydreamed and languished. She looked at herself and still could not recognize herself in the anguish of this body compressed by the binding of clothing. And she was still ashamed to admire her body.

How pure and fragrant is innocent, free flesh! Her whole maidenly body smells captivating, and especially sweet are the smells of her knees and shoulders, and still sweeter is the spicy, moist aroma emanating from those deep and sensitive depressions, overgrown with fine, curling little hairs, that lie between the splendor of her breasts and the elastic power of her shapely arms.

But the aromas rising from her body still seemed partly alien to Irina, mixed with the crushed smells of clothing, with the metallic fragrances of perfume, with the overabundant exhalations of sweat. And she was still ashamed to breathe in the aromas of her darling body.

This body was bared and liberated, but it still wasn't nude and free, and her boldness had not yet ripened to carry it to meet the lusts of a pure and intrepid seeker—to meet his dream and his passion.

It was fortunate that summer was then beginning. She insisted on being allowed to go alone to a distant wilderness. She secluded herself in the deserted spaces and lived as she wished.

There, unseen by anyone, becoming like a resurrected dryad or water sprite, Irina passed long days nude, under the open sky. She would walk into deserted waters and spend a long time giving herself up to the broad, cold embraces of the depths, which quickened the beating of her fiery heart. She would lie on the warmed riverside sand, running her tanned fingers through its light, dry friability. She would walk along soft and hard soils, along bedewed grasses and softly dry mosses, along the sticky bottoms of rain puddles, now dirtying her nude soles with warm earth, now washing them clean with cool waters.

And she became lithe, slender, strong, tanned to bronze. Her chest breathed deeply and powerfully, and her voice acquired a bright ring and a power that could be heard afar. Under her elastic skin the play of her powerful muscles became joyful and beautiful. Her skin became more elastic, unyielding, and dense, and the branches of forest bushes no longer scratched her thighs, calves, and back so sharply, and her naked soles boldly ran across the sharp stones of paved roads. All her perceptions of the external became precise and sensitive, as if the whole world had opened up, expanded, become multicolored and begun to resound with never before seen or heard ecstasies—her blessed world. A free world!

For sixty-six days Irina did not once put on any clothing other than a light mantle sometimes in the cool evenings, and not once did she put shoes on her feet.

And there came the sixty-seventh day. A torrid day at the end of July, morning.

Irina was quietly walking along a narrow valley in the forest. Against the luminous green of the grasses and mosses and the dark green of the foliage, her body shone with gold and flame, displaying on its surface innumerable warm, shimmering tones, created by the combination of the blood that glimmered through her skin, the fiery kisses of the lofty Dragon, the frolicsome touches of the winds, and the abyssal embraces of the waters. And this body seemed to have been composed out of the primordial red clay.

When Irina was passing in the shade of the trees, the foliage, penetrated by light, cast upon her body a trembling, rippling web woven of skimming, shimmering little circles of molten gold. Dappled in this way, Irina smiled joyfully and abashedly, as if the hot sunlight that came to meet her steps and poured out over her breast and stomach were tickling her. The green reflections on her golden body, which shone with a multihued gilding, made her look like a forest maiden who had primordially risen up out of the bowels of the earth. And her eyes sparkled and shone with a sylvan, primordially clear laughter.

This was the sixty-seventh day, the beginning of a torrid and passionate day. She exulted in a joyful assurance that he, the desired and awaited one, would come today.

And there, walking out of the forest, he appeared in a transparent gap in the branches, youthful, and beautiful, and not at all like the poet of our days.

"Is it he?" Irina thought questioningly, and surveyed with regret his luminous summer clothing, made simply and well, because he had come from the big city, from far away, driven by the dream of finding her, the beautiful maiden who had withdrawn from people, the one whose body had the color of the primordial clay.

Irina stopped in the shade of the trees, to the side of the road along which he would pass—and he diverged from his road and headed toward the marvelous tree under which the nudity of the dauntless and unashamed maiden shone with the bright, burning shimmering of torrid flashes.

A maiden who had been promised to someone.

"To him?" she thought.

"To me?" he thought.

And they looked straight into one another's eyes. They felt an ecstasy that resembled fear, and a momentary shame burst out like flashes of cold, dark-blue lightning, a shame that suddenly quickened the pounding of both their hearts, one beating in harmony with the other, because two torrid, two fiery dark waves rose up, swaying two bright rubies on their summits, two tautly ardent flowers.

If the rose of the nude maiden's lips smiles on the torrid swarthiness of her face, then what a white flashing is uncovered when they lightly open!

If heat lightning trembles in the two skies of the nude maiden's bottomless eyes, flickering dark-blue through her long, smoky, arrowlike eyelashes, then that dark-blue coldness is transformed into a dark-blue flame, and all of her, the bared maiden, is the burning bush.

Unplaited, her heavy braids fell to the sides of her head, they fell behind her shoulders, they are streaming behind her shoulders, and rippling is their dark laughter.

And she heard his first words: "If you are waiting for me, I have come to you, darling tsarevna."

Joy laughs sweetly, and her joyful body trembles ambrosially. The heat lightning flickered, and she said reed-pipe words, she dropped golden chimes to the flowers: "Am I really a tsarevna? A tsarevna has a diadem, but I am only a forest maiden."

He smiled, and he spoke, and he looked at her with clear eyes, as one sky looks at another: "You have come here as a white maiden of rippling ribbons, you have arisen here as the golden tsarevna of the blue heights. You are not of the forest, because your light figure is embraced and your skin is scorched by the impotent lust of the evil Serpent, who hurls his furious arrows—only arrows, but you are for me, that which can be kissed for my lips, that which can be embraced for my embraces, and I am to repose in your lap as it sways, because I am now before you."

"Yes," Irina said, "you have come to me, and I will not ask your name, so that a white swan will not lead you away across unknown waves to the shrine of your Grail."[3]

And she embraced his neck with one arm, and led him away at a swift run to the valley where no one could come, no one could see. Led away by her at a swift run, he felt on his neck the trembling of the slender nerves of her arm and the heaviness of her arm that pulled him, the torrid fascination of power, the enchantment of her arm.

There in the unknown valley the clear sun shone, there in the unknown valley, the ambrosial and pure Edenic air of a primordial paradise, nurtured by the good earth, poured into his broadly breathing breast—because at the entrance into the unknown valley she had pulled off his boring city clothing, the evil shrouding of his youthful body, and thrown it aside. And his body was white, beautiful, and shapely, and it was not like the bodies of the poets of our days, our dim and depraved days.

And she embraced him, and kissed him, and wanted his love and kisses and embraces and caresses.

And if there were skies and the earth, they were primeval and new. And did the sun shine to four skies—the two skies reflected closely and blissfully in two other skies—did the sun of the lofty azure shine?[4] And did coolness stream from the river to two breasts that were pressed one to another—his white breast on the swaying of her swarthy breasts—did the living, sweet coolness stream with a fresh wafting that was delightful for swift and happy sighing? Trees and grasses, riverbanks and waves, rustling and noises, warmed stones and cold lizards—what lay ahead and what was sweeping by? And all of life was in the harmonious rhythm of two bodies.

So innocent was the enchantment of their kissing that they lay for a long time embracing, and kissing, and saying ambrosial words, but not tasting the ultimate and sweetest happiness.

Bending to his white shoulder, Irina opened her laughing mouth and pressed her teeth onto the skin of his shoulder, and with a gentle bite awoke in him the frenzy of sensuality. Feeling on his neck her intertwined arms and on his face her quick, moaning breath, he wound his arms about her body, and linked his hands behind her back, and firmly embraced her, and passionately pressed himself, shuddering, to her body.

Having delighted in the first caresses, they lay next to each other, languidly flaming and feeling the sweet languors of the first shame. And again they united their embraces, and kisses, and the caresses of the desired consummations.

Made apparent to the unknown valley, the torrid day lengthened, but for them, torrid, youthful, and beautiful, time burned away. And the sky rolled up as a tent close above their heads, and the earth was a bed of delights, and the earth was for light running, games, and dances. And in the river there was water for cooling sport, and resounding, splashing spray rose up over the water, splitting into rainbow colors. They would walk out again onto the bank, where there was soft clay under their feet, and friable sand, and grass that caressed their feet—and they would entwine their arms, and go round and round in circles, and dance, and rush at a swift run, and fall onto the soft bed of grasses in the broad shade of the trees, to renew the joy of sweet consummations.

The day lengthened, and time burned away, and their desires and passion were inexhaustible—but what are you, poor body of a person? Weariness takes possession of you and inclines you to the lassitude of death. Already their breathing was becoming fitful, and the beating of their hearts uneven, and their arms and legs spread out impotently on the earth, and their languid eyes looked but didn't look.

But overcoming their fatigue, they pressed close to each other and united their bodies and their lusts for the final caresses. They took delight for the last time, they united the remnants of their passionate powers and burned them up in a blessed flame.

They lay exhausted. Her head pressed down to his shoulder, sweeping it with her braids in black streams. Her swarthy arm, impotently stretched out, lay across his white body. They lay exhausted.

And it was day no longer, and the sunset had already burned away, and the skies were covered by a cold dark blueness, and white mists started to sway above the river. From behind the tops of the distant trees, there beyond the river, the clear, round moon rose up and looked impassively at their motionless bodies. It had completed all its living rounds, exhausted all its sighs of love, and was now dragging along forever, cold and impassively sad.

It had come to know the peace of the final consolation. And as it consoled, it cast its dead spells.[5]

Then the one whose name I will not name, the one who wanders all around and never shows a person her earthly face, came out of the silent forest and drew near to the sleeping ones. She sat above them for a long time and looked at their tired faces. Under her motionless gaze their beautiful bodies were inert and cold. And she languished and sighed, like you, like you, my dear one . . .

She questioned herself: "Does it really have to be?"

She answered herself with another question: "Why?"

She finally decided in agreement with herself: "I will weave new mantles for them and will release them to their earthly days, to the creation of a new life."

She took a small vessel from her neck and opened it unhurriedly—but fateful decisiveness was already present in all her movements—and sprinkled them with water so cold that their shapely bodies trembled for a long time. With spellbinding movements of her hands, on a loom made of moonbeams, she swiftly wove a broad, soft fabric out of an unknown thread, and a second one just like the first, and she covered Irina and the one who was with her with the two delightful garments.

When their breathing became even and the beating of their harmonious hearts became deep and even and strong, she left, casting secret spells, leaving behind on the dew a trace that feebly glittered in the moonlight.

And they retained the sign of her sadness.

1908

THE ROAD TO DAMASCUS

(WRITTEN WITH ANASTASIA CHEBOTAREVSKAYA)

I.

From the turbulent debauchery of a frenetic life to a quiet union of love and death—the dear road to Damascus . . .[1]

In the evening of a quiet spring day, when droshkies were rumbling by on the cheerfully noisy streets, when fierce ragamuffins and faded women were selling naive lilies of the valley, Klavdia Andreyevna Kruzhinina emerged from a doctor's office, red and trembling from shame and despair, completely crushed by what she, a young girl, had been forced to hear. It seemed to her that everyone, the patients waiting in the reception room and the maid in the anteroom, were looking at her with mockery that stung her heart with serpent's bites.

After all, who would want her, so plain and quite uninteresting, bashful, awkward, always flustered in the presence of men?

For a long time now, the mirror had caused her to despair, the disgusting, truthful piece of glass that mercilessly reflected only that which is: a face not only plain but devoid of any charm. The plainness of her face was not relieved even by her few separate pleasant and sweet features. Deep, intelligent eyes that vividly reflected every movement; endearing dimples on her cheeks and chin; thick waves of hair, black as an autumn night—all these scattered beauties were in sad disharmony with the general gray tone of her face and all the gracelessness of her figure.

After all, who would want her? Who would call her his wife?

With the merciless frankness of the cynic that his profession had made him into, the doctor hurled merciless words at her.

Klavdia Andreyevna babbled disconcertedly, "But doctor, how can this be? Does this really depend on me? I have no fiancé."

The doctor shrugged his shoulders. "You can't argue with nature," he said indifferently. "No medicine is going to help you."[2]

II.

In that state of discomfiture and shame when your legs tremble and fail and you don't know what to do, Klavdia Andreyevna walked through the streets. The familiar intersections and crossings led her to a fourth-floor apartment overlooking a courtyard. This is where her friend Natalya Ilinichna Oprichina lived, cow-eyed and buxom, a wonderful person and excellent comrade.

Klavdia Andreyevna told her everything. If even a little time had passed, even a single day, perhaps she would have become ashamed to tell even her friend about this. But now it seemed to come out all by itself. All the more since Oprichina understood from Klavdia Andreyevna's unhappy, upset face that something unexpected and very unpleasant had happened and started asking her questions. Klavdia Andreyevna sat down, smiled with discomfiture and shame, and started telling her in detail and conscientiously, like a lesson she had learned by heart.

She told her story and started crying. Oprichina paced the room with heavy steps that caused the little pieces of glass on the table candleholders to jingle lightly. She was thinking.

"In my opinion," she said, "there's nothing to cry about, but you have to take action. You don't have your eye on anyone?"

Klavdia Andreyevna confessed in a plaintive voice, "There's nobody."

Oprichina said, "All our men are so nasty, and it's outrageous and unfair that they're happy to run after any pretty little face even if she's as stupid as an ass, but no one wants to look at the plain ones."

She stopped suddenly and went up to Klavdia Andreyevna with the look of someone who has suddenly devised something very felicitous and ingenious.

"You know, I can help you. I have just the person. . . . Well, in a word, it's a certain good friend of mine. He likes to have dealings with innocent girls. I'll arrange it for you."

III.

A few days later, Klavdia Andreyevna was sitting in a private room in an expensive restaurant with an exquisitely dressed gentleman a little over forty. The conversation wasn't going smoothly. A light but expensive supper had been served—oysters and champagne. Klavdia Andreyevna was embarrassed, but she was trying valiantly to hide it. Sergei Grigorievich Tashev, her companion, was complimenting her intellect, her wit, her education.

"It's been a long time since I've spent such a pleasant evening. You are the most intelligent of all the women I know in St. Petersburg."

Klavdia Andreyevna looked at his suspiciously black hair, his too upright figure, the unpleasant outline of his straight-cut mouth with the closely clipped, bristly black mustache above it. She felt that he was saying all this because it was impossible to praise her appearance, but nevertheless it was necessary to say some pleasant words that would draw them together.

Sometimes it would suddenly seem to her that this was all a dream, an invention. She—plain, slouching, in her eternal black dress, shabbily adorned "for the occasion" by a little light-blue neck scarf, she who never went to restaurants, who didn't know how to carry herself or how to turn on the electricity or cope with artichokes. And this strangely alien room with its irritating red wallpaper, with its conventional mirrors, with an upright piano in the corner and a garnet velvet portière, behind which something else was hidden—what? a washstand? a bed? And the elegant gentleman with his yellow-white, almond-like teeth, with the carefully combed part above his creased face, with wrinkles around his mouth and eyes, with his excessively exquisite (in her opinion) clothes, and the amazing dark-garnet dickey on his cambric shirt.

What had brought them together here? Why were they, so alien and distant, unacquainted with each other only yesterday, sitting here alone, the two of them, separated by heavy garnet portières from the street, from the city, from everything external, customary, and habitual?

This strange, piquant atmosphere acted on Klavdia Andreyevna like a dizzying, evil hallucination. The white narcissi and scarlet carnations in a crystal bowl in the middle of the table exhaled their fragrance in the warmed air. The wine, sparkling so pleasantly, offering welcome warmth and lifting the spirit, golden and joyful in the tall, spherical wineglasses.

She forgot all the absurdity of the tangled connection of events and why she had come here, she forgot, she lost the memory of that, dropped it into the golden tears in the glasses, and she sat there joyful, answering questions, talking, even laughing at a funny story about a professor she knew.

Tashev said as he finished his anecdote, "I don't know how cultured people can visit such places. For example, I may boast, for my part, that I have never once possessed a woman without love."

Klavdia Andreyevna shuddered, perhaps from the too-cold wine, in which pieces of unmelted ice floated. Tashev continued, "A woman with whom we are in love may be plain; after all, what is beauty if not a conventional idea? But she must maintain tender charms, the fascination of what is eternally feminine, mysterious, and instinctive. Delicate, ineffable threads must stretch between her and the man before they are united by what we call love."

His face, yellowish and pale, became animated and turned red. His eyes began to dance, and his unpleasantly big teeth sparkled more often from beneath his protruding, bright carmine upper lip.

IV.

Oysters, cold and slippery, on a large round platter. Klavdia Andreyevna timidly rolled two of them onto her plate and waited in embarrassment for her companion to arm himself with his knife and show her what to do with this dish she'd never seen before.

"With lemon or without?" he asked, obligingly offering her a little crystal plate holding yellow discs and a small gilt fork.

Suddenly she felt that she was turning red from the roots of her hair to her shoulders, as people turn red when they realize the hopelessness of their situation. He must have understood; he took his knife, deftly used it to open the shell, and quickly upended the slippery lump into his mouth.

Klavdia Andreyevna felt gratitude and even something like goodwill toward him. He had saved her from the first agonizing moments. But what would happen next?

It was eerie and intriguing, and the whole time it seemed to be happening in a dream, in a fog. Again the wine, golden goblets, golden slices of pineapple on a crystal plate, and again, dim through the fog, conversations about beauty, about women, about love.

"None of us knows what beauty is, we just strive to find out. But then that's not the point.

> Today you are not at all beautiful,
> But you're somehow especially sweet—"

Tashev declaimed. He loved to show off his knowledge of modern poets and foreign literature, and he attended all the premieres and gala performances.[3] How did he have time for it all! To give university lectures, preside over all sorts of scholarly and half-scholarly meetings, to go on business trips abroad, to write a book.

V.

Next door in a large room there was a real bacchanal going on. They could hear the sounds of the *maxixe*, the cakewalk, fragments of Gypsy and operetta motifs.[4] A broken, hysterical voice at times tried to draw out a high-pitched phrase, "I'll flood your lips with burning kisses . . . ," but each time it broke off at the same place and squealed sorrowfully, "I can't, I can't!"[5]

Someone was complaining about something in a quite drunken voice, someone was being consoled, someone was exchanging loud kisses, trying to drown out the sound of the kisses with bursts of laughter. It must have been a crazy, motley, and drunken company!

As he poured wine into Klavdia Andreyevna's goblet, Tashev said, "Listen to what fun those people are having, and you and I haven't even finished drinking our first bottle of champagne. I drink to interesting, intelligent women, with the same beautiful eyes as my enchanting companion."

And with an unexpected movement, he bent over quickly and kissed Klavdia Andreyevna's hand.

The unexpectedness disconcerted her but did not amaze her. After all, this is what she was waiting for, what she had been preparing for, as two hours ago, with beating heart, she had ascended the stairway of the first-class restaurant, with its carpet under bronze rods. And she so seldom had her hand kissed! From that kiss, fugitive and unexpected, a tremulously glowing thread reached out from him to her, an invisible but significant thread.

He moved closer to her, so that there was no longer any space between them on the narrow little sofa; he placed his yellowish hand, with its dark, distinctly visible hairs, on her small, swarthy wrist, and said, now in an intimate tone to which he tried to lend a tinge of soulfulness:

"The only deficiency in our emancipated women is that despite their freedom of thought they still do not want the same kind of freedom for the body. In my opinion, the harmonious development of the personality must unite in itself both the one and the other."

Klavdia Andreyevna looked at the swarthy, alien face, listened to these dusty words, familiar to her from novels, and somehow stopped feeling the strangeness of her situation and of her closeness to this man who was completely alien to her and whom she was seeing for only the second time in her life. A dull, apathetic indifference took possession of her.

"It's all the same, it's all the same," flashed in her weary, befogged head.

Life, so gray, so ruthless, would crush her any day now, all the same. And there flashed before Klavdia Andreyevna's eyes a dismal stretch of cheerless years, her youth passing without any enthusiasms, in tiresome worries about salary, in petty mortifications and vain attempts to fall in love, to find "a guy"—a friend, a husband.

VI.

The drunken hum next door suddenly reminded her of last year, when at Shrovetide she was riding in a third-class train carriage at night, summoned by a telegram to Kaluga, where her younger brother, a university student, had shot himself. A merry, drunken couple had found themselves a place on the neighboring berth—a workman with a harmonica and a woman who might have been a prostitute, his girlfriend for the night.

That whole horrible night Klavdia Andreyevna, benumbed, as if overcome by heavy fumes, never closed her eyes, and the whole night the harmonica squealed, the workman shouted with gusto, and the drunken prostitute yelled drunken songs.

Klavdia Andreyevna was on her way home to her family. That family gathered only when some misfortune happened to one of its members—death, exile, going off to war. Now they were preparing to bury her younger brother. This is how they would all gather at these sad moments of life, all of them plain, all failures, all with their own poison in their soul; they would silently crowd next to the coffin or the train, not knowing how to say anything consoling to each other. Like a crowd of chimeras, gray and dismal, they would stand, exchanging dull glances and gray words.

On that night of lassitude, she forgot all this and in dull numbness listened to the drunken squealing, the invective, the kisses, the shrill harmonica. Wasn't it all the same—it seemed even then—any day now life would smother her, wasn't it all the same?

She turned over on the hard bench and suddenly started coughing from the fumes of cheap tobacco. On the other side of the low partition, the prostitute laughed hoarsely.

"Someone's hacking over there, must be a fine young lady," her disgustingly husky voice could be heard.

A scrawny lad with a green face and a prickly, gray-eyed gaze leaned out for a moment from behind the partition. He pricked Klavdia Andreyevna with his gaze, and suddenly his face became contemptuously bored. He turned away.

From behind the partition she could hear his drunken, insolent voice: "An ugly snout, and she's hacking like one, not like a beauty."

"Snoutification!" the prostitute squealed hoarsely.

The sharp sting of the insult pierced right through the poor heart of the grieving girl.

VII.

Now she recalled that night and that insult, and again her heart began to ache with a shameful pain. It was a pain that seemed to flood her whole body, her whole, suddenly blushing body, and it suddenly struck the nerve of a tooth that had begun hurting the other day, which she had planned to have filled but didn't manage to.

Tashev looked sympathetically at her face, suddenly distorted by pain.

"What's wrong?" he asked, bending over her and inundating her with a light aroma of wine.

"My tooth has started to hurt," she said.

And pitiful, small tears gushed from her eyes. Involuntarily. She babbled: "It's nothing. It will pass in a minute."

Tashev said something; she could hardly hear him through the crimson fog that was making her head spin, and she could hardly understand what she heard.

"Take some water and rinse your teeth."

She hardly realized that she was submitting to him and walking somewhere, and he was supporting her caressingly and solicitously by her left elbow. The heavy crimson folds of the portière were swaying right before her eyes.

"There's water here. Please allow me to help you."

He threw back the heavy folds. He turned on the switch, and suddenly a cramped alcove was illuminated by the dim light of an electric bulb: the gray marble of a washstand with beautiful copper faucets, and a bulky, insolently huge bed.

It was so shameful to stand next to this bed. He poured out water for her. She took it into her mouth, onto the painful tooth. The pain died down. Klavdia Andreyevna babbled incoherently, "Thank you. I feel better. It's passed."

She turned to leave the alcove. She was met by a smile and his gleaming, unpleasantly large teeth.

"Wait a moment, calm down, don't hurry," Tashev said.

He was panting slightly, and his eyes were gleaming with cunning, passionate sparks. Klavdia Andreyevna felt the touch of his hot hand on her waist.

He was whispering, "You are tired. Lie down for a while. Take a rest. This will calm you down better than anything."

He bent over quite close to her. With caressing but insistent gestures he moved her to the soft sedation of the too elegant bed.

A shamefaced horror suddenly seized her. With a wild movement she pushed Tashev away and rushed out of the alcove, all red and trembling.

She grabbed her hat. Tashev kept repeating in bewilderment, "Klavdia Andreyevna, what on earth is this? What's wrong with you? Just calm down. I really don't understand. It seems that I . . ."

With trembling hands, fumbling, Klavdia tried to pin her hat on. The pin fell out of her trembling hands, and its large, blue-glass head clinked and gleamed on the parquet floor.

Tashev, muttering something and evidently angry, went up to Klavdia Andreyevna. She squealed in fright, grabbed her light cape, and rushed out of the room. She could hear behind her the fragments of Tashev's exclamations: "I don't understand! It's simply outrageous! But why?"

The restaurant footmen looked in amazement at the young lady as she ran past them impetuously.

VIII.

Klavdia Andreyevna walked quickly, almost running, through the noisy city streets. She ran along her usual route to the building where Oprichina lived, and she had already gone halfway up the stairs when suddenly, just as impetuously, she turned back and again found herself on the street.

She would walk for a while and then stop. She straightened her hat, which had fallen off, pinning it with her only remaining hatpin. She got on the first streetcar that came and sat there dully, with no thoughts, red-faced, obviously unhappy, until everyone started to get out and someone in the darkness said in a bored, evil voice, "We're here. It's the end of the line."

She got out. She looked around.

The outskirts of the city. Small gray houses. The crooked slabs of a narrow sidewalk. Scraggly but cheerfully green grass between the stones of the pavement, visible even through the evening mist.

She walked haphazardly. She walked—tired, quiet, silent. All around it was night, and silence, and half-darkness, and sadness on the earth, and a desolate blueness above the earth.

It seemed that someone was crying, someone forgotten and unnecessary. The moist spring air was quiet and sad. It smelled of water. A reed-pipe moan reached her from somewhere nearby in the night silence.

IX.

Suddenly Klavdia Andreyevna distinguished that it was the sounds of a violin. Someone was playing, as if the violin was weeping over someone's dear remains, resting in peace. Klavdia Andreyevna started walking in the direction from which these sounds were reaching her.

There it is—a poor, quiet house, all dark. A wicket gate. From the courtyard the thin lament of the grieving violin reached her.

Klavdia Andreyevna went into the courtyard. A weak light could be seen through a window curtain in the depths of the courtyard. Klavdia approached the window along the rickety boards of a narrow walkway. She stood and listened by the open window for a long time.

The reed-pipe howls died away on a high, long, moaning note. She could hear the violin being laid onto the table with a quiet knock, and she could hear quick, uneven steps going back and forth.

Whether a light wind had pulled the edge of the curtain away or whether Klavdia Andreyevna herself had slightly moved it away with the tips of her trembling fingers—she caught sight of the musician.

He was a young man in a student's pea-jacket, with a nervous, pale, haggard face, with thick hair that curled tightly and obstinately, sticking out in a matted shock above the steep, obstinately protuberant forehead, with choppy movements and an awkward, harsh gesture of his dry hands that rapidly tousled his hair. The student was walking, dashing around the room—and in his movements there was anguish, and in his face a languor that was painful to the point of death.

The bottomless black gaze of his eyes stopped for a moment on Klavdia Andreyevna's face, but it was clear that the student could not see her, a random girl who had come here at night from who knows where. And in the bottomless black gaze of his eyes was concealed languor, a person's last, insane languor.

X.

In the whole atmosphere of the poor rented room, the run-of-the-mill lair of a loner, there was something ineffably significant. It was the sudden, strange, doleful disorder of a place where there are people dying.

On the table, among the books and the usual junk, between a box of cheap cigarettes and a half-drunk glass of tea, lay a note that was placed too correctly and had apparently just been written. The table drawer had been pulled out a little bit, and this somehow struck the eye, as if there was something significant about it.

But perhaps it seemed that way to Klavdia Andreyevna because hardly had she caught sight of this slightly pulled-out drawer than the student went up to it and, slouching awkwardly, began rummaging in it.

Klavdia waited with avid curiosity to see what he would pull out of the drawer. Insistently, like an evil hypnotic suggestion, along with the heavy beating of the blood in her temples, there repeated a single word, as ordinary as the streets: "Revolver, revolver."

And the evil suggestion, the evil premonition, was justified. The student walked away from the table, and in his hand Klavdia Andreyevna caught sight of the steel gleam of a weapon, small and elegant as a child's toy.

With a sharp gesture of his free hand the student tousled his obstinate curls, and he raised the revolver to his temple.

His eyes widened. The hand swayed strangely in the air, trying to fix the muzzle of the revolver on the proper place.

Then he lowered his hand, looked into the muzzle of the revolver, once again tousled his hair sweepingly, and shouted abruptly and loudly: "Basta!"

And with a decisive movement he swung the revolver toward his head.

A sudden feminine howl caused him to flinch. He peered out.

XI.

Opening the curtain with an impetuous gesture of both hands, Klavdia Andreyevna screamed desperately: "Darling, darling! Why? Don't do it!"

The student saw that an unknown, plain girl was crawling into his window, awkwardly clutching at the window frame, catching on something with her dress—an awkward girl with a hat sitting crookedly on her disheveled hair, with a red, excited, unhappy face, drenched in tears, distorted by sobbing grimaces.

She was crawling in, so ludicrous, funny, and tear-stained, and repeating tearfully and piteously, "My darling, don't do it, don't do it!"

The student stuck the revolver into the drawer, rushed to the window, and muttering something incoherently, helped his unexpected guest to climb over the windowsill.

Full of the exciting emotions of recent days, she rushed to him, embraced him, wept, and repeated endlessly, "My darling, my beautiful one, don't do it—live, love me, live, I am also unhappy."

"Forgive me," the student said, "please calm down. Maybe you'd like some tea?"

Klavdia Andreyevna started laughing, although she was still crying. She said, "No, no, I don't need anything. And we don't need that toy. Look, if you have reached the point where you no longer have anything to live for—in your soul, nothing—look, the same is true of me, and if we want to, couldn't we, couldn't we really create life according to our will—life, and love, and death? Listen to me."

She spent a long time telling him about herself, disconnectedly, in detail, with child-like frankness. She told him everything. And again she returned to the insults that burned her heart with the pricks of a thousand bee stingers. Laughing and crying, she said, "He says, 'An ugly snout, and she's hacking like one'—that was me coughing from his cheap tobacco. And she says, 'Snoutification.' And they both laugh. Ugly snout! Well, so what, so what!"

The student tousled his shaggy hair, with a sharp, habitual gesture cast up his hands somehow too high, and said in a consoling voice, "Well, to hell with that. I've got quite an ugly snout myself."

And suddenly they both started laughing. And there was no longer a fatal languor in his eyes or in her soul. He went up close to her and embraced her impetuously, and kissed her resoundingly, gaily, and youthfully on her joyfully trembling lips. He said, "To hell with that nonsense!"

And he angrily closed the table drawer.

And she kept kissing him and repeating, "My darling, my darling! Love me, love me, kiss me—we will live together and die together."

It's easier together.
And if we fail to walk on,
We'll die together on the road,
We'll die together.[6]

So, having run away from the turbulent frenzy of an unrighteous life, they came to their longed-for Damascus, into a union of a love that is as strong as death and a death that is as ambrosial as love.

1910

THE KISS OF THE UNBORN CHILD

I.

At a large joint-stock company, a nimble office boy with closely cropped hair, wearing a tight jacket with two rows of small bronze buttons, a jacket on which no dust was visible because it was gray, peeked through the door of a room where five women typists were working—tapping, sometimes simultaneously, on five loudly chirping typewriters—and grabbing hold of the doorframe and swinging on one foot, he said to one of the young ladies:

"Nadezhda Alexeyevna, Mrs. Kolymtseva wants you to come to the telephone."

He ran off, and his footsteps were inaudible on the gray mat that had been laid along the narrow corridor. Nadezhda Alexeyevna, a tall, gracefully built young woman of about twenty-seven, with quiet, assured movements and with that calmness in her deep gaze that is given only to those who have lived through difficult days, unhurriedly finished the end of the line she was typing, got up, and went downstairs, to the room where the telephone was, next to the anteroom. She was thinking, "What's happened now?"

She had already gotten used to the fact that if her sister Tatyana Alexeyevna wrote to her or called her on the telephone, it almost always was because something had happened in her family—the children were sick, her husband had some unpleasantness at work, something had happened at the children's school, they were in severe need of money. Then Nadezhda Alexeyevna would get on a streetcar and set off for the distant outskirts of the town, to help, to console, to rescue. Her sister was about ten years older than Nadezhda Alexeyevna, she had gotten married long ago, and although they lived in the same town, they seldom saw each other.

In the cramped telephone booth, where for some reason it always smelled of tobacco, beer, and mice, Nadezhda Alexeyevna took the receiver and said, "Hello. Is it you, Tanechka?"

Nadezhda Alexeyevna heard the voice of her sister, weeping and agitated, exactly as she had expected to hear it.

"Nadya, for the love of God, come as soon as you can, we've had a terrible disaster, Seryozha has died, he shot himself."

Without having time to take fright at the unexpected news of the death of her fifteen-year-old nephew, the darling boy Seryozha, Nadezhda Alexeyevna said confusedly and incoherently, "Tanya, darling, what are you saying! How horrible! But why? When did it happen?"

And without waiting for or listening to an answer, she hurriedly said, "I'll come right now, right now."

She dropped the receiver without even remembering to put it back on the hook, and quickly went to see the administrator to request the rest of the day off for family reasons.

The administrator allowed her to go, although he gave her a disgruntled look and grumbled, "You know that this is the busiest time, right before the holidays. All of you always have some emergency, right at the most inconvenient time for us. Well, all right, go, if it's so urgent, but just remember you have work waiting for you here."

II.

A few minutes later Nadezhda Alexeyevna was sitting in the street-car. It was about a twenty-minute ride. During that time Nadezhda Alexeyevna's thoughts returned to the same thing they were always drawn to in those moments of life when unexpected incidents, almost always unpleasant ones, so frequently disturbed the boring flow of her days. Nadezhda Alexeyevna's feelings were vague and subdued. Only from time to time did a sharp pity for her sister and for the boy suddenly grip her heart painfully.

It was terrible to think that this fifteen-year-old boy, who just a few days ago had come to see Nadezhda Alexeyevna and had had a long conversation with her, that the formerly cheerful *gimnazia* student Seryozha had suddenly shot himself. It was painful to think about how his mother, who even without this had been wearied by her difficult, not entirely fortunate life, was grieving and crying. But there was something else, perhaps even harder and more terrible, weighing on her whole life, that prevented Nadezhda Alexeyevna from giving herself up to these feelings, and her heart, pressed upon by an anguish of long standing, could not sweetly wear itself out in the torments of sorrow, pity, and terror. It was as if the source of relieving tears had a heavy stone weighing it down, and only scanty, infrequent little tears sometimes appeared in her eyes, whose usual expression was indifferent boredom.

Once again, her memory returned Nadezhda Alexeyevna to that same passionate, fiery circle she had traversed. She recalled a few days from several years ago, days of self-oblivion and passion, of a love that boundlessly surrendered itself.

The days of the luminous summer were like a holiday for Nadezhda Alexeyevna. The sky appeared to her a joyful blue above the meager open spaces of the countryside surrounding the Finnish dacha settlement, and brief summer showers made an amusingly cheerful sound.[1] The smell of resin in the warm pine forest was more sweetly intoxicating than the fragrance of roses, which didn't grow in this region, so gloomy but nonetheless dear to the heart. The greenish-gray moss in the dark forest was a sweet bed of bliss. The forest brook, flowing among gray, clumsily scattered stones, prattled as joyfully and resoundingly as if its transparent rill was rushing straight to the fields of happy Arcadia, and the coolness of these resounding streams was cheerful and joyful.

The happy days rushed by so quickly for Nadezhda Alexeyevna in the cheerful rapture of being in love, and the final day came, which of course she did not realize was the last happy day. Everything all around was just as cloudless, and luminous, and simple-heartedly cheerful. The broad forest shade, fragrant with resin, was just as cool and pensive, and the warm moss under her feet was just as joyfully tender. Only the birds had already stopped singing—they had built their nests and hatched their young.

Only on the face of her darling one there was a kind of dim shadow. But it was because that morning he had received an unpleasant letter.

That is what he said himself: "A horribly unpleasant letter. I'm in despair. How many days I'll have to go without seeing you!"

"Why?" she asked.

And she hadn't yet had time to turn sad. But he said: "My father writes that Mother is ill. I must go."

His father had written something completely different—but Nadezhda Alexeyevna did not know about that. She didn't yet know that love can be deceived, that lips that have kissed can speak a lie as if it were the truth.

Embracing and kissing Nadezhda Alexeyevna, he said: "I have to go, there's nothing to be done! What a bore! I'm sure it's nothing serious, but all the same I simply must go."

"Yes, of course," she said, "if your mother is ill, how can you not go! But write to me every day. I will miss you so much!"

As always, she accompanied him to the edge of the forest, to the main road, and went home by a forest path, a little saddened, but so certain that he would soon return. But he did not return.

Nadezhda Alexeyevna got several letters from him. They were strange letters. There was a sense of embarrassment and reticence, there were incomprehensible hints that raised alarm. And yet the letters came. Nadezhda Alexeyevna began to guess that he had stopped loving her. And suddenly she found out from strangers, in a chance conversation at the end of that summer, that he had already gotten married.

"Why, of course, didn't you hear about it? Last week they went straight from the altar to Nice."

"Yes, he's a lucky man—he snapped up a wife who's beautiful and rich."

"A large dowry?"

"I'll say! Her father has . . ."

She didn't stick around to hear what the father had. She walked away.

She often recalled what happened next. She didn't want to recall—Nadezhda Alexeyevna tried to chase away these memories, to smother them within herself. It was so difficult and degrading—and so unavoidable—then, in those first difficult days, when she had learned about his marriage, having felt herself to be a mother there, among those dear places, where everything still reminded her of his caresses, having just felt the first movements of a new creature, to already think about its death. And to kill the unborn child!

No one in the house found out. Nadezhda Alexeyevna thought up a plausible pretext for leaving home for two weeks. Somehow or other, with great difficulty, she gathered the amount of money she needed to pay for the evil deed. They performed this terrible deed, the details of which she so disliked recalling later, in a foul clinic, and she returned home, still half-sick, emaciated, pale, and weak, hiding her pain and horror with pitiful heroism.

The recollections of the details of this deed were persistent, but all the same Nadezhda Alexeyevna somehow was able to deny them enduring power over her memory. She would quickly, hastily call it all to mind, shudder from horror and revulsion, then hurry to distract herself from these scenes.

But what was relentless and what Nadezhda Alexeyevna could not and did not want to struggle with was the darling and terrible image of the unborn child, her child.

When Nadezhda Alexeyevna was alone and sitting quietly, her eyes closed, the little boy would come to her. It seemed to her that she could see him growing up. These sensations were so vivid that at times it seemed to her that year by year, day by day, she was living through everything that a real mother of a living child experiences. At times it seemed to her that her breasts were full of milk. Then she would give a start when she heard the noise of some object falling, afraid that her little boy had hurt himself.

Sometimes Nadezhda Alexeyevna wanted to talk to him, to pick him up, to caress him. She would stretch out her hand in order to stroke the soft, luminous golden hair of her son, but her hand encountered emptiness, and behind her back she seemed to hear the laughter of the child, who had run away and hidden somewhere.

She knew his face, the face of her child, although unborn. She could see his face clearly: the darling and terrible combination of the features of the man who had taken her love and abandoned it, who had taken her soul and drunk it up and forgotten it, his features that despite everything were still dear—the combination of those features with her own.

The cheerful gray eyes—those are from his father. The delicate shells of his little pink ears—those are from his mother. The soft outline of the lips and chin—those are from his father. The round, tender shoulders, like the shoulders of a young girl—those are from his mother. The golden, slightly curly hair—that is from his father. The endearing dimples on his rosy cheeks—those are from his mother.

And so Nadezhda Alexeyevna analyzes it all, the little hands, the little feet, and she recognizes it all. She knows it all. She recognizes his habits: he holds his hands this way, he crosses one leg over the other this way—he got that from his father, although the unborn child never saw his father. If he laughs, looks to the side, blushes tenderly and shyly—that's from his mother, the unborn child took that from his mother.

It was sweet and painful. As if someone cruel and dear were rubbing salt into the deep wound with a tender, pink little finger—it hurt so much! But it was impossible to chase him away.

"And I don't want to, I don't want to drive you away, my unborn little boy. At least live in the way you can. At least I will give you this life."

Only a life in dreams. He was entirely in that life. Darling, poor unborn child! You yourself won't feel joy, you won't laugh by yourself for yourself, you yourself won't cry about yourself. You are living, but you do not exist. In the world of the living, among people and objects, you do not exist. So alive, and darling, and luminous, and you don't exist.

"That is what I have done to you!"

And Nadezhda Alexeyevna thought: "He's still small now, he doesn't know. He'll grow up, he'll come to understand, he'll compare himself with children who have been born, he'll want a living life and he'll reproach his mother. Then I will die."

She did not notice and did not consider that her thoughts would seem insane if judged by common sense, that horrible and insane judge of our deeds. She did not think about the fact that that small, formless, wizened little fetus that she had discarded had remained a soulless lump of material, dead matter, which had not been given animating form by the human spirit. No, for Nadezhda Alexeyevna the unborn child was alive and torturing her heart with unending torment.

He was luminous, in luminous clothes, with little white hands and feet, with clear, innocent eyes, with an immaculate smile, and when he laughed, he laughed joyfully and resoundingly. It's true that when she wanted to embrace him, he would run away and hide, but he didn't run far, and he would hide somewhere nearby. He would run from her embraces, but then again he himself would often wind his warm, tender little arms around her neck and press his delicate lips to her cheek, at those moments when she would sit quietly with her eyes closed. Only he never once kissed her right on the lips. "He'll grow up and he'll understand," Nadezhda Alexeyevna thought. "He'll grow sad, he'll turn away, he'll go away forever. Then I will die."

And now, sitting in the monotonously rumbling streetcar, among strangers wrapped in their coats, holding their holiday packages on their knees, Nadezhda Alexeyevna closed her eyes and again saw her little boy. Again she looked into his clear eyes, heard his delicate prattle—she didn't listen carefully to the words—and in this state she reached the place where she had to get off.

III.

Nadezhda Alexeyevna got out of the streetcar and started off along the snowy streets, past the low stone and wooden houses, past the gardens and fences of the remote outskirts of the town. She walked alone. The people who came her way were strangers. Nadezhda Alexeyevna did not have her own person, darling and terrible, with her. And she thought: "My sin is always with me, and I have nowhere to get away from it. Why am I living? After all, even Seryozha has died!"

She walked, and the dull anguish was in her heart, and she did not know how to answer her own question. Why am I living? But why should I die?

And she thought: "He is always with me, my little one. He is already growing up—he's eight years old, and there is a lot for him to understand. Why doesn't he get angry at me? Does he really not want to play with the little kids here, to go sledding? All the delight of our earthly life, everything that I too relished so luminously, all that delight, so enchanting even if it is deceptive, the delight of life on this dear earth, in this best of all possible worlds, is he really not enticed by it?"

Now as Nadezhda Alexeyevna walked down the strange, indifferent street alone, her thoughts no longer dwelt on herself and her little boy. She remembered the family of her sister, to whom she was going: her sister's husband, buried in his work, her always weary sister, the mob of kids, noisy, capricious, and constantly demanding this or that, the poor apartment, the lack of money. The nephews and nieces, whom Nadezhda Alexeyevna loved. And the *gimnazia* student Seryozha who had shot himself.

How could this have been expected? He was such a cheerful, lively boy.

But now Nadezhda Alexeyevna remembered a conversation with Seryozha the previous week. The boy was sad and agitated. They were talking about something they had read in the Russian newspapers, hence something horrendous, of course. Seryozha said, "Things are bad at home, and you pick up a newspaper—it's all horror and nastiness."

Nadezhda Alexeyevna answered something she herself didn't believe, just in order to distract the boy from his sad thoughts. Seryozha smirked in a cheerless way and said, "Aunt Nadya, just think how bad it all is! Just think what is going on around us! After all, it's terrible if the best of people, in his old age, runs away from his home and dies somewhere! He just saw more clearly than the rest of us the horror in which we all live, and he couldn't endure it. He went away and died.[2] It's terrible!"

Later, after a silence, Seryozha said the words that had frightened Nadezhda Alexeyevna then:

"Aunt Nadya, I'll tell you frankly, because you are a darling and you will understand me—I really don't want to live in the midst of everything that's going on now. I know that I am just as weak as everyone, and what can I do? I'll just be pulled into this vileness little by little. Aunt Nadya, Nekrasov was right: 'It's a blessing to die while you're young.'"[3]

Nadezhda Alexeyevna was very frightened and talked to Seryozha for a long time. It seemed to her that he believed her at last. He smiled cheerfully, the way he used to smile, and said in his former carefree tone: "Well, all right, we will live and we will see. 'The movement of progress is starting now, and the end of it we cannot tell.'"

Seryozha loved to read Nekrasov, not Nadson or Balmont.[4]

And now Seryozha does not exist, he shot himself. He really did not want to live and watch the majestic march of progress. What is his mother doing now? Kissing his waxen hands? Or spreading butter on bread for the kids who've been hungry since morning, frightened and teary-eyed, so pitiful in their worn-out little dresses and jackets with holes in the elbows? Or is she simply lying on her bed and crying, crying endlessly? She's lucky—lucky if she is able to cry! What in the world is sweeter than tears!

IV.

Now finally Nadezhda Alexeyevna reached their house, went up to the fourth floor along the narrow stone staircase with its steep steps, went up quickly, almost running, so that she was out of breath and stopped to rest before ringing the doorbell. She breathed heavily, held the narrow iron strip of the banister with her right hand in its warm knitted glove, and looked at the door.

The door was covered in felt, upholstered with oilcloth, and on this oilcloth there were black strips going crisscross, either as a decoration or for support. One of these strips had been torn away in the middle and was hanging down, the oilcloth had been torn through in this place, and the gray felt was sticking out. And for some reason this suddenly aroused pity and pain in Nadezhda Alexeyevna. Her shoulders started shaking. She quickly covered her face with her hands and started crying loudly. It was as if she had suddenly gotten weak; she quickly sat down on the top step and cried for a long time, covering her face. Under her warm knitted gloves, abundant tears flowed from her closed eyes.

It was cold, quiet, half-dark on the staircase, and the firmly shut doors, three on a single landing, were motionless and mute. Nadezhda Alexeyevna cried for a long time. Suddenly she heard familiar, light steps. She froze in joyful anticipation. And he, her little one, embraced her neck and again pressed up to her cheek, moving away her hand in its knitted glove with his warm little hand. He pressed his tender lips to her and quietly said: "Why are you crying! You know you are not to blame!"

She was silent, and she listened, and she didn't dare to move and open her eyes, for fear that he would go away. Only she dropped her right hand, the one that he had moved, onto her knees, and covered her eyes with her left hand. And she tried to hold back her tears, in order not to frighten him with her unattractive female crying, the crying of a poor earthly woman.

And he said to her again: "You are not to blame for anything."

And again he kissed her cheek. And he said to her, repeating Seryozha's terrible words: "I don't want to live here. I thank you, darling mama."

And again he said: "It's true, believe me, darling mama, I don't want to live."

These words, which were so terrible when Seryozha said them, were terrible because they were said by a person who had received the living image of a human being from an unknown power and was obligated to preserve the treasure he had been given and not to destroy it. Now these same words on the lips of the unborn child were joyful for his mother. Very quietly, afraid of frightening him with the coarse sound of earthly words, she asked: "My darling, have you forgiven me?"

And he answered: "You are not to blame for anything. But if you wish, I forgive you."

And suddenly Nadezhda Alexeyevna's heart was filled with a premonition of unexpected joy. Not yet daring to hope, not yet knowing what would happen, she slowly and fearfully stretched out her hands—and she felt him, the unborn child, on her knees, and his arms lay on her shoulders, and his lips pressed to her lips. She kissed him for a long time, and it seemed to her that the luminous eyes of the unborn child were looking right into her eyes, luminous as the sun of a serene world, but she did not dare to open her eyes, so as not to die for having seen that which a human being is forbidden to see.

When the child's embraces unclenched, and she heard the light steps on the staircase, and her little boy went away, Nadezhda Alexeyevna got up, wiped away her tears, and rang the doorbell of her sister's apartment. She went in, calm and happy, to help the people prostrated by sadness.

1911

THE LADY IN SHACKLES

A Legend of the White Nights

TO N. I. BUTKOVSKAYA[1]

A certain Moscow Maecenas (they say that these days, Maecenases are to be found only in Moscow) has a magnificent picture gallery, which after the death of the owner will become the property of the city, but for now is known to only a few and is difficult to gain access to. In this gallery hangs a painting by a Russian artist of little fame but great talent, a superbly executed painting with strange subject matter. In the catalogue the painting is labeled with the title *A Legend of the White Nights*.

The painting depicts a youthful lady in an exquisitely simple black dress, wearing a wide-brimmed hat with a white feather, sitting on a bench in a garden that has just started its spring blossoming. The lady's face is lovely, and its expression is enigmatic. In the uncertain, enchanted light of a white night, a light that has been conveyed splendidly by the artist, it seems at times that the lady's smile is joyful; but sometimes this smile seems to be a pale grimace of terror and despair.

Her arms are not visible; they are folded behind her back, and from the way the lady is holding her shoulders, one might guess that her hands are bound. Her feet are bare. They are very beautiful. On her feet one can see golden bracelets, shackled with a short golden chain. This combination of the black dress and the white, unshod feet is beautiful but strange.

This picture was painted a few years ago, after a strange white night spent by its creator, the young painter Andrey Pavlovich Kragayev, with the lady depicted in the painting, Irina Vladimirovna Omezhina, at her dacha near St. Petersburg.

It was at the end of May. The day was warm and enchantingly clear. In the morning, that is at the time when working people are preparing to have lunch, Kragayev was called to the telephone.

The familiar voice of a youthful lady said to him, "It's me, Omezhina. Andrey Pavlovich, are you free tonight? I will be expecting you at my dacha at exactly two o'clock in the morning."

"Yes, Irina Vladimirovna, thank you kindly," Kragayev was about to begin.

But Omezhina interrupted him.

"So, I'll be expecting you. At exactly two o'clock."

And she immediately hung up. Omezhina's voice was unusually cold and flat, like the voice of a person who is preparing for something significant. This, along with the brevity of the conversation, surprised Kragayev quite a bit. He was accustomed to conversations on the telephone, especially with ladies, always being lengthy. Irina Vladimirovna, of course, was no exception in this regard. For her to say a few words and then hang up was unexpected and new, and aroused his curiosity.

Kragayev resolved to be punctual. He ordered an automobile ahead of time; he did not have one of his own.

Kragayev was rather well acquainted with Omezhina, although not particularly close to her. She was the widow of a rich landowner who had died suddenly a few years before this spring. She also had her own independent fortune. The dacha she had invited Kragayev to visit was her own property.

At one time, there were strange rumors about her life with her husband. They said that he beat her often and cruelly. They were amazed that she, a wealthy woman, would endure this and not leave him.

They had no children. People said that Omezhina was unable to have children. And this seemed even stranger to everyone—why then did she live with him?

Kragayev's watch read exactly two o'clock and it was already becoming quite light when his automobile, slowing down, came near the enclosure of Omezhina's villa, where he had had occasion to visit several times the previous summer.

Kragayev felt a strange excitement.

"Will there be someone else there or am I the only one invited?" he thought. "It would be more pleasant to be alone with a sweet lady on this enchanting night. Didn't she tire of all these people during the winter!"

There was not one carriage visible by the gateway.

It was absolutely quiet in the dark garden. The windows of the house were not illuminated.

"Should I wait?" the driver asked.

"No," Kragayev said decisively, and paid him.

The wicket gate next to the dark gateway was open a little bit. Kragayev went in and closed the wicket behind him. For some reason he looked back. He saw a key in the wicket gate and, obeying a kind of vague premonition, he locked it.

He walked quietly along the sandy paths to the house. Cool air was coming from the river, the first, early birds were chirping feebly and uncertainly here and there in the bushes.

Suddenly a familiar voice, again strangely flat and cold as it was in the morning, called to him.

"I'm here, Andrey Pavlovich," Omezhina said.

Kragayev turned in the direction from which he heard the voice, and he saw the mistress of the house on a bench in front of a flowerbed.

She was sitting and smiling, looking at him. She was dressed exactly the same way as he later depicted her in the painting: the same black dress of an exquisitely simple cut, with no jewelry; the same black hat with a wide brim and a white feather; her arms were folded in the same way behind her back and seemed to be bound; her white feet were visible in the same way, calm on the damp yellow sand of the path, and on them, clasping her slender ankles, feebly glimmered the gold of two bracelets shackled with a golden chain.

Omezhina was smiling the same indeterminate smile that Kragayev later transferred to the portrait, and said to him, "How do you do, Andrey Pavlovich. For some reason I was sure that you would come at the appointed hour without fail. Forgive me, I cannot offer you my hand—my hands are tightly bound."

Noticing a movement by Kragayev, she laughed mirthlessly and said, "No, don't trouble yourself. You should not untie me. This is how it has to be. This is how he wants it. This is again his night. Sit down here, next to me."

"Who is *he*, Irina Vladimirovna?" Kragayev asked in surprise, but cautiously, as he sat down next to Omezhina.

"He, my husband," she answered calmly. "Today is the anniversary of his death. He died at this very hour. And each year on this night and at this hour I again surrender myself to his power. Each year he chooses the person into whom his soul will enter. He comes to me and tortures me for several hours. Until he gets tired. Then he goes away, and I am free until the next year. This year he has chosen you. I see that you are amazed. You are ready to think that I am insane."

"For goodness' sake, Irina Vladimirovna," Kragayev began.

Omezhina stopped him with a light movement of her head and said, "No, this is not madness. Listen, I will tell you everything, and you will understand me. It cannot be that you, such a sensitive and responsive person, such a splendid and subtle artist, would not understand me."

When a person is told that he is a subtle and sensitive person, he is of course prepared to understand anything you like. And Kragayev felt he was beginning to understand the spiritual state of the young woman. It would have behooved him to kiss her hand as a sign of sympathy, and Kragayev would have been delighted to bring Omezhina's slender little hand to his lips. But since this was inconvenient, he contented himself with pressing her elbow.

Omezhina answered him by gratefully inclining her head. Smiling strangely and uncertainly, so that it was impossible to tell whether she was very amused or wanted to cry, she said, "My husband was a weak, evil person. I don't understand now why I loved him, why I didn't leave him. He tortured me, at first timidly, later more openly and viciously with every year that passed. He invented a range of different ways to torment me, but soon he fixed on a single torture, very simple and ordinary. I don't understand why I endured all this. I didn't understand then, and I don't understand now. Perhaps I was waiting for something. Whatever the case, I was weak and vicious, like a submissive slave, in his presence."

And Omezhina started telling Kragayev calmly and in detail how her husband tortured her. She spoke as if about someone else, as if it were not she who had endured all these tortures and mockery.

Kragayev listened to her with pity and indignation, but so quiet and flat was her voice and such a vicious contagion breathed in it that suddenly Kragayev felt in himself a savage desire to throw her to the ground and beat her as her husband had beat her. The longer she spoke and the more he learned the details of that vicious torture, the more clearly he felt in himself this increasing vicious desire. At first it seemed to him that what was speaking in him was his annoyance at the shameless frankness with which she was conveying her entire agonizing tale to him—that it was her quiet, almost innocent lewdness that was evoking in him this savage desire. But soon he realized that this malicious feeling had a more profound cause.

Was it truly the case that the soul of the dead man was being embodied in him, the disfigured soul of an evil, weak torturer? He was horrified, but he soon felt how that momentarily acute horror was dying out in his soul, how the lust for torture, the evil and petty poison, was flaming up more and more imperiously in his soul.

Omezhina said, "I endured all this. I never once complained to anyone. And even within my soul I did not murmur against it. But there was a day in the spring when I was just as weak as he was. The desire for his death entered my soul. Whether the beatings he was inflicting on me then were particularly painful or whether it was spring with those transparent white nights that was affecting me—I don't know where this desire came from. It's so strange! I was never malicious or weak. For several days I languished with this base desire. At night I would sit down by the window, look into the quiet, vague light of the northern city night, clench my hands with anguish and malice, and think insistently and viciously: 'Die, you damned one, die!' And it happened that he suddenly died on this very day, at exactly two o'clock in the morning. But it wasn't I who killed him. Oh, do not think that I killed him!"

"For goodness' sake, I don't think that," Kragayev said, but his voice sounded almost angry.

"He died all by himself," Omezhina continued. "Or perhaps I drove him to the grave by the strength of my evil desire? Perhaps sometimes the will of a person can be that powerful? I don't know. But I did not feel any remorse. My conscience was completely calm. And so it continued until the following spring. In the spring, the brighter the nights became, the worse I felt. Anguish tormented me more and more powerfully. Finally, on the night of his death he came to me and tortured me for a long time."

"Ah, he came!" Kragayev said with a sudden malicious glee.

"Of course, you understand," Omezhina said, "that this was not a corpse coming from the cemetery. He was, after all, too well-bred and urbane a person for such pranks. He found another way to arrange it. He took possession of the will and soul of a person who, like you now, came to see me on that night, who tortured me cruelly and for a long time. When he went away and left me exhausted by torture, I cried like a little girl who's been thrashed. But my soul was calm, and again I stopped thinking about him until the following spring. Now every year, when the white nights set in, anguish begins to torment me, and on the night of his death my torturer comes to me."

"Every year?" Kragayev asked in a voice choked with malice or excitement.

"Every year," Omezhina said, "there is someone who comes to me at this hour, and each time it is as if the soul of my husband is implanted into my chance tormentor. Then, after a torturous night, my anguish passes, and I return to the world of the living. This has happened every year. This year he wanted it to be you. He wanted me to wait for you here in this garden, in these clothes, with bound hands, barefoot. And so I am submissive to his will. I sit here and wait."

She looked at Kragayev, and on her face was that complicated expression that he later transferred into his painting with such artistry.

Kragayev stood up rather too hurriedly. His face had become quite pale. Feeling a terrible malice, he grabbed Omezhina by the shoulder and shouted in a savage, hoarse voice, not even recognizing the sound himself: "This has happened every year, and this night it will be no different for you. Go!"

Omezhina got up and began crying. Kragayev, squeezing her shoulder, dragged her to the house. She walked submissively after him, trembling from the cold and the dampness of the grains of sand under her bare feet, hurrying and stumbling, feeling painfully at every step the jerking of the golden chain and the bumping of the golden bracelets. And so they went into the house.

1912

LITTLE FAIRY TALES

(Selection, 1898–1906)[1]

THE HAMMER AND THE CHAIN

A sturdy hammer, full of excellent intentions, made of the best iron, was chatting with an iron bar that was lying on the anvil. They were talking about earthly imperfections and about the evil insults that some heap upon others.

"Fetters are a shameful remnant of barbarism," the hammer said, and tried to persuade the iron never to become a chain.

Listening to him on the burning anvil, under the heat of the forge, the iron became soft and melted. But then the burly blacksmith swung the hammer high and brought it down heavily onto the iron. Red sparks rained down, and the poor iron bar began to moan.

"What is this, you've decided to beat me yourself?" it asked.

"Yes, I am beating you, and you will endure it. That is how things are set up, and I have been placed higher than you in the world, in order to strike at you."

The hammer kept coming down heavily on the iron bar, saying weightily, "Away with cruelty! The cruel are contemptible!"

When the iron had been forged into the links of a long, durable chain, the hammer turned away with contempt.

"All turncoats are like that," he said. "Soft as wax at the beginning, but in the end, they are not ashamed to serve as shackles."

And the chain quietly jingled its durable rings and whispered: "That is how it must be, that is how everything is set up. A few more blows to my links—and I will be delighted to wind around the body of an accursed convict."

BULLIES

Tom Thumb met a boy the size of a fingernail and pummeled him. Tom Fingernail stood there, squeaking pitifully.

A boy the size of two thumbs saw this and beat up Tom Thumb. "Don't fight!" he said. Tom Thumb started squealing.

A boy the size of an elbow came along and asked:

"Tom Thumb, what are you crying about?"

"Boo-hoo! Tom Two-Thumbs roughed me up," Tom Thumb said.

Tom Elbow chased down Tom Two-Thumbs and beat him painfully. "Don't," he said, "bully the little ones!"

Tom Two-Thumbs started crying and ran to complain to a kindergarten boy. The kindergarten boy said: "I'll give him a thrashing!" and thrashed Tom Elbow. And a second-grader pummeled the kindergartner for this.

The kindergartner's mama stood up for him and roughed up the second-grader.

The second-grader started shouting. His papa came running and beat up the kindergartner's mama. A policeman came and took the second-grader's papa to the police station.

That's where the fairy tale ended.

CHOO

A certain little boy was always mimicking everybody. If somebody laughed, he would shout, "Hee-hee." If somebody sneezed, he would say "Choo." One day the boy walked on some damp grass. He came home and sneezed. His mama asked, "Why are you sneezing?"

And the boy said, "So, Mama, choo! So."

Mama said, "You have a cold. You walked on some damp grass, didn't you?"

The boy said, "No, Mama, choo! I didn't."

Mama felt the boy's feet and said, "Then why are your boots damp?"

The boy started crying and said, "Mama, I didn't walk—choo!—on the damp grass, it was—choo!—my boots that did it!"

THE VOYAGER STONE

There was a road in the city paved with stones. A wheel knocked a little stone out of it. It thought, "Why should I lie there with the others, it's cramped—I'll be on my own."

A little boy ran up and grabbed the stone.

The stone thought, "I wished for it, and I got to move—all you have to do is wish."

The boy threw the stone at a house. The stone thought to itself, "I wished to fly, and I flew—it's very simple, I get my way!"

The stone hit a window—the glass broke and shouted, "Oh, you damned ruffian!"

And the stone thought, "You should have gotten out of the way in time! I don't like to be hindered—everything has to be how I want it, that's who I am!"

The stone fell on the carpet and thought, "I had a little flight, and now I'll lie down and rest a while."

They took the stone and threw it out onto the pavement.

It shouted to the other stones, "Hey, there, brothers—I've been to the palace, but I didn't like being there with the lords and ladies, I wished to be with the common people."

THE BAD BOY AND THE QUIET BOY

Once upon a time there was a Bad Boy.

He had two aunts: a clever aunt and a good, kind aunt.

When the Bad Boy didn't understand something, he would run to the clever aunt and she would explain it; when the Bad Boy did something naughty, he would run to the good, kind aunt and she would protect him.

One day the Bad Boy was sitting with his clever aunt. A Quiet Boy walked by.

The clever aunt said to the Bad Boy, "Run quickly and bite the Quiet Boy on the leg."

The Bad Boy rejoiced. He set off running. But he was a coward. He ran up to the Quiet Boy, but he didn't dare to bite him.

So the Bad Boy bent over, bit himself on the leg, and ran off to his good, kind aunt, shouting and crying, "Good, kind aunt, a nasty brat, the Quiet Boy, bit me."

The good, kind aunt believed him and said, "Bring that worthless Quiet Boy to me."

They brought him. The good, kind aunt said, "Oh, oh, oh! You worthless brat, Quiet Boy, how did you dare to bite? Good, kind boys never bite."

The Quiet Boy burst into tears and said, "I won't ever bite."

And they put him in a corner, and they patted the Bad Boy on the head.

This is how it often happens.

DEATH TAKEN CAPTIVE

In the olden times there lived a valiant and invincible knight.

One day he happened to take death itself into captivity.

He brought her to his strong castle and put her in a dungeon.

Death didn't mind, she just went on sitting there—but people stopped dying.

The knight rejoiced and thought: "Things are good now, but it's troublesome, she has to be guarded. It would be better to destroy her outright."

But the knight was a just knight—he could not put death to death without a trial.

So he came to the dungeon, stood by the little window, and said, "Death, I want to chop off your head—you have done much evil in the world."

But death just sat there silent.

So the knight said, "I'm pronouncing sentence on you—defend yourself if you can. What do you have to say in your defense?"

Death answered, "I have nothing to say to you for now, but let life speak on my behalf."

And the knight saw life standing next to him—a buxom, ruddy, but hideous wench.

And she started saying such nasty, unholy words to him that the valiant and invincible knight began to tremble, and he hastened to open the dungeon.

Death set off—and people once again were dying. The knight too died at his appointed time—and he never told anyone on earth what he had heard from life, the hideous, unholy wench.

THE WAND

There is a kind of marvelous wand in the world—no matter what you touch with it, it all instantly becomes a dream and disappears.

So if you don't like your life, take the wand, press the end of it to your head—and you will suddenly see that it was all a dream, and you will start living all over again in a completely new way.

And you will totally forget everything that happened in that dream.

That's the kind of wonderful wand there is in the world.

THE LAMP AND THE MATCH

A lamp was standing on the table.

They took the glass shade off it; the lamp saw the match and said, "Keep away, little kid, I'm dangerous, I'm about to be ignited. I get lighted every evening. After all, without me it's impossible to work in the evenings."

"Every evening!" the match said. "To get lighted every evening— that's horrible!"

"But why?" the lamp asked.

"You know you can only fall in love once!" the match said, flared up—and died.

THE DROP OF WATER AND
THE SPECK OF DUST

A raindrop was falling, a speck of dust was lying on the earth.

The drop wanted to be united with a solid entity—it was tired of floating freely.

It united with the speck of dust—and it settled on the earth as a lump of mud.

EQUALITY

A big fish chased down a little one and wanted to swallow it.

The little fish began to squeak: "This is unjust. I want to live too. All fish are equal before the law."

The big fish answered, "Why, I am not disputing the fact that we are equal. If you don't want me to eat you, then please, go ahead and swallow me, be my guest—swallow me, it's okay, have no fear, I'm not disputing it."

The little fish tried, this way and that, but it couldn't swallow the big fish.

It sighed and said, "You win—go ahead and swallow me!"

THE THREE GOBS OF SPIT

A man was walking along, and he spit three times.

He left, and the gobs of spit remained.

And one gob of spit said, "We are here, but the person is gone."

And the second one said, "He has left."

And the third one said, "He only came here in order to place us here. We are the goal of human life. He has left, but we remain."

THE FUTURE ONES

No one knows what's going to happen.

But there is a place where the future shines through the azure fabric of desire. It is a place where those who have not yet been born repose. It is delightful, peaceful, and fresh there. There is no sadness, and instead of air, an atmosphere of pure joy is spread out, in which the unborn children breathe easily.

And no one leaves this land before they want to.

There were four souls there who at the very same moment conceived the desire to be born on our earth.

And in the azure fog of desires, our four elements appeared to them.

And one of the future ones said:

"I love earth, so soft, warm, and solid."

And the second one said:

"I love water, eternally falling, cool, transparent."

And the third one:

"I love fire, cheerful, bright, purifying."

And the fourth:

"I love air, striving outward and upward, the light air of life."

And so it came to pass.

The first one became a miner—and at work the mineshaft caved in and buried him.

And the second one shed tears like water, and finally drowned himself.

And the third one burned up in a blazing house.

And the fourth one was hanged.

The innocent, pure elements. . . . The folly of those who desire . . .

Oh, delightful place of nonexistence, why does the Will lead people away from you!

THE DEATH-LOVING CORPSIE

Once upon a time there was a death-loving corpsie. He went walking through the fertile lands, grinning and rejoicing most happily. The other corpses started trying to dampen his enthusiasm, to reprove him, saying, "You should lie there as quiet as a mouse and wait for the Last Judgment—you should lie there, repenting your sins."

But he said, "Why should I lie there—I'm not afraid of anything."

They said to him, "You sinned so much on the earth, they'll sort it all out and send you to Tartarus, to the pits of hell, to fiery Gehenna, to the terrible torments, for ever and ever and ever— they'll boil you there with boiling pitch, the unquenchable fire will blaze up, and the demons, exceeding fearsome demons, will rejoice at our torments."

But the death-loving corpsie just kept on laughing: "Never fear," he said, "You can't scare me with that—I'm a Rooshian."

THE SUN-RAY IN THE DUNGEON

The sun-rays came to the Sun to get their traveling orders. One sun-ray said, "I'll go to the palace today."

The second said, "I'll go strolling along Nevsky Avenue."

The third said, "And I'll take a walk through the fields."

The fourth said, "And I'll go bathing in the stream."

They grabbed up all the good places and were about to run off; but the Sun shouted: "Wait, brothers, there's another little place— a dark dungeon where a poor prisoner is sitting."

All the sun-rays started whining: "It's damp in the dark dungeon, it's dirty in the dark dungeon, it smells bad in the dark dungeon—we don't want to go into the dark dungeon."

The Sun caught one little sun-ray by its hair and said, "You were very naughty yesterday, you peeped into places you weren't assigned to—go spend at least five little minutes in the dark dungeon."

The poor little sun-ray burst into tears, but there was nothing to be done, it's impossible not to carry out the orders of the Sun. It spent five little minutes with the poor prisoner in the dark dungeon—the sun-ray was sour, spiteful, and frowning. But even that was a great holiday for the poor prisoner.

DEATHLINGS

Death gave birth to some children, put them in her skirts, carried them around and shook them and asked, "Who needs deathlings? Five kopecks a pair."

Who needs deathlings! Nobody would take them even for free. People said, "You gave birth to them, so you feed your own little brats."

Death said to the people, "What am I going to feed them? They're not just any deathlings, they're noble, you can't feed them just anything."

Coming toward Death was the spawn of hell, Sir General; his mug was Lenten, but his mustache was twisted upward like the German KakaKaiser's.

Death says to him: "Hi there, spawn of hell, Sir General! Don't you need some deathlings? Since I respect you so much, I'll give them to you cheap."

The spawn of hell, Sir General, was so overjoyed that his spleen squeaked. He said with great expectation:

"I have plenty of thrusters and grinders, runners and stompers, but a deficit has arisen: it smells like not enough heroic spirit's been supplied."

Death said to him, "Oh, you spawn of hell, Sir General, don't you grieve about that. Take my deathlings for that—they have enough spirit-smell for ten Roossias. When one of my deathlings breathes—it stinks for a thousand miles all around."

The spawn of hell, Sir General, all his joints rejoiced. He sniffs the deathlings with rapture, on his hips he puts his hands, with eyes lifted, there he stands, sends the deathlings to Far East lands, and says a parting word to them:

"Deathlings, hurry, don't be late—for spirit-smell the Far East waits, drag our brave troops to fatal war—be Rooshian heroes for your mother, the whore."[2]

1898–1906

NOTES

INTRODUCTION

1. Andrei Belyi, "Istlevaiushchie lichiny," in *O Fedore Sologube: Kritika. Stat'i i zametki*, ed. [compiled by] Anastasiia Chebotarevskaia (St. Petersburg: Nav'i Chary, 2002; reprint from St. Petersburg, 1911), 149 (first published in *Kriticheskoe obozrenie*, 1907).

2. Two translations of *The Petty Demon* are currently available in English, by S. D. Cioran (Ann Arbor: Ardis, 1983, reprinted 2009; includes an excellent selection of articles edited by Murl Barker) and by Ronald Wilks (*The Little Demon*, London: Penguin, 1994). There is also a version by Andrew Field (New York: Random House, 1962).

3. See Omry Ronen, "Toponyms of Fedor Sologub's *Tvorimaia Legenda*," in *The Joy of Recognition: Selected Essays by Omry Ronen*, ed. Barry P. Scherr and Michael Wachtel (Ann Arbor: Michigan Slavic Publications, 2015; originally published in *Die Welt der Slaven* [1968], Jahrgang XIII, Heft 3, 307–16); Irene Masing-Delic, *Abolishing Death: A Salvation Myth of Russian Twentieth-Century Literature* (Palo Alto, CA: Stanford University Press, 1992); and Lukasz Wodzyński, "The Quest for 'Pure Fame': Fedor Sologub's *A Legend in the Making* and the Modernist Ambivalence About Literary Celebrity," *Slavic and East European Journal* 61, no. 4 (2017): 778–801. The novel was translated by John Cournos (London: Martin Secker, 1916) and by S. D. Cioran (Ann Arbor, MI: Ardis, 1979).

4. Stanley J. Rabinowitz, *Sologub's Literary Children: Keys to a Symbolist's Prose* (Columbus, OH: Slavica, 1980), 6. This book remains one of the key studies of

Sologub in English. See also Vassar Williams Smith, "Fyodor Sologub (1863–1927): A Critical Biography" (PhD diss., Stanford University, 1993). Jason Merrill has recently published a series of articles on Sologub's work, particularly his drama (see the Selected Works). My understanding of Sologub's life and career has been informed by an excellent online biography (in Russian), accessed at http://sologub.narod.ru/bio1.htm. I have been unable to find a published version of this biography or to determine the name of its author. Another excellent biography in Russian is Mariia Savel'eva, *Fedor Sologub* (Moscow: Molodaia gvardiia, 2014), in the "Lives of Remarkable People" series. I have also drawn on the notes to Fedor Sologub, *Sobranie sochinenii*, 6 vols., ed. T. F. Prokopov (Moscow: NPK Intelvak, 2001).

5. M. M. Pavlova, "Tvorcheskaia istoriia romana 'Melkii bes,'" in Fedor Sologub, *Melkii bes*, ed. M. M. Pavlova (St. Petersburg: Nauka, 2004), 661.

6. Given the vastness of Sologub's corpus of short prose, I have not used any rigid principle of selection but have tried to cover the range of his favored genres and themes. I have not included the canonical stories "Light and Shadows" ("Svet i Teni," 1894), "The Sting of Death" ("Zhalo smerti," 1903), or "The Poisoned Garden" ("Otravlennyi sad," 1908), because they have been recently translated into English and included in anthologies. The most recent English-language edition of stories by Sologub is *The Kiss of the Unborn and Other Stories*, translated and with an introduction by Murl G. Barker (Knoxville: University of Tennessee Press, 1977). The pioneering translations of Sologub's stories were *The Sweet-Scented Name, and Other Fairy Tales, Fables, and Stories*, ed. Stephen Graham (Westport, CT: Hyperion, 1977; reprint of 1915 edition by Constable, London), and *The Old House and Other Stories*, ed. John Cournos (New York: Knopf, 1916). Individual stories have appeared in anthologies in the intervening years. The most notable among these is *The Dedalus Book of Russian Decadence: Perversity, Despair, and Collapse*, ed. Kirsten Lodge (Sawtry, UK: Dedalus, 2007), which includes numerous poems by Sologub and three stories, "The Sting of Death," "The Poisoned Garden," and "Light and Shadows." On the early translations of Sologub by Cournos and Graham, see A. B. Strel'nikova and A. V. Sysoeva, "Sbornik rasskazov Fedora Sologuba 'The Old House and Other Tales' v perevode Dzhona Kurnosa: Voprosy retseptsii i konkurentsii," *Russkaia literatura* 2 (2020): 122–31. Cournos was of Russian origin. He met Sologub and attempted to bring him out of Russia after the Bolshevik Revolution of 1917.

7. O. N. Chernosvitova, "Materialy k biografii Fedora Sologuba," ed. M. M. Pavlova, in *Neizdannyi Fedor Sologub*, ed. M. M. Pavlova and A. V. Lavrov (Moscow: Novoe literaturnoe obozrenie, 1997), 236.

8. See also the poems included in *The Dedalus Book of Russian Decadence*, as well as passages Sologub excluded from the published version of *The Petty Demon*, which are provided in an appendix to the Ardis edition. Savel'eva explains that Sologub removed prolonged scenes of corporal punishment "that offended the

taste of the first readers of the manuscript" (Savel'eva, *Fedor Sologub*, 85). Margarita Pavlova has discussed Sologub's playing along with rumors about his "reputation as a sadist, erotomaniac, satanist, and necrophiliac." M. Pavlova, *Pisatel'-inspektor: Fedor Sologub i F. K. Teternikov* (Moscow: Novoe literaturnoe obozrenie, 2007), 339. These rumors appear to be based more on Sologub's literary works than on any reliable evidence from his life. See also Sologub's unfinished narrative poem "Solitude," subtitled "The History of a Boy Onanist," published by Margarita Pavlova in *Novoe literaturnoe obozrenie*, no. 3 (55) (2002): 14–31, and in *Pisatel'-inspektor*, 389–410. The sensual nature of Sologub's writings inspired a series of erotically charged letters and postcards to him from female readers, beginning with the publication of *The Petty Demon*. T. V. Misnikevich, "Fedor Sologub, ego poklonnitsy i korrespondentki," in *Erotizm bez beregov: Sbornik statei i materialov*, ed. M. M. Pavlova (Moscow: Novoe literaturnoe obozrenie, 2004), 349–90.

9. Chernosvitova, "Materialy," 230.

10. *Bad Dreams* (*Tiazhelye sny*) was translated by Vassar W. Smith (Ann Arbor, MI: Ardis, 1978).

11. Anastasiia Chebotarevskaia, "Fedor Sologub. Biograficheskaia spravka," in *Russkaia literatura XX veka (1890–1910)*, ed. S. A. Vengerov (Moscow: Mir, 1915). Reprinted in Fedor Sologub, *Melkii bes. Stikhotvoreniia. Rasskazy. Skazochki*, ed. E. V. Peremyshlev (Moscow: Olimp; OOO ACT, 1999), 488. In his lifetime, Sologub expressed disdain for the practice of biography or autobiography and insisted that a writer's works contained all that the public needed to know. Chebotarevskaya's sketch is thus the only "authorized" biography of Sologub. On Sologub's resistance to biography, see M. M. Pavlova and A. V. Lavrov, eds., *Neizdannyi Fedor Sologub* (Moscow: Novoe literaturnoe obozrenie, 1997), 244n.1 and 303–4n.2.

12. "Ne postydno li byt' dekadentom" (1896), in Pavlova, *Pisatel'-inspektor*, 494–501, this passage on 499–500. See also the discussion by Pavlova in the same book, 154–56. Pavlova argues that the ideas in Sologub's essay were influenced by Oscar Wilde and the French Symbolist Jean Moréas and were in polemical dialogue with Max Nordau, whose 1892–1893 book *Degeneration* links Decadent aesthetics with mental illness. Sologub was interested in the Futurist movement and was associated for a time with the Ego-Futurist Igor Severyanin.

13. Wodziński, "The Quest for 'Pure Fame,'"789. David Bethea has drawn a convincing parallel between the plotline of Lyudmila in *The Petty Demon* and the narrative of Humbert Humbert in Vladimir Nabokov's 1955 novel *Lolita*, arguing for Sologub's novel as an unacknowledged subtext for Nabokov's. David Bethea, "Sologub, Nabokov, and the Limits of Decadent Aesthetics," in his *The Superstitious Muse: Thinking Russian Literature Mythopoetically* (Boston: Academic Studies Press, 2009).

14. Pavlova and Lavrov, eds., *Neizdannyi Fedor Sologub*, 303.

15. A. V. Lavrov, "Fedor Sologub i Anastasiia Chebotarevskaia," in *Neizdannyi Fedor Sologub*, ed. M. M. Pavlova and A. V. Lavrov (Moscow: Novoe literaturnoe obozrenie, 1997), 290–302, this passage on 290. Lavrov's essay, in its balance and objectivity, is the best source on Chebotarevskaya that I have encountered. Lavrov has also published an excellent account of the life of Anastasia's sister Aleksandra, as an introduction to letters to her from Ivanov. "Pis'ma Viacheslava Ivanova k Aleksandre Chebotarevskoi," in *Ezhegodnik rukopisnogo otdela Pushkinskogo Doma na 1997 goda*, ed. T. G. Ivanova (St. Petersburg: Pushkinskii Dom, 2002), 238–95.

16. See Colleen McQuillen, *The Modernist Masquerade: Stylizing Life, Literature, and Costumes in Russia* (Madison: University of Wisconsin Press, 2013), 55–56, 219n.46.

17. Fedor Sologub, introduction to Anastasiia Sologub-Chebotarevskaia, *Zhenshchina nakanune revoliutsii 1789 g.*, ed. Fedor Sologub (Petrograd: Byloe, 1922), 15, 17.

18. Online biography, chapter 17. The title of the union, *Soiuz deiatelei iskusstv*, is very hard to translate, as the word *deiatel'* can mean "doer," "worker," "agent," or just "figure." I have chosen "practitioner" rather than the more standard "worker," because the latter has a Soviet coloration.

19. This word is also the title of an 1817 ode by Alexander Pushkin that was one of the reasons for his exile to the south of Russia in 1820–1824.

20. Cited in Konstantin L'vov, "Stezhki blestiashchikh paradoksov. Zhizn' i poeziia Fedora Sologuba," *Radio Svoboda*, October 19, 2020, https://www.svoboda.org/a/30888968.html.

21. A vivid account of the bureaucratic tortures of the Sologubs in their efforts to leave Russia is given by the poet Vladislav Khodasevich, *Necropolis*, trans. Sarah Vitali (New York: Columbia University Press, 2019), 147–48. Khodasevich also provides a touching description of how Sologub "used a dream to overcome reality" during the deprivations of War Communism: "Over a span of twelve days in the spring of 1921, unyielding, unvanquished, in cold and in hunger, he wrote a merry, boisterous cycle of poems that should have been unthinkable under the circumstances: twenty-seven pieces in the style of the French bergerette [pastoral poem]" (149). Sologub himself noted that these poems were all written "in order to give [Anastasia] amusement." Fedor Sologub, "Pominal'nye zapisi ob An. N. Chebotarevskoi," in *Neizdannyi Fedor Sologub*, ed. M. M. Pavlova and A. V. Lavrov (Moscow: Novoe literaturnoe obozrenie, 1997), 381.

22. Chernosvitova, "Materialy," 223. Her sister Aleksandra also suffered from depression and drowned herself in the Moscow River in 1925. See Lavrov, "Pis'ma Viacheslava Ivanova," 249–50.

23. Sologub, introduction to *Zhenshchina*, 21–22.

24. Cited in L'vov, "Stezhki blestiashchikh paradoksov."

25. Sologub was able to publish a few books in 1921, at the beginning of the comparatively liberal period of the New Economic Policy. See Savel'eva, *Fedor Sologub*,

211–12. On the All-Russian Union of Writers, which existed from 1920 to 1932, see Savel'eva, *Fedor Sologub*, 214–24.

26. Cited in L'vov, "Stezhki blestiashchikh paradoksov."

27. Rabinowitz, *Sologub's Literary Children*, 12.

28. Rabinowitz, *Sologub's Literary Children*, 15.

29. Fedor Sologub, *Stikhotvoreniia*, ed. M. I. Dikman (Leningrad: Sovetskii pisatel', 1975; Biblioteka poeta, Bol'shaia seriia), 217.

30. Tzvetan Todorov, *The Fantastic: A Structural Approach to a Literary Genre*, trans. Richard Howard (Cleveland: Case Western Reserve University, 1973), 25.

31. D. S. Mirsky, *A History of Russian Literature, Comprising A History of Russian Literature and Contemporary Russian Literature*, ed. and abridged by Francis J. Whitfield (New York: Knopf, 1949), 446. See Rabinowitz's stylistic analysis of this story, *Sologub's Literary Children*, 30–31.

32. Mirsky, *History of Russian Literature*, 446; Anastasiia Chebotarevskaia, "'Tvorimoe' tvorchestvo," in *O Fedore Sologube*, ed. [compiled by] Anastasiia Chebotarevskaia (St. Petersburg: Nav'i Chary, 2002), 146.

33. Olga Matich, *Erotic Utopia: The Decadent Imagination in Russia's Fin de Siècle* (Madison: University of Wisconsin Press, 2005), 6. Matich's book is an essential source on the Symbolist milieu in general, on Russian Decadence, and on "life creation." It is not primarily focused on Sologub.

34. Jason Merrill, "Authorial Intent vs. Critical Reaction: Fedor Sologub's *Hostages of Life* and the Crisis of Russian Symbolism," *Slavic and East European Journal* 61, no. 4 (2017): 754–77, this passage on 757n.9. This article illuminates Sologub's position vis-à-vis the other Symbolists in the wake of the 1910 "crisis of Symbolism."

35. Chebotarevskaia, "'Tvorimoe' tvorchestvo," 138.

36. "The White Dog" is in dialogue with several poems by Sologub that impersonate the voice of a dog, most notably "The Lord's moon is high" ("Vysoka luna gospodnia," 1905), "We are captive beasts" ("My—plenennye zveri," 1905), *The Dog of the Gray-Haired King* (*Sobaka sedogo korolia*, 1906), and the cycle *When I Was a Dog* (*Kogda ia byl sobakoi*, 1913–1914). Sologub's evocation of the dog's perception of the world through smells is yet another precursor of Bulgakov's *Heart of a Dog*.

37. Bethea, "Sologub, Nabokov, and the Limits of Decadent Aesthetics," 349, 360.

38. "Polotno i telo," in Sologub, *Sobranie sochinenii*, vol. 2, 543. On the significance of nudity for Sologub and for other Symbolist artists, see McQuillen, *Modernist Masquerade*, 192–203.

39. "Mechta Don Kikhota (Aisedora Dunkan)," in Sologub, *Sobranie sochinenii*, vol. 2, 511. Chebotarevskaya also wrote about Duncan's significance. Elena Obatnina finds it telling that Sologub's relationship with Chebotarevskaya rapidly developed soon after he published his essay on Duncan. Elena Obatnina, "Realisticheskii podtekst simvolistskoi p'esy Fedora Sologuba 'Nochnye pliaski,'"

in *Fedor Sologub: Biografiia, tvorchestvo, interpretatsii*, ed. M. M. Pavlova (St. Petersburg: Institut russkoi literatury [Pushkinskii Dom] Rossiiskoi Akademii Nauk, 2010), 324. This essay provides valuable background on Chebotarevskaya's feminist beliefs.

40. O. V. Tsekhnovitser, "Simvolizm i tsarskaia tsenzura," *Uchenye zapiski Leningradskogo gosudarstvennogo universiteta. Seriia filologicheskikh nauk*, issue 11, no. 76, ed. I. G. Iampol'skii (Leningrad: Leningradskii gosudarstvennyi universitet, 1941): 275–319; this passage on 313. I would like to thank Jason Merrill for providing me with a copy of this article.

41. Adrian Wanner, *Russian Minimalism: From the Prose Poem to the Anti-Story* (Evanston, IL: Northwestern University Press, 2003), 68–84. See also N. V. Barkovskaia, "'Skazochki' F. Sologuba i 'Sluchai' D. Kharmsa," http://www.d-harms.ru/library/skazochki-sologuba-i-sluchai-harmsa.html; and Pavlova, *Pisatel'-inspektor*, 201–14.

42. My analysis here has been inspired by that of Ivanov-Razumnik, who writes that Sologub "told us what he heard" from life in his novel *The Petty Demon*. Ivanov-Razumnik (pen name of Razumnik Vasilievich Ivanov, 1878–1946), "Fedor Sologub," in *O Fedore Sologube*, ed. [compiled by] Anastasiia Chebotarevskaia (St. Petersburg: Nav'i Chary, 2002), 21.

TO THE STARS

1. See Note on Transliteration and Translation Issues for information on the dacha. In the 1890s, when this story takes place, the word *dacha* could connote a range of houses from humble to sumptuous, normally used as summer retreats for city dwellers, and often grouped into settlements on the outskirts of major cities. Seryozha's family appears to be well-to-do but not aristocratic, and their dacha is a comfortable house with an extensive garden.

2. In his history of the dacha, Stephen Lovell explains: "Locations near the coast offered the . . . invigorating exercise of sea bathing, an activity that was claimed to yield benefits both physical and moral. Not only did it make the human organism generally more robust, conscientious parents could also safeguard their children against the 'English sickness' of masturbation by immersing them, morning and night, in the cold salt water." Stephen Lovell, *Summerfolk: A History of the Dacha, 1710–2000* (Ithaca, NY: Cornell University Press, 2003), 102. Seryozha's yellowish face (14), small stature, poor health, and the "pleasure he had never experienced before" (22) imply that his obsession with the stars is a metaphor for masturbation. This type of obsessive secretive activity also appears in Sologub's 1894 story "Light and Shadows," in which both a child and his mother succumb to a compulsive urge to make shadows on the wall with their hands.

3. The "bathing house" that Seryozha refers to is a semipermanent, tentlike structure based on the shore but extending into the water, in which people could splash in the water without being seen by the public. Men and women would be separated into different pavilions for modesty's sake, but it was possible to swim out from under the walls of the structure into open water, which is what Seryozha mischievously does later in the story.

4. The student's reference to the "end of the century" evokes the general sense of fin-de-siècle ennui and anxiety but also the aesthetics of Decadence and Symbolism, of which Sologub was a prime exponent in Russia. The student has probably been reading Max Nordau's *Degeneration* (1892–1893), which was a popular analysis that attributed a multitude of ills to the "end of the century." Sologub had a polemical attitude toward Nordau's work.

5. Seryozha is making a servile bow with his leg "scraped" backward.

6. The "luminous, heavy curtain with which the sun covers the stars" is a reference to poems by Fyodor Tyutchev (1803–1873), most notably "Day and Night" (1839), in which the day is described as a covering of golden fabric that has been thrown over "the mysterious world of the spirits." It is not likely that Seryozha is familiar with Tyutchev, but he was an important precursor for Symbolist poets such as Sologub. In his poetry and prose, Sologub elaborates the contrast between day and night into his mythology of the sun as the evil Dragon that hides the truth, which is revealed at night.

7. A droshky is a light, open, four-wheeled carriage on springs.

BEAUTY

1. Elena's fetishization of beauty is reminiscent of the philosophy of Jean des Esseintes, the hero of Joris-Karl Huysmans's 1884 novel *À Rebours* (*Against the Grain*), a key text for both French and Russian Symbolists.

2. "White acacia" is the common Russian term for *Robinia pseudoacacia*, or black locust. Its flowers are typically cream-white, and I have translated the name of the plant here as "white acacia" to preserve the visual sense of whiteness that is so important for Elena's surroundings.

IN CAPTIVITY

1. The expression "petty demon" may allude to Sologub's masterpiece, the novel *The Petty Demon*, which began publication in 1905, the same year "In Captivity" was published.

2. The *gimnazia* was the secondary school that prepared students for university study. Paka is surprised to see the boy's *gimnazia* badge because he has decided

that the boys are peasants, but peasant families could not afford to send their children to the *gimnazia*.

3. Russian children's ideas about Native Americans were influenced by the novels of James Fenimore Cooper (1789–1851), whose works began to be translated into Russian in the 1840s and maintained their popularity into the Soviet period.

4. "Arguses" refers to *argus panoptes*, a many-eyed giant in Greek mythology who often serves as a watcher or guardian.

5. "Winged words" is a Homeric expression for the apt words of epic poetry. In English the phrase retains its connotation of words that are particularly apposite. In Russian it refers more particularly to common quotations from history, the Bible, classic authors, etc. Later in the story the boys embody the metaphor of words in flight by inscribing them on their arrows. A further hint to the nature of the words the boys learn is given by Antoshka's reference to the peasants saying "something about their mother." The rich Russian tradition of obscene language is called *mat*, a word derived from the word for "mother," since obscenity is often directed at the mother as a normally sacrosanct target.

6. Since the boys are coming to take away the evil fairy that looks like Paka's mother and restore him to his real mother, Paka is afraid that if they have already eaten dinner wherever his real mother is, then she will not serve dinner when they are reunited, and he will miss dessert.

7. At the turn of the century, French erotic novels were notoriously published in yellow covers.

THE TWO GOTIKS

1. The All-Seeing Eye of God, or Eye of Providence, depicting an eye within a triangle, is a Christian symbol. It was commonly included in decorations on the walls of Russian Orthodox churches and on icons. Throughout this story, I have had to change the literal sense of the text in order to approximate the many puns. In this case, the pun hinges on the sound equivalence in Russian between *glaz* ("eye") and *glas* (the Biblical word for "voice" in Isaiah 40:3). I have replaced "The voice of one crying in the wilderness" with "The voice of one eye crying in the wilderness." Like Lyutik, Sologub was an avid punster. Punning is the humorous flipside of the poet's gift of soundplay or paronomasia.

2. The Guelphs and Ghibellines were two rival factions in medieval German and Italian politics, favoring the pope and the holy Roman emperor, respectively. Marshal-Admiral the Marquis Heihachiro Togo (1848–1934) was commander in chief of the imperial Japanese Navy during the Russo-Japanese War of 1904–1905. In May 1905 his forces destroyed the imperial Russian Navy's Baltic Fleet at the Battle of Tsushima. Lyutik's pun is based on the similar sound of *Ghibelline* and the Russian word *gibel'*, meaning "ruination," "death," or "doom."

The name *Togo* is similar to a common Russian pronoun, so it is also ripe for punning.

3. Maresuke Nogi (1849–1912), general in command of the Japanese Third Army, captured the Russian-held Port Arthur in Manchuria in early 1905. The word *nogi* means "feet" in Russian, so the original pun involves the Japanese under Nogi walking into Port Arthur.

4. The references to strikes, walkouts, and obstructions are connected to the widespread civil disturbances in Russia in 1905 in the wake of the country's defeat in the Russo-Japanese War.

IN THE CROWD

1. The details of the anniversary celebration in the fictional Russian town of Mstislavl are closely based on the disaster of Khodynka Field on May 30 (O.S. May 18), 1896. As part of the festivities accompanying the coronation of Nicholas II, a crowd gathered on a field outside Moscow, expecting the distribution of presents. Thanks to monumentally poor planning by the authorities, there was a human stampede in which 1,389 people died. Chukhloma and Medyn are obscure provincial towns; mentioning them in the same breath as Paris and London adds to the satirical tone of the story's opening pages.

2. "It's a family affair, we'll settle it ourselves" is the title of an 1849 play by Aleksandr Ostrovsky (1823–1886), which is based on Moscow merchant life.

3. The Safat River is a mythical location in Russian knightly tales, possibly derived from the biblical valley of Jehoshaphat, the "valley of judgment."

4. The woman's appearance as "noseless" is probably due to a symptom of tertiary syphilis in which the bridge of the nose collapses, known as "saddle nose."

DEATH BY ADVERTISEMENT

1. In the original, the name of the paper company is spelled "Margarette Mill." Around the turn of the century, the Vienna firm Theyer & Hardtmuth manufactured a line of stationery called Margaret Mill.

2. Leiner's restaurant was opened in 1877 (some sources say 1885) on Nevsky Avenue, in an early nineteenth-century building known as Kotomin House. By the 1890s it was frequented by an artistic crowd, including actors from the Alexandrinsky Theater.

3. In stark contrast to the normal etiquette, Rezanov and the woman use the intimate *ty* form of the second-person pronoun with each other from the start. There is no way to reproduce this in English, so I have inserted the words about their "intimate tone." Just as one speaks to God with the intimate form, Rezanov is speaking to his "death" in this way.

4. The passages displayed in italics are versified in the original. This passage and the next one in italics are from Sologub's 1906 poem "Tikhaia kolybel'naia" (Quiet lullaby), first published in 1907 under the title "Sleep and death (lullaby song)."

5. This line appears as "And light my death will be / And sweeter than a poison" in Sologub's 1905 poem "Ia k nei prishel izdaleka" (I came to her from far away). Sologub used the title *Sweeter than Poison* for a novel published in 1912. In the poetic lines I have used the article "a" in order to preserve the meter.

6. This line is from Sologub's 1907 poem "Chto bylo, budet vnov'"(What happened once will happen anew).

THE WHITE DOG

1. The word *scutched* refers to the processing of flax. This is in character for the viewpoint of a woman working in the garment industry. Similarly, later in the story the word *goffered*, which also refers to the processing of textiles, is used to describe a man's forehead as the seamstress Alexandra perceives it.

2. In Russian, in addition to describing the sound a crow makes, *to caw* means "to prophesy doom."

3. The word translated here as "shape-shifter," *oboroten'*, is an important concept in Russian folklore, deriving from the verb *oborotit'*, "to turn." It refers to a creature that can magically change its form, often from human to animal and back, but also changing gender. It is usually associated with a demonic influence. The *oboroten'* plays an important role in the works of Nikolai Gogol, as well as in Sologub's novel *The Petty Demon*. "The White Dog" is in dialogue with a number of Sologub's poems that impersonate the voice of a dog. See Introduction, note 36.

THE SADDENED FIANCÉE

1. The phrase translated here as "created sadness," *tvorimaia pechal'*, echoes the title of Sologub's trilogy *The Created Legend* (*Tvorimaia legenda*, written 1907–1911, published as a trilogy in 1914). The trilogy begins with the words, "I take a piece of life, coarse and barren, and I create out of it an ambrosial legend, for I am a poet." See Introduction.

2. Aisa is an alternative name for Atropos, one of the three Fates in Greek mythology. She is the one who decides how each mortal will die and uses shears to cut the thread of life.

3. The task that Nina is promising to take up for her "fiancé" appears to be a political assassination.

THE SIXTY-SEVENTH DAY

1. This story was published in 1908 in the journal *The Golden Fleece*, signed with the initials "F. T." It led to a criminal prosecution of the journal on a charge of pornography. The story was not reprinted in Sologub's *Collected Works*. See Introduction.
2. A *kokoshnik* is a traditional headdress of Russian women.
3. This alludes to the plot of Richard Wagner's 1850 opera *Lohengrin*, which is in turn based on medieval German romance. The heroine Elsa disobeys her lover Lohengrin's injunction not to ask his name, so he is taken from her in a swan-boat to the castle of the Holy Grail, and she dies. Sologub's 1911 story "Lohengrin" plays with the plot of the same opera.
4. Somewhat confusingly, the "four skies" here apparently refer to the four eyes of the two lovers, as Irina's eyes were called "two skies" earlier in the story, perhaps because of their blue color.
5. The description of the moon here may be indebted to the opening of Oscar Wilde's 1892–1894 play *Salome*, in which the page to Herodias says, "Look at the moon. How strange the moon seems! She is like a woman rising from a tomb. She is like a dead woman. One might fancy she was looking for dead things." In Russian as in the original French of Wilde's play, the word for "moon" is of feminine gender and has feminine pronouns. Oscar Wilde, *The Importance of Being Earnest and Other Plays*, ed. Peter Raby (Oxford: Oxford University Press, 1995), 65.

THE ROAD TO DAMASCUS

1. When this story was published in Sologub's *Collected Works* in 1914, it was accompanied by a note from Sologub, "Written together with Anastasia Chebotarevskaya." For more on Sologub's wife Chebotarevskaya, see Introduction. The "road to Damascus" refers to the conversion of Paul the Apostle, recounted in Acts 9, Acts 22, and Acts 26. For Sologub and his milieu, the phrase would have an added meaning, thanks to Valery Briusov's 1903 poem "V Damask" (To Damascus), in which the road to Damascus is the road to sexual ecstasy.
2. The doctor appears to be advising Klavdia Andreyevna to have sexual relations in order to relieve unspecified symptoms, probably considered to be of "hysterical" origins. Having no prospects of marriage or a serious relationship, she is brought to despair by his "prescription." There is a long history of marriage and intercourse being prescribed as a treatment for hysterical symptoms in women. See Rachel P. Maines, *The Technology of Orgasm: "Hysteria," the Vibrator, and Women's Sexual Satisfaction* (Baltimore, MD: Johns Hopkins University Press, 1999).

3. These lines are from a 1910 poem, "Utro" (Morning), by Iurii Nikandrovich Verkhovskii (1878–1956), a close associate of Sologub and Chebotarevskaya. The male poetic voice addresses a young woman in a somewhat patronizing tone that is consonant with Tashev's attitude to Klavdia Andreyevna: "But your figure is just as lithe and shapely, / Just as strong are your shoulders and breast, / And your young step is proud . . . / Forget your melancholy, forget it."

4. The *maxixe* was a popular dance originating in Rio de Janeiro, also called the Brazilian tango, which was popularized in the United States and Europe around the turn of the century. The cakewalk, a dance developed by Black Americans before and after emancipation, also became popular in Europe in the early twentieth century.

5. The words "I'll flood your lips with burning kisses" are from the romance "Ne ukhodi, pobud' so mnoiu" (Do not leave, stay with me a while) (1899), music and lyrics by N. V. Zubov. The original words are "I'll cover your lips with kisses," but I have altered the words to keep the meter of the original. The motif of fire and burning appears later in the song.

6. The poetic passage is from Sologub's 1897 poem "V pole ne vidno ni zgi" (Not a thing is visible in the field), about a person who hears a call for help on a dark night and thinks, "What can I do? / I myself am poor and small, / I myself am deathly tired, / How can I help?" and hears the reply given in the story.

THE KISS OF THE UNBORN CHILD

1. The territory that is now Finland was part of the Russian Empire. In his history of the dacha, Stephen Lovell writes, "In the 1880s . . . it was nothing out of the ordinary for Petersburg dachniki to venture far into Finnish territory, renting often rather modest houses in a long string of settlements that extended all the way to Vyborg" (Stephen Lovell, *Summerfolk: A History of the Dacha, 1710–2000* [Ithaca, NY: Cornell University Press, 2003], 60). The dacha settlement represented a holiday space that was neither city nor countryside, but a social grouping something like a suburb, hence the sociability that allowed for summer romances such as Nadezhda's. The adjective here, *chukhonskii*, was used in tsarist St. Petersburg to refer to people belonging to one of several Finno-Ugric groups; there is no precise English equivalent, so the term is usually translated as "Finnish." Sologub himself spent time at dachas in both Finland and Estonia.

2. Seryozha is referring to the death of Lev Nikolaevich Tolstoy (1828–1910), one of Russia's greatest writers, who at the age of eighty-two left his home after bitter family arguments and undertook a sort of pilgrimage, visiting the monastery

of Optina Pustyn as well as a convent in which his sister lived as a nun. He continued his journey, was taken ill, and died at the small railway station of Astapovo. Sologub wrote a substantial article about Tolstoy ("Edinyi put' L'va Tolstogo," 1898; later reworked after Tolstoy's death) and in 1912 wrote with his wife a dramatization of Tolstoy's novel *War and Peace*.

3. Seryozha is quoting an 1868 poem by Nikolai Nekrasov (1821–1878), "Do not sob so madly over him." The phrase is literally "It's good to die while you're young," but I have slightly altered the sense to preserve the anapestic meter. Sologub's sister-in-law Olga Nikolayevna Chernosvitova, who cared for him in his last years, wrote that as a child, "All [Sologub's] sympathies were on the side of the oppressed people and their defenders. Such an attitude explains the future Symbolist's extreme enthusiasm for the poetry of Nekrasov, almost all of whose works he knew by heart, and whom he esteemed much higher than Lermontov and Pushkin." O. N. Chernosvitova, "Materialy k biografii Fedora Sologuba," ed. M. M. Pavlova, in *Neizdannyi Fedor Sologub*, ed. M. M. Pavlova and A. V. Lavrov (Moscow: Novoe literaturnoe obozrenie, 1997), 239.

4. "We will live and we will see" is a literal rendering of an idiomatic Russian expression roughly equivalent to "Time will tell." I have preserved the literal meaning because it includes the idea of the continuation of life, so pertinent to the story. The lines about progress are again Nekrasov's, from his satirical narrative poem "The Contemporaries" (1875). As in the previous passage, I have slightly altered the sense to preserve the anapestic meter. The literal sense of the full quatrain is, "Just wait a bit! Progress is moving, / And we cannot see the end of its movement: / What is considered shameful today / Will be worthy of a crown tomorrow." In the early twentieth century, Semyon Nadson (1862–1887) and Symbolist poet Konstantin Balmont (1867–1942) would have been more currently popular poets than Nekrasov, who fully belonged to the nineteenth century. But Nekrasov seems to have captured Seryozha's imagination with his progressively oriented poetry.

THE LADY IN SHACKLES

1. Natal'ia Il'inichna Butkovskaia (1878–1948) was an actress and director of plays in the experimental, avant-garde venues the Stray Dog Café and the Ancient Theater in St. Petersburg, and the publisher of books by theater innovator Nikolai Nikolaevich Evreinov (1879–1953). She was married to the set designer A. K. Shervashidze (1867–1968), with whom she emigrated in 1920. Evreinov directed Sologub's plays *Vanka the Steward and the Page Jean* (*Van'ka-kliuchnik i pazh Zhean*, 1908) and *Night Dances* (*Nochnye pliaski*, 1909).

LITTLE FAIRY TALES

1. These tales appeared in various journals in 1898–1906 and in two collections, *Kniga skazok* (Book of fairy tales) (Moscow: Grif, 1905) and *Politicheskie skazochki* (Little political fairy tales) (St. Petersburg: Shipovnik, 1906). Of the tales translated here, three appeared in *Politicheskie skazochki*: "The Death-Loving Corpsie," "The Sun-Ray in the Dungeon," and "Deathlings." I have tried to select tales that can be most successfully translated, as many of them are heavily dependent on the nuances of Russian and Sologub's wordplay and use of dialect.

2. "Deathlings" appeared in the 1906 *Politicheskie skazochki*, 19–20. It was not republished in the Shipovnik *Sobranie sochinenii* and does not appear in the 2001 *Sobranie sochinenii*. The translation of this fairy tale is complicated by the fact that the word *dukh* can mean both "spirit" and "smell."

PUBLICATION HISTORY OF THE STORIES

"To the Stars": *Severnyi vestnik*, no. 9 (1896); *Teni* (1896); *Sobranie sochinenii*, vol. 3, *Zemnye deti* (St. Petersburg: Sirin, 1913–1914).

"Beauty": *Sever*, no. 1 (January 3, 1899); *Sobranie sochinenii*, vol. 4, *Nedobraia gospozha* (St. Petersburg: Sirin, 1913–1914).

"In Captivity": *Severnye tsvety assiriiskie. Al'manakh IV* (Moscow: Skorpion, 1905); *Sobranie sochinenii*, vol. 3, *Zemnye deti* (St. Petersburg: Sirin, 1913–1914).

"Two Gotiks": *Literaturnoe prilozhenie k gazete "Slovo,"* no. 9 (April 2, 1906); *Sobranie sochinenii*, vol. 7, *Dni pechali. Rasskazy* (St. Petersburg: Sirin, 1913–1914).

"The Youth Linus": *Vesy*, no. 2 (1906); in the collection *Istlevaiushchie lichiny* (St. Petersburg: Grif, 1907), under the title "The miracle of the young Linus"; *Sobranie sochinenii*, vol. 11, *Kniga prevrashchenii* (St. Petersburg: Sirin, 1913–1914).

"In the Crowd": *Novaia illiustratsiia*, nos. 3 and 4 (February 5 and 19, 1907); *Birzhevye vedomosti*, nos. 9865 and 9867 (April 26 and 27, 1907); *Sobranie sochinenii*, vol. 7, *Dni pechali. Rasskazy* (St. Petersburg: Sirin, 1913–1914).

"Death by Advertisement": *Zolotoe runo*, no. 6 (1907); *Sobranie sochinenii*, vol. 7, *Dni pechali. Rasskazy* (St. Petersburg: Sirin, 1913–1914).

"The White Dog": *Put'*, no. 2 (1908); *Sobranie sochinenii*, vol. 7, *Dni pechali. Rasskazy* (St. Petersburg: Sirin, 1913–1914).

"The Saddened Fiancée": *Obrazovanie*, no. 7 (1908); *Sobranie sochinenii*, vol. 7, *Dni pechali. Rasskazy* (St. Petersburg: Sirin, 1913–1914).

"The Sixty-Seventh Day. A Novella": *Zolotoe runo*, no. 7–9 (1908).

"The Road to Damascus": The almanac of the publishing house Shipovnik, St. Petersburg, 1910, book 12; *Sobranie sochinenii*, vol. 12, *Kniga stremlenii* (St. Petersburg: Sirin, 1913–1914). In the commentary to the *Sobranie sochinenii*, the author provides a clarification: "Written together with Anastasia Chebotarevskaya."

"The Kiss of the Unborn Child": *Utro Rossii*, no. 297 (December 25, 1911); *Sobranie sochinenii*, vol. 14, *Neutolimoe* (St. Petersburg: Sirin, 1913–1914).

"The Lady in Shackles. A Legend of the White Nights": *Ogonek*, no. 21 (May 19, 1912); *Sobranie sochinenii*, vol. 14, *Neutolimoe* (St. Petersburg: Sirin, 1913–1914).

"Little Fairy Tales": These tales appeared in various journals in 1898–1906 and in two collections, *Kniga skazok* (Book of fairy tales) (Moscow: Grif, 1905) and *Politicheskie skazochki* (Little political fairy tales) (St. Petersburg: Shipovnik, 1906); *Sobranie sochinenii*, vol. 10, *Skazochki i stat'i* (St. Petersburg: Shipovnik, 1910).

R

RUSSIAN LIBRARY

The Voice Over: Poems and Essays by Maria Stepanova, edited by Irina Shevelenko

The Symphonies by Andrei Bely, translated by Jonathan Stone

Countries That Don't Exist: Selected Nonfiction by Sigizmund Krzhizhanovsky, edited by Jacob Emery and Alexander Spektor

Homeward from Heaven by Boris Poplavsky, translated by Bryan Karetnyk

Stravaging "Strange" by Sigizmund Krzhizhanovsky, translated by Joanne Turnbull with Nikolai Formozov

CPSIA information can be obtained
at www.ICGtesting.com
Printed in the USA
JSHW011602130123
36240JS00001B/1

9 780231 200059